CW01151484

A Northern Family Saga

TRAIL OF THE VIKING FINGER

JOHN BEAN

Copyright © 2016 John Bean

The moral right of the author has been asserted.

Apart from any fair dealing for the purposes of research or private study, or criticism or review, as permitted under the Copyright, Designs and Patents Act 1988, this publication may only be reproduced, stored or transmitted, in any form or by any means, with the prior permission in writing of the publishers, or in the case of reprographic reproduction in accordance with the terms of licences issued by the Copyright Licensing Agency. Enquiries concerning reproduction outside those terms should be sent to the publishers.

This is a work of fiction. Names, characters, businesses, places, events and incidents are either the products of the author's imagination or used in a fictitious manner. Any resemblance to actual persons, living or dead, or actual events is purely coincidental.

Matador
9 Priory Business Park,
Wistow Road, Kibworth Beauchamp,
Leicestershire. LE8 0RX
Tel: 0116 279 2299
Email: books@troubador.co.uk
Web: www.troubador.co.uk/matador
Twitter: @matadorbooks

ISBN 978 1785893 056

British Library Cataloguing in Publication Data.
A catalogue record for this book is available from the British Library.

Printed and bound by CPI Group (UK) Ltd, Croydon, CR0 4YY
Typeset in 11pt Minion Pro by Troubador Publishing Ltd, Leicester, UK

Matador is an imprint of Troubador Publishing Ltd

MIX
Paper from
responsible sources
FSC FSC® C013604

Dedicated to the memory of our ancestors who jointly gave us Englishness. May their descendants maintain it.

Bjorne/Byrne Family Tree of main characters

Key: m. Married bro. Brother sis. Sister dtr. Daughter

1066
Bjorne Dagson
m. Brietta *dtr.* of Cedric & Hild son 1.Alan Byrne. son 2. Johannes *dtr.* Gwenda. Bjorne is now Walter Byrne

*bro.*Ragnar Dagson
m. Margit *dtr.* of Edgar the butcher

Ragnar is now Edgar Svenson *m.* Margaret

Einar Hairfair

1089
Alan Byrne
sires son Thomas from Freyja

Thomas *m.*Freda. son William

A Gt.grandson of Ragnar is Reginald Ragnar.
In Jewelry-making with Ivor Fairhall

Ivor Fairhall
Gt-grandson of EinarHairfair

1215
John Byrne
Grandson of William *m*.Freda. son 1.John William. son 2.Walter.
Dtr. Gwenda

Walter *m*.Edwina Rawlinson.
son 1.Henry. son 2. Edward

1288
John William,
son Alfred *m*.Kathy

Richard Byrne
son of above (&sis. Elizabeth) *m*. Catherine

Rufus Byrne *m*. Mary.
son Alan *m*. Catherine Hood. son 1. Bryan. son 2. Richard, sis. Johanna, sis.Edwina – mother of Stephen Blake.

Ivor Fairhall
m. Elizabeth Byrne

1415
Bryan Byrne
m. Elizabeth Turner. Twins Bryan John and Edwina . son 2 Thomas.

Thomas's son l. was William. son 2, Arthur.

1528
William *m*. Ellinor Burton.
Dtr Jane. son Abraham.

Cedric Byrne.
son 1. Richard. sis. Kathleen. Son 2. Cedric *m*. Ellen

1638
Richard, first m. to Mary.
son Bryan *dtr* Emily
Bryan Byrne fathers John

David (son of John)

Richard *m*.Ellen,
son 1. Bryan. son 2. Cedric

Richard, 2nd *m*. Maryanne

Seamus Byrne

1740
Bryan *m*. Anne.
son William. *Dtr*. Matilda

Seamus Byrne II *m*. Beatrice,
son Thomas *dtr*. Maryanne

Arthur Byrne *m*. Joan Pryke

1785
William *m*. Ellinor Bell.
son. John Frederick, *dtr*. Elizabeth

John Frederick *m*. Margaret Bevis.
Dtr Mary, Son Frederick William Byrne

Mary Byrne *m*. Alan Smith.
son 1. George. son 2. Charles

1840
Frederic William *m*. Catherine Lawson.
son 1. David Lawson. Son.2 Edward John. *Dtr*. Elizabeth

David Lawson *m*. Sophie Thompson.
son. Brian Lawson. *Dtr*. Alice

1885
Brian Byrne *m*. Joan 'Byrne'.
son 1. William John. *Dtr*. Ellen. son 2.Richard Frederick. son 3. John Alan

John Alan *m*. Madge Hoskins.
son Kenneth. *Dtr*. Margaret

1920
William John *m*. Elizabeth Hartley.
son Edward William Byrne

Preface

Those who are readers of Edward Rutherfurd's historical novels may compare *Trail of the Viking Finger* to his works, not least his first, *Sarum,* with its 10,000 year storyline. In all seven of his novels he invents several fictional families and tells the stories of their descendants. Over a minimum of five hundred to in excess of a thousand pages he weaves them in and out of historical situations where they react with each other as well as with historical personalities.

In contrast, *Trail of the Viking Finger* deals with the descendants of one family only, the Byrnes, whose founder was a Danish Viking, Bjorne the Red. Over a 900 year storyline their inherited DNA displays several physical and behavioural characteristics which recur irregularly in succeeding generations and sometimes not until two or three generations later. The most noticeable physical characteristic was the bent fingers which developed in middle life and are commonly referred to as the Scandinavian or Viking Disease and is now known medically as Dupuytren's Contracture.

Another difference from Rutherfurd's captivating historical novels is that in keeping with modern reading custom this novel is more concise. As Carl Jung wrote, *History is not contained in thick books but lives in our very blood.* Nevertheless it still gives details of the lives of specific Byrne families – which could be brutally violent in the medieval period. These are mainly selected to show how they reacted to the social and political events that marked the different periods, e.g. the Black death, the Peasants' Revolt and the English Civil War. The Byrne families encountered all lived in Yorkshire until 1783 and then in Northumberland and Tyneside until 1885, both areas that were heart of the Danelaw just prior to when this novel commences in 1066. It should not be overlooked that as a result of marriage (a basic custom in the period covered) Anglo-Saxon and ancient Celtic blood comes into our story. The author supports the view that when we talk of 'Anglo-Saxon' immigrants the majority were Angles and Jutes, i.e. from Jutland in Denmark.

I was inspired to write this historical novel as a result of preparing my own family tree, which I managed to trace back to a Brian Beane born at Saxton in Elmet – near York – around 1570. Nearly all locations, many Christian or forenames and occupations that are given in this novel are those of my family over the generations. My great, great, great grandfather, William Bean (no 'e' on the end by now) *did* leave the Yorkshire farm in 1783 in company with his sister as did William Byrne with his sister in this novel to make their way to Northumberland.

My great, great grandfather, John Bean, was a miller in Newcastle.

It is stressed that although many forenames (which tended to be repetitive over many generations before the 20th century) are taken from my family tree, all characters in this book are ficticious.

Some six years ago I undertook an unsuccessful operation in the West Suffolk hospital for the swollen tendons and inward curving little fingers in both hands – Dupuytrens Contracture. In 2012 I had my DNA tested by the laboratory of Oxford Ancestry which is run by Professor Bryan Sykes. The result said that I carry the Y- chromosome recognised as being of Anglo-Saxon or Danish Viking origin. In an explanatory note it said that 'at the present time it is impossible to distinguish between the DNA of Danish Vikings and Anglo-Saxons.' The Norse Vikings from Norway were quite distinct from those of Danish origin.

Whether or not some fictitious Bjorne the Red beaten by the Saxons at the Battle of Stamford Bridge in 1066 is an equally fictitious ancestor of mine is pure conjecture.

Chapter One

'It's in his Blood'

Teddy Bill hastened to finish his porridge. Made to eat it by his Aunty Jenny for breakfast every morning he was rather bored with it. Today was special. The quicker he finished his porridge the sooner he would be able to go out and join Uncle Henry. The threshing machine had turned up. He had seen it for himself as it came puffing up from Dorking, billowing smoke over Ranmore Common. It was operated by a contractor who visited many Surrey farms following harvest time. With its rakes, shakers and pairs of fans (or fanners as the farm workers called them), the threshing machine – of the latest 1928 design – took its power by belts from the steam engine.

'Shut the gate boy! Shut the gate,' cried Uncle Henry, 'Otherwise the dogs will be chasing the rats into our garden and even into the house.' 'Now young lad,' said John Weatherston, the farmer who Henry Hartley worked for, 'You stand over there and don't get too near the threshing engine belts. If you see any rats come your way from the corn stack whack em with your stick and let the dogs have em.'

The Jack Russells knew by instinct to keep clear of the moving belts, with the bitches often being quicker in grabbing a rat by the throat and killing it in seconds. One who initially escaped the dogs came tearing towards Teddy Bill, who hit it so hard with his stick that it was momentarily stunned, just long enough for a Jack Russell to finish it off. Jenny Hartley had arrived to see the threshing machine start up. She saw Teddy Bill's quick action with the rat but made no comment. That evening before turning in, both of them exhausted, she said quietly to Henry: 'I was rather shocked at the hatred on young Teddy Bill's face as he whacked that rat. I have never seen him like that. He's always been such a gentle boy and looks it with his auburn hair and blue eyes.'

'Yes, several of the men said to me afterwards that they had never seen such strength in a four-year-old boy. Don't know where that comes from and I wouldn't like to cross him when he's eighteen. He's a rum 'un, is our Edward William.'

Jenny Hartley had adopted Edward Byrne when his mother, Elizabeth Byrne, had died of tuberculosis in 1927 at the young age of thirty. Nobody in the Byrne family had come forward to look after the two-year-old 'Teddy Bill' as Jenny soon called him, but as Elizabeth had been her younger sister she had volunteered to do so.

'Well, I have already got a boy of sixteen and a girl of fourteen (Edward's cousins) so they will help look after him, particularly as he grows older,' was Jenny's answer to the problem.

Edward's father William John Byrne was born in Gateshead. In 1914 he volunteered to be a soldier in the Northumberland Fusiliers and by the end of the year he was in the trenches on the Western Front. Within a few months he was gassed and never fully recovered. It took twelve years to kill him and he took his last choking breath in June 1928, just a year after losing the love of his failing life, Elizabeth Hartley.

Young Edward Byrne had a sister, Daphne, who on the death of their mother was looked after by their father's younger brother John Byrne and his wife Madge who lived only a mile or so from their elder brother's rented house in Swanley.

The grandparents, Brian Lawson Byrne and his wife Joan were unable to look after their two orphaned grandchildren, as Brian was now suffering from the results of a stroke and his wife was trying to hang on to the good living that she and Brian enjoyed prior to the great slump which had ruined his engineering business and other investments. In any case she had not really forgiven her son William for marrying the family cook, Elizabeth Hartley. This was after they had come South and eventually taken up residence in a Surrey country hall near Esher. William had berated his mother for her snobbery telling her: 'You've forgotten we were all born and raised with working people on Tyneside. You have now joined the nouveau riche and insult your own son, and your own people, let alone my dear Elizabeth.'

Brian Byrne and family had moved from Tyneside in 1885 to live in Manchester for four years. He began to work for Lord Lever and helped in engineering work in the setting up of Port Sunlight on the Mersey, where Sunlight Soap was founded. When the work was completed, mainly at the instigation of his wife Joan he moved to London then Surrey, allegedly so that he could develop a small engineering company he had bought in Bermondsey.

* * *

Winter began to set in up on Ranmore Common. The first snow arrived and young Edward Byrne was taken for a toboggan ride by Aunty Jenny's daughter Jane. 'Hang on Teddy Bill,' she cried, pushing the toboggan to the top of the hill before jumping on. 'We could go all the way down to Dorking without stopping. But we won't because we would have to walk back in the snow, and you're too small for that.'

In reply he just said 'Yes'. But he thought she's only being kind to me and I love her. But when the snow goes I will walk down and back by myself and show them what I can do.'

Among Aunty Jenny's proud possessions was a gramophone. But as far as young Edward knew there were only two records that were ever played in the winter evenings, usually by cousin Jane. Her favourite was 'Nobody Cares if I'm Blue' sung by an American with Jack Hylton's Band. Edward much preferred the other record, usually played by Aunt Jenny herself. It was the 'Blue Danube Waltz' by Johann Strauss.

It was spring time and Edward was approaching his fifth birthday. He did not really know why: possibly because he was too young – but he again had this overwhelming desire to be out on the common and walk and walk and walk. Uncle Henry said it was something in his blood.

His cousin David had been given a vintage Triumph motorbike which was older than he was. Assisted by his father over the winter, he had spent many hours tinkering with it to give it a more consistent performance. He was told he could ride it around the common but not to go on the road down to Dorking with it, nor to frighten the sheep and cattle with its noise.

Seeing Edward striding along as fast as his little legs would go, David pulled alongside him.'Jump on behind me, Teddy Bill, and hang on to my waist. We're off for a spin! Mind your legs on the exhaust pipe or it will burn them.'

Edward accepted the offer with eagerness. This was a new experience for him. He felt exhilaration as the common flashed by and had to hold tightly on David's waist as they went over bumps and between bushes and trees. David kept away from the main woods and a good distance from the farm and any fields where he knew animals would be. He knew that otherwise his father would take the bike away for a month or more.

It so happened that his mother was just entering the cottage as he drove up at a more cautious speed to put the bike away in their shed.

'David, what are you doing when you are supposed to be working on the farm? And what are you doing with a five-year-old boy on the back!?'

'Mr Weatherston has given me a couple of hours off, Mum. As for Teddy Bill, I only took it slowly and he loved it as he hung on to me properly. Didn't burn his legs either on the exhaust.'

'Well next time you tell me first, or your father, if you are planning to give Teddy Bill a ride.'

As he lay in bed that night, young Edward's mind went over that motor bike ride. It was the most exciting thing he had done. His left leg did hurt a bit where he had burnt it on the exhaust. He had thought it best not to mention it to David, and certainly not to Aunty Jenny, in case he could not go riding on the bike again.

* * *

It was now Easter 1930. Henry and Jenny had arranged for three days off from the farm, starting Good Friday through to Easter Sunday. Jenny's brother Tom Hartley and his wife operated a Thames red sail barge out of Charlton and it was arranged that Jenny, Henry, daughter Jane and young Edward would join them on the barge for three days while it went to Gravesend and back. David took their place in helping out with the cows at milking time.

Good Friday started with all four walking to the church in Dorking for the first Good Friday service, then quickly on to the railway station. They took a train to Croydon and from there a bus to Charlton. Their midday meal was eaten on the train and consisted of boiled egg sandwiches prepared by Jenny and washed down with milk from the farm dairy.

It was the first time that Edward had seen the barge, or a ship of any sort. As he was lifted up on board he thought it could be as big as the Titanic had been. There was a dusty smell of wheat coupled with that of horse manure. Uncle Tom said to Edward, 'Most times we carry horse manure from London's taxi cabs up to Ipswich where the Suffolk farmers put it on the land. We then bring back a second quality grain to feed them horses. If we continue to have more and more motor taxis the horse-drawn ones will disappear and I don't know what me and Aunty Nell, my missus, will do then.'

'We've got some dry goods to take to Gravesend, so we'll set off in the morning when the tide and the wind is right. We have only got two sleeping places here, as much room as possible must be for the cargo. You lot will all sleep together and keep nice and warm, and me and the missus will sleep at the bow, that's the sharp end to you, where we always do. If you want to go to lavy and it's a number two, don't pull the chain until we get down river a bit. Otherwise the LCC (London County Council) will be after us if they find any smelly bits washed ashore.'

'Meanwhile,' said Nell, 'we will have some tea. We got winkles and brown bread and butter and Tom has got some beer he brewed for those who wud like it after.' Edward was given half a small cup of beer. He sipped it, but grimaced and said he did not like the taste.

'You will probably change your mind, Teddy Bill, when you get older,' said a smiling Aunty Jenny.'But I don't think you will be one of those who let the beer do the talking and get them in trouble.'

Edward thought about this advice but did not know what to say in reply. So he just smiled and said nothing.

As Tom had planned to set off at 6. 30 in the morning, they all retired around 9. 30pm. Edward slept between his Aunty Jenny and cousin Jane. It had been a busy and tiring day, particularly for a small boy. As he lay there feeling both warm and pleased that Jane was cuddling him, he knew that the others had gone straight to sleep. Within fifteen minutes he had joined them.

Edward was awakened by the movement of the barge. He clambered over Jane, pulled his trousers on and raced up on deck. In the dim morning light he could see Uncle Tom pulling on the sails to catch the best wind while Aunty Nell held the tiller. Seeing him, Tom shouted: 'You be careful of this boom, boy. I don't want to see you knocked in the river, 'cos I can't swim and there would be no one to save you.'

'I will do what you tell me Uncle Tom, 'cos I want to learn and be a sailor when I grow up.' Aunty Nell took one hand off the tiller and waved to Edward giving him a big smile.

Aunty Jenny had to call him three times before he would even come down and have his breakfast. It was a streaky bacon sandwich left ready for them by Nell. Edward grabbed his sandwich and shot back up on deck, where he stayed for five hours before the barge, making good time, reached Gravesend. Having tied up alongside the harbour Tom announced:

'There's a good fish and chip shop here that's always open on a Saturday dinner time. If we put five bob in the kitty that should cover it.'

'I'll put another shilling in,' said Jenny, 'because our Jane will have an adult portion now and Teddy Bill can have man-size chips.' They all looked at Edward and laughed. He looked pleased.

There had been a couple of light showers on the way down to Gravesend but for early April it was a warm afternoon. They decided to sit out on deck and eat their fish and chips, washed down with several cups of tea. Henry, Jenny and daughter Jane were telling Tom and Nell how much they had enjoyed the barge trip so far.'It's a hard enough life being a farm labourer and a dairy maid who has seen better days. But you can see that although you enjoy running this barge, it's very hard work for just the two of you.'

Having eaten every one of his chips, Edward was gazing out at the wideness of the Thames now that they had left London.'Hello Teddy Bill, are you still with us?' asked Henry.'Do you still want to be a sailor when you grow up?' With, a serious face, Edward turned to the family group.'Now I can see the water is wide like the sea, I know I have been at sea before. So I will be a sailor when I grown up.'

In a serious voice Jenny said: 'What do you mean, young Edward, that you have been at sea before? You have never been near the sea until today. You say such odd things sometimes, my boy.'

Turning to Tom and Nell, Henry said: 'Although all of us at home love this boy, now and again he says and does some strange things, and remember he is still only five. They are not bad but odd things we don't really understand. He is now going to the infant school down in Dorking, which is nearly a three mile walk for him. He had only been there a month when his teacher complained to us that he was fighting with a boy a year older than him and that our little Teddy Bill had nearly gone berserk and she had to pull him off. Now that could develop into a bad thing.'

'Why did you do that Edward?' asked his Aunt Nell.

'He said that I was only a daft little farm boy with ginger hair. I didn't really know I was hitting him until the teacher pulled me off. Anyway, me and him are friends now.'

* * *

Some two months had passed since the enjoyable short holiday (the only one for the year) they had spent on the barge, when Jenny Hartley needed to go shopping in Dorking. Bread and many groceries were supplied from an elderly Ford van that came up three times a week from Dorking. Milk and eggs were supplied from the farm. She needed to get new underpants and socks for Henry, clothing for herself and perhaps get a new dress, if the price was right. When finished she would meet Teddy Bill at school (she had promised to call him 'Edward' outside the school) and he would carry one of the smaller parcels for her.

Jenny was feeling happy after her shopping expedition, mainly because she had been able to pick up a nice blue dress exactly her size which had been reduced in a sale. Meeting 'Edward' outside the school she told him that before going home they would go into Woolworths where he could choose a toy that did not cost more than a shilling. After looking at a model aeroplane, a tank and a railway engine, but being told 'No, they are much more than a shilling Teddy Bill,' he stopped by a counter which was full of lead model soldiers and farm animals.' Look,' said Aunty Jenny, 'there are some British soldiers, like your daddy, and some German ones he fought. You could have three of them for a shilling.' Edward picked up two British and one German soldier, turned them around, then put them back.'No Aunty Jenny I think I'll have these three for a shilling. It's a pig and a cow to be part of my farm, and a soldier to make sure no nasty person steals them.' The 'soldier' he had chosen was a Viking, wearing a winged helmet.

Little did young Edward William Byrne, the Hartley family, or any of those in the Dorking shop, know that in the next hundred years life and the nation's structure was to change more than it had in the previous one thousand. The reasons for some of these changes would be as obscure or pointless as the horns placed on a Viking helmet by the Victorians.

Chapter Two

Viking Roots

Bjorne Dagson, also known as Bjorne The Red because of his red beard, and his younger brother Ragnar struggled to reach Jorvik by dawn. If not, they and the other thirteen Viking survivors from the defeat at Stamford Bridge knew that it was likely they would be slaughtered by armed Saxons. It was a time when there was little difference in ruthlessness in battle between Saxon, Norman or Viking. If they stayed in the open country they knew they would join Harald Hadrada, King Harald III of Norway, in Valhalla with two thirds of his followers.

With four of their number being wounded, Bjorne thought that it would be almost impossible to fight their way to the coast where the residue of the Viking fleet was still offshore. In their favour it was likely that Vikings still had a strong presence in Jorvik as they had defeated a northern English army just five days earlier. What they did not know was that Harold Godwinson, the English Saxon king, had departed from the Yorkshire battle field of September 25th as quickly as he had arrived from London. Now there were very few Saxon soldiers left who could have barred the way for Vikings to reach the few ships left of Harald Hadrada's fleet. It was said that he had arrived with 300 ships and only twenty-four were required to take his surviving followers back to Norway and Denmark

To complicate the picture there were some Saxons, who had supported Tostig Godwinson (King Harold's bother), who had been killed at Stamford Bridge supporting Harald Hadrada.

Bjorne The Red and his fellow survivors, travelling mainly by night, reached Jorvik (later shortened to York) around seven in the morning of September 27th. They had thrown away their helmets and did their best to hide weapons under their jerkins. They had combed their beards and hair and cleaned themselves, as was Viking custom, as much as they could. The main gate had been opened for normal business and mingling among locals they slipped through, being greeted with 'God Dag' by Viking settlers and looks of curiosity from Saxon and Celtic inhabitants. Harold Godwinson's rapid return to the south was to meet the threat of William of Normandy who had landed near Hastings to claim the English throne. In reality it was another challenge from the Norsemen, even if now they spoke French. William was a direct descendant of Rollo who in AD 876 led his Norsemen in the colonising of that part of Northern France which become Normandy. The Norse language was spoken at Bayeux until around 1030.

William the Bastard, Jarl of Rouen, thought that he had a better right to the English Kingdom than Harold Godwinson. This was based on the fact that William's father and the previous English King, Edward the Confessor were first cousins. Perhaps more important was that William considered it payback time for Harold for breaking his marriage proposal to William's daughter. William took considerable pride in his Norse ancestry and respect for the Danish Vikings. In his speech to his army before the battle of Hastings he proclaimed: 'Let anyone, whom our predecessors, both Danes and Norsemen, have defeated in a hundred battles, come forth and show that the race of Rolf ever suffered a defeat from his time until now, and I will submit and retreat.'

(*This and other detailed information on the Viking era comes from the English translation of the Heimskringla by Snorre Sturlason*)

With a large contingent from Flanders and Brittany, William's forces numbered 10,000, against Harold's 7,000. Less than half were his Housecarls, well armed and well trained full-time soldiers, the remainder being the fyrd – poorly armed working men called up in time of danger. Unfortunately the discipline of the fyrd did not match their courage, which led them to fall for the trick enacted by William's men of pretending to panic and retreat. The outcome was Harold's encirclement with his best men, his death, and annihilation of most of his followers. It was not long after William became King that he abolished English laws and retained those of the Danes, first introduced when Canute was our King some thirty years earlier. The law of the Danes and Norsemen still prevailed in Norfolk, Suffolk and Cambridgeshire. When William heard of this, together with other laws of his new Kingdom, he offered approval and gave orders that it should be observed throughout the kingdom. Apparently, he stated that this was because his ancestors, and those of all the barons of Normandy had been Norsemen from Norway or Denmark. However, although Saxon control and property ownership was much reduced, William eventually listened to the English people's objections and at the urgent request of his barons allowed them to retain much of the laws of Edward the Confessor.

* * *

Bjorne , Ragnar and the other survivors from the defeated Viking army split up once inside the city and were given refuge amongst most established Anglo-Scandinavian citizens of Jorvik.

Two of the wounded had died of infections in their wounds within ten days of their arrival.

Jorvik's origins are said to have gone back well before the coming of the Romans, who called it Eboracum, which evolved from a Celtic name for a large hamlet on the site. In the 7th century the Anglians called it Eoforwic. In AD 867 it was captured by the Danish Viking Halfdan and with the surrounding area it had remained as the Kingdom of Jorvik. As nearly all Danes and most Norwegian royalty had become Christians, Bjorne and the remaining survivors of the slaughter at Stamford Bridge made a point of attending services addressed by the Archbishop Ealdred, who was to hold his post for another three years. Thus they had no major problem in being accepted. But with King William and his Norman Barons in control, all that was about to change *and drastically.*

As was their inherent custom, Bjorne and Ragnar and nearly all the survivors were eager to earn their keep by working for established 'Jorvikers'. Language presented no problem as Danes and Saxons spoke basically the same language. Bjorne helped a smallholder who rented a strip of land outside the wall on which he grew vegetables, mainly cabbage and broad beans. They even kept two lambs there, bringing them in at night, which they were fattening up. Prior to the defeat of Hadrada and then the growing rumours of the severity of rule they could expect under the Normans, much commerce and support for agriculture was carried on outside the city walls. Ragnar and two others found work with a smithy, not only in sharpening tools and, secretly, weapons, but in fashioning metal brooches and ornaments. At first they were given basic runic inscriptions. By the turn of the year this was then followed by the ring-chain interlace pattern, often terminating in an animal-mask, a skill Ragnar had begun to develop back in Danemark before he went a 'Vikinging'. Bjorne had tried his hand at this artistic work, but lacked Ragnar's patience to develop the skill.

By the spring of 1068 the Normans had still not entered Northumbria, which had remained as an Earldom with the backing of the archbishop, Ealdred.

Bjorne, Ragnar and most of the Viking survivors of Stamford Bridge still dreamt of getting back to Danemark or Norway. Back in his home in Sonderborg, Bjorne had been unofficially engaged to his childhood sweetheart, Benta, who lived in the nearby important trading town of Hedeby. This was mainly due to its position on a river on the south east corner of Jutland, which gave easy access south to Germany as well as the rest of Scandinavia. It was surrounded with reasonably good agricultural land, where one of Bjorne's uncles had a holding. Benta's family lived in a gabled house looking on to a wood-paved street. Most of the houses, including those at Sonderborg, were of stave construction in which tree trunks are split vertically and placed in the ground and the walls of wattle then plastered with a mixture of mud, dung and horse hair. The roofs were thatched with straw, reeds or covered with turves. Similar houses were built in Jorvik and to this day houses of the same basic construction, but with some improvements, can be found in East Anglia, another area of Danish Viking settlement.

A plan was made to get away to the coast that summer and steal a boat that was seaworthy and get to the North Sea coast of Jutland. If the boat had no oars, they would make them. Ragnar, although dedicated to his brother, was not enthusiastic over this plan. He had developed a relationship with a Northumbrian girl and there was talk of marriage. Her parents would object if she was taken away to Danemark. Of the thirteen Vikings who came with Bjorne and Ragnar after their defeat at Stamford Bridge, two died of their wounds and three wanted to stay in Northumbria. That left eight, with only four additional to Bjorne really wanting to get back to Danemark at present with all the risks involved.

As a compromise Bjorne, with a reluctant Ragnar and four others, took two days off and went to the coast searching for a small boat which would hold ten to twelve men. They found one (without oars) which was similar to the normal Viking construction. It had several areas between the clinker-built overlapping planks which needed sealing with bitumen, or fat if bitumen could not be found. Although it did not seem to belong to anybody, they buried it above the high water mark, with a view to coming back several times before the autumn really set in to get it sea-worthy. They came back on two occasions that year but were reduced to five regulars: Bjorne and Ragnar, plus Sven Olafsen, Harald the Limper and Einar Hairfair. They were staying overnight because of the time spent in uncovering and recovering the boat, let alone the work that had to be carried out. Bjorne felt happier that Ragnar was becoming more supportive of the plan. To encourage him he said in a matter of fact way:

'You can see who are the crafstmen here. It's you and Sven. My work is that of a novice'

'If you had a couple of pigs to look after or there was need to kill an enemy, you and Harald would show your worth,' grunted Ragnar.

With nearly two years having passed since William and the Norman Knights became established, several rebellions, mainly in the South and Midlands, had been put down with considerable indiscriminate bloodshed. It was Ragnar who said to his brother: 'William the Bastard has already built a fort here in Jorvik and Anglo-Saxons as well as Anglo-Vikings who hold any local position find they are being squeezed out by Normans.'

Bjorne considered this comment for a few moments before saying: 'This is likely to lead to a major battle here in Northumbria, which as a trained warrior means I will have to pick up arms again. I don't want to, but I feel it will have to happen.'

As the winter set in the grip on York by the Normans become stronger. Being treated equally as serfs by the new overlords brought those of Saxon, Danish and Norse Viking, and even Celtic origins together. They were all Northumbrians or Jorkists now.

By February 1069 the Northumbrians besieged the newly built Norman castle, with the result that the Norman commander, Robert Fitz Richard was killed. Inspired by this, plus the quantity of ale consumed in the alehouses, some thirty or more men came to Bjorne's lodgings, calling out:

Bjorne Redbeard, you're an old Berserker. Come with us with your friends to defend our city. The Norman pigs will be back in force.'

Bjorne strode out, with his right hand on the hilt of his sword.'My friends, we are still too few and not yet strong enough to meet the mounted Norman knights in face to face battle. They will exterminate us all. Rape our women and kill our children. We must take our chance to pick them off singly or in twos and threes and disappearing off to the hills if necessary.'

Some agreed with this advice, others scorned him and shouted, Now you think you're a farmer you've lost your courage.

Most of the latter were killed the following month when King

William himself led the sacking of the city. Churches including the Minster were plundered by the Normans and the rebels who survived had to flee. Bjorne Dagson, his brother Ragnar, Sven Olafsen, Harald the Limper and Einar Hairfair all met in the lowly lodging house where Bjorne had stayed since the Stamford Bridge massacre. This was the home of long established Northumbrian Saxons, Cedric and his wife Hild who made a living by cloth weaving and dyeing. Its apparent poverty was a reason why it had not been pillaged. Their late-teenage daughter Brietta had the slightly darker hair and graceful walk of a Celt, whose genes must have run among those of either Cedric or Hild. She was very taken with Bjorne and his trustworthy manner. On many occasions in the small hours of the night he would lie in his cot by the dye house wondering if Benta was still in love with him – or perhaps she was married to someone else in Sonderborg or Hedeby? With increasing frequency he asked himself 'Would it be better to forget Benta and ask Cedric for his daughter's hand in marriage? I feel that Brietta already loves me. I could easily let myself love her if it wasn't for Benta and my duty to her.'

The purpose of the meeting at Cedric and Hild's house was to find out if they would be prepared to come with them to Danemark, if the boat could be made seaworthy. Knowing that the former Vikings had something important to discuss, Hild had cleaned the house up as best as she could and made sure they had a good supply of rush lights. Cedric checked that there was still enough ale from his last brew. They toasted each other 'to the good will of Jorkists and Northumbrians, new and old' before Bjorne opened the meeting.

'It seems that William's Normans have subdued the English in the south. He will now concentrate his knights and followers in a reign of terror to suppress us in Northumbria, particularly in Jorvik. We are working on making a boat seaworthy to take a number of us former Vikings back to Danemark. We have room to take you and your family, Cedric, on the understanding that we would help you return when it became more peaceful.'

'If I may interrupt,' said Ragnar, 'as you know I am living at the house of Edgar the Butcher and his family and I have hinted at this already. His daughter Margit and I want to get married and she has said she would come with us. With their three boys and another young girl the rest of the family would prefer to stay here. I have sworn them to secrecy.'

'That's good news that you and Margit wish to marry,' said a smiling Hild. 'We will all come to the wedding!' They all shouted their approval, with the men banging their tankards on the table. Directly the noise stopped a blushing Brietta said, 'I would like to come to Danemark too.'

This was greeted with momentary silence as they all looked at Cedric.

'Hild and I are staying here, come what may. As she is still an unmarried girl we cannot let Brietta go to Danemark, however much we respect Bjorne, his bother Ragnar, and their good friends.'

As Bjorne went to reply to Cedric he could not fail to see the tears that were now welling up in Brietta's eyes.

'I am honoured that the charming Brietta, a credit to her parents, should wish to come with us. Speaking for myself, I was about to be betrothed to a fair lady in my home town before I made the fateful visit, with other Vikings, to this pleasant land. I cannot break my word to her until I find out whether she wishes to join with me in marriage. Until that is resolved I can say no word, or take no action, however much I feel, that would make things more complicated for the dear girl Brietta who must stay with her parents.'

'Thank you Bjorne,' replied Cedric, 'I thank you for your honesty on this matter.'

'Before we go,' said Ragnar as tankards were being drained, 'With the ice and snow of the winter and now the heavy rain, not much progress has been made on the boat. However, the present troubled events mean that we must make our small longship ready by early September.'

* * *

It was a fine day in August when Ragnar and Margit were married in the old Saxon church which had now become a minster. His brother was the best man and Brietta was the only bridesmaid. They were all wearing their best clothes, which were mainly in Vikings and Saxons favourite red and blue colours. Cedric told the family and close relatives who had heard rumours of the plans of the 'Viking friends' to depart home to Danemark to say nothing of their intentions.

The service was conducted by Archbishop Ealdred who, between bouts of acute coughing, said that the marriage was an example that others could take in the coming together of the peoples of Northumbria or even Britain as a whole. A month later Ealdred was dead. Some said he died of a broken heart. Having originally backed Harold Godwinson, who he crowned as King of England, he later gave his allegiance to William who he crowned as King in Westminster Abbey at Christmas 1066.

Late August, just ten days after the wedding of Ragnar and Margit, the five former Vikings, plus one of the original thirteen went to the coast to unearth the boat once more. Someone had obviously located it because it showed that attempts had been made to remove some of the top planking, probably thinking it was just suitable for firewood. Fortunately, whoever it was must have been disturbed.

After a discussion with Ragnar, Bjorne said: 'We must finalise on the seaworthiness of our little longship and get away in five days time, which will be September 2nd. It is no good taking up all the time in burying it again, even though somebody knows it is here. Can I have two volunteers who will stay on guard here whilst arrangements are made to bring as many weapons we can gather and food to last seven of us fourteen days?'

Sven Olafson and Harold the Limper, armed with the axes they were using for working with, plus two short swords they always carried, agreed to be the guardians.

Another twist on the kaleidoscope of history that was bringing so many different patterns to the life of 'Yorkists' and Northumbrians took place on September 8th in this eventful year. Danes under King Sweyn II entered the Humber with a fleet. He was accompanied by Edgar of Wessex who claimed England's throne. From the north bank of the Humber they marched on Jorvik, but the Normans decided to discourage Sweyn and Edgar from making it their HQ by a show of burning the city. However, the flames burnt out of control, killing many Normans and destroying the Anglo-Saxon minster where Ragnar and Margit had married. King William was supervising the building of the New Castle by the river Tyne when he was informed of Sweyn's campaign. Gathering every available Norman and Saxon supporter in the area he quickly made his way to Jorvik, where he spent the winter.

Two days before King Sweyn and Edgar of Wessex had come up the Humber to land near Hessle, only some fifteen miles to the north-east near Barmston, Bjorne, Ragnar, Margit and the four other Danish escapees were loading the little longboat ready to depart for Danemark. Their provisions included dried peas, lentils and broad beans, many of them grown by Bjorne on his strip of rented land, and bread which they had wrapped in cloth to protect it from mould. With the increasing trouble besetting Jorvik, a month previously he had decided to slaughter the two sheep he had raised, giving one to Cedric for his family. With the one he had kept he made sure that each joint was well covered in salt to preserve it.

Despite the onset of squally showers driven by an easterly onshore wind they decided they could wait no longer. A make-shift sail – made from two old sheets taken from a desolate house whose occupants had been killed that March when William attacked the City – was hoisted and they began to move north virtually parallel with the shore. The six men took an oar each, which had been made by Ragnar with the help of Harald the Limper. They slowly began to get away from the shore but still in a northerly direction instead of the east-nor-east Bjorne considered necessary for reaching Jutland.

After three hours of rowing it was realised that the wind had swung more to a south-easterly, which had helped to get their craft further into the North Sea. Having taken a rest with rowing it was realised that they were again heading for the shore. This time it was Flamborough Head. The sail was furled, the tiller pushed right over, and strong rowing was again commenced.

Their efforts had been rewarded and they had just managed to get round the Head when Ragnar saw something that caused his heart to miss a beat. There was at least a hand-span depth of water at the bottom of the boat, more than could have been driven in by the wind upon the wave tops.

'Bjorne!' he shouted, 'Look at this water! If Sven and I keep rowing as a pair, you and the rest must keep bailing it out.'

A fired-clay gourd was kept on board for this purpose, but soon had to be aided by the use of their tankards. By non-stop actions the water level was kept constant. Taking a deep breath Bjorne put his head below the water level. Sitting back on his bench he said quietly, 'We have trouble here. It looks like the second plank above the keel is coming away. That's because not all the timber we used had dried sufficiently. We have no option. Let's hoist our sail again, put the tiller right over to starboard and keep rowing. We must beach her before we all drown.'

Turning to Margit he said, ' Dear Margit, if Ragnar has no objections you must be in charge of the water pot – and as fast as you can. The rest of us must keep rowing hard. It's getting dark and soon we won't be able to see the shore.'

With a smile Margit replied, 'And if someone wants a short rest from the oars I will have a go.'

Bjorne smiled. Ragnar bent over and kissed her forehead.

All six rowers were nearing exhaustion. The wind was right, the current was right and the incoming tide was right. The problem was that they had to keep pulling the extra weight of water which half-filled the boat no matter how fast Margit bailed water out. Near collapsing, they suddenly felt the keel running over a shingle beach between two cliffs.

With Bjorne in front (being the strongest) they pulled the

wrecked boat up above what they suspected was the high water line, then collapsed against the side opposite the wind. After a few minutes silence, Ragnar, clearing his throat, looked straight at Bjorne in the fading light and said, 'Bjorne, this is really down to you. You took charge in rebuilding this leaking hulk, and when I said that some of the planking was not really up to the quality needed to reach Danemark you said, as always, 'that will do'. We respect you for your strength and fighting ability – Oh, and also to fatten lambs for us to eat, but your unpractical ways will let us down.' There was silence for several seconds. Then a quiet growling voice came from Bjorne's direction.'If you were not my brother and not sitting there next to your wife, I would enable you to swallow your teeth.'

There was further silence which was so penetrating that it seemed to last half an hour. In reality it was not much more than five minutes. It was broken by the voice of Margit.'You must all be hungry, noble warriors. At least the sea has washed off the preserving salt from Bjorne's fine lamb. If my dear husband has been left any teeth to eat with by his brother, I will give him the first piece.'

They all laughed, including Bjorne. With the wind dropping most of them, huddled together with Margit in the middle, slept well after the day's exertions. The exception was Bjorne. He lay there thinking of his brother's comment that he lacked attention to detail and concentration. He thought of the days when he was a boy and an instructive task given to them by the elders was to build a small boat. It became a joke that any boat he built, no matter how small, would sink before leaving the harbour. Thus at the age of nine he was left to look after the pigs, which he was happy to do.

Bjorne had inherited more of the genes of his mother's family than his father's – Ragnar was the other way round. Although as a youth Bjorne appeared to spend much of his time in a dreamland, he could respond, when he felt like doing so, to critical comments with a quick wit. With his pleasant looks, inherited from his mother, this could suddenly change to reveal a deep-seated anger. At the age of only thirteen years he had snatched his father's sword and attempted to strike down an older youth who said he was just a pretty boy who would never be accepted as a Viking. Although an inner fear of violence was normally there, such was the explosive power of his anger that by his seventeenth birthday Bjorne the Red was accepted not just as a Viking, but as a Berserker. The fit of madness that the berserker experienced was often referred to as berserkergang (going berserk). Men who were thus seized showed strength which seemed impossible to human power.

According to the sagas their teeth chattered and the face swelled and became redder. The great rage developed, under which they howled like wild animals, bit the edge of their shields and cut down everything and everybody they met, friend or foe. Bjorne's father was far removed from the concept of a Berserker. His fighting was that of necessity and not of desire. His love of tools from an early age had led to him becoming a carpenter, equally content in building a longboat or fashioning table bowls inscribed with runes chosen for artistry rather than an historic saga. These were the qualities inherited by his youngest son, Ragnar.

* * *

As dawn gave way to the full light of day they could see to the North a long expanse of desolate cliffs and beaches. Those with the best eyesight thought they could see a small township near a rising cliff, perhaps ten miles away.'That's probably Skartborg,' said Einar Hairfair.'The Normans are building a big castle on that cliff overlooking the town.'

'If we go there we will look very obvious and the Normans would certainly give us trouble,' said Ragnar.'With winter round the corner and the boat being beyond sufficient repair we can't stay here. What do you suggest Bjorne?'

'Our only choice is to get back to Jorvik. Get our weapons out of the boat and all food that is still eatable. We will have a good meal before we start. We have three helmets between us that we managed to find when we first discarded them after Stamford

Bridge. I will have one, so draw lots for who is going to have the other two. We will only wear them if we see Norman horsemen about to charge us. Ragnar and friends, do you agree with me on this?'

'A point of detail,' replied Ragnar,' I think we should not just leave the old boat here but drag it up the track between these cliffs to those distant bushes well away from the beach, so no one will know we have been here without a reason to be searching for us.'

'A good idea,' said Bjorne. The others agreed. It took half-an-hour to drag the boat up the track and into the bushes before they decided to have their extended breakfast. Margit said she did not feel hungry,' But I will have something later.' No one, not even Ragnar, saw her previously sneaking into some bushes to be sick. This was because with the aid of a net he had been otherwise occupied in catching two plovers and an oyster catcher to augment supplies.

They could see some people working in a field some distance away. Margit said it was probably one of the last fields to be harvested for wheat. The barley would be in by now.'If we go to the south I believe we will come to Driffield. My father has a sister who lives there and I went with him and mother two years back. There is a good road there which goes to Stamford Bridge and then into Jorvik.'

'It must be only an hour or so before midday,' said Bjorne, butting in.'So let's get moving and try what you said Margit. We can alter our route should we have to.' This was met with everyone's approval.

As they moved off Ragnar said 'We must look more like serfs or cottagers so that those who meet us will believe us when we say we are going on for final harvesting work. We must hide our weapons as best as possible. I have already got my helmet down the back of my jerkin, which makes me look like a hunchback.'

This was greeted with laughter. They would not have laughed if they knew they were on a convergent path that meant they would meet up with King Sweyn and his Viking and Saxon army.

* * *

Twice they passed greetings with peasant farm workers, leaving Margit and Ragnar, as they looked less Danish, to say they were on their way to Driffield where they had a job. Passing through a small village in the late afternoon they were again accosted by some villagers.'Haven't you heard! A big army of Vikings and Saxons from Wessex have landed and are probably in Driffield now. They are going to sack Jorvik! Best not go to Driffield until it's all over.'

Directly they were out of earshot of the villagers Bjorne said, 'The way I look at it we have two choices. We can carry on to Driffield and join up with Sweyn's men and hope we can be carried into Yorvik by them without being killed in the fighting. Or we can swing north now, move along the edge of the moors then come down to enter Jorvik by a north gate that's only used by local people on foot and usually has no guard over it. That will be the opposite side from where Sweyn is likely to attack.'

All agreed that they should take the northern route, although it would take longer.

As they made their way in the direction of the North Moors they kept a continual look out for any signs of Norman horsemen. They knew that William must have several outrider teams whose main function would be to follow Sweyn's movements. Fortunately, they only met a few serfs, none of whom had heard the news of Sweyn's army. Margit asked them to not mention they had seen her husband and friends if any Norman scouts came along. They readily agreed to say nothing.

Dusk was approaching when just off the track they were following they saw a dilapidated barn, which they thought probably housed cattle in the winter months. As the rain of the last two hours showed no sign of lifting, they decided this would have to be their home for the night. The men took it in turns to keep lookout, each being fully armed and wearing one of the helmets.

Refreshed by a good night's sleep, they set off at dawn, having augmented their shrinking rations with some turnips stolen from a nearby field. Luck was with them as only once did they see some

Norman horsemen in the far distance who were going away from them. Fortunately they had not appeared to have seen them.

* * *

King Sweyn II, who was part Norse and part Dane in parentage, was actually born in England. He walked with a limp, was courageous but never really successful in battle. He managed to break into Jorvik, in spite of William having fired much of it once again in order to diminish its use as an HQ for Sweyn in the forthcoming winter. Although Sweyn and Edgar of Wessex managed to have temporary control of much of the North, William was able to commence his harrowing initially to the west and north of Jorvik.

King William, with much of his Norman forces still intact, offered Sweyn a considerable bribe to return to Danemark with his Vikings and desert Edgar and his Saxons. That winter the people of Northumbria, particularly the sector that was to become known as Yorkshire, suffered the full murderous forces of William's harrowing of the land so that crops could not grow and the killing of those who tried to oppose it. This included the devastation of Durham and the land up to the Tyne. It was the fifth morning since the seven survivors had beached their boat on the sea shore. Their rations were now virtually extinct and they got by with what they could steal, including a chicken. The decision to reach the edge of the North Moors and follow a track to the west proved to be correct. The trees growing along the moor edge provided good cover, although it slowed them down. They passed just north of Pickering then turned south near Appleton, which they reached just before dusk. It was here that Harald the Limper stole the chicken. A plump white hen who only managed a few clucks before Harald had rung its neck.

'We can't camp here for the night,' said Bjorne, 'It's too open and not far enough away from the owner of our supper. We definitely saw Normans in Pickering and he or she may have spotted us and informed them. Fortunately, there's a good moon tonight. Let us press on for a good hour and find a copse off the road where we can hide up and light a small fire and cook the hen.'

They walked on for twenty minutes and suddenly saw a solitary figure, dressed like a serf as far as they could see in the dark. Seeing them at the same time he shot off the road and ran away over a field that he was obviously familiar with. The seven pressed on for another half hour as the moonlight began to be obscured by passing clouds.

'Look right.' whispered Ragnar.'I've been looking there and it's not just a clump of trees but a small wood, I hope.'

Following Ragnar they worked their way through the wood for at least two hundred paces. Everyone scoured around to find small pieces of broken branches that were reasonably dry. Einar always carried some fine kindling with him as well as flints, as did the quiet Sven Olafsen, and in ten minutes he had a small fire going.

After eating the well-smoked chicken, with the last of a few beans each, Bjorne said 'we should now put that fire out. We can only be about three leagues from Jorvik and therefore must not signal our presence for anyone else who comes along the road.'

After drinking from a stream that ran through the wood and filling up the two flasks they still had, they set off south again aiming to bypass the small village of Bulmer. Suddenly they heard the sounds of horses hooves at a gallop. The wood was still obscuring the curved track so they could not see who they were, but knew they must be Normans.

Bjorne pushed Margit into a ditch and told her to cover herself up with ferns and brambles.

'Men, to your arms and put the helmets on. Quick, move into that sodden field. Yes Ragnar, away from Margit. Mounted Norman knights are not so agile in the mud.'

Because of the need to hide their weapons the six Danes had no spears or shields. They did have swords, shorter than normal but just as sharp, as well as knives and axes. They had just reached the middle of the sodden field when they saw four mounted Normans come round the curve of the track. They each had lances and shields, which they raised in attack mode on seeing the Vikings. Bjorne stopped dead in his tracks and still without moving he stared at the on-coming horsemen muttering to himself and reddening in the face and neck. The Normans were about to meet a Viking Berserker.

The lead Norman came straight for Bjorne with his lance lowered. With an upward thrust of his sword Bjorne shattered the lance as the horse came level, with his knife he stabbed the horse straight in the heart, upon which the poor beast collapsed on the spot to die. Falling to the ground in his unwieldy armour the Norman was at the Viking's mercy, and was despatched with a thrust of the knife between the breast armour and the helmet, severing the jugular.

The three other Normans rode around Bjorne to attack the four Danes who were in an open semi-circle some twenty paces beyond Bjorne. With his sword in his hand Sveyn Olafsen, Ragnar's friend, received the full penetrating thrust from a lance and fell down vomiting blood to die within a minute. As the Norman turned his horse, more slowly than he expected in the churned up field, Ragnar managed to bring his sword down with his maximum power on to the top of the rider's right leg. His armour gave the leg considerable protection from being severed, but there was enough power and inflicted pain to bring him to the ground. As Ragnar leapt upon the prostrate Norman he did not see the third horseman bearing down on him. But Bjorne did and noticed that his visor was fully open. With enormous strength he threw his axe which embedded itself in the Norman's face. Shrieking with pain and blinded by blood, he rode off the field and, unlikely to survive, was not seen again. Meanwhile, on the first charge of the three Normans, Harald the Limper, Einar Hairfair, and Sven Olafsen waving their swords, decided the best way to deal with the two Normans aiming to put them down was to keep zigzaging on the sodden ground as they could turn quicker than the horses. Harald, not being as nimble as Einar, was caught a glancing blow on his head from a lance – but Harald had drawn the long straw to wear a helmet, and the point of the lance skidded off. Frustrated by Harald, Sven and Einer, this Norman knight attacked Ragnar, wounding him in the arm, which he had hardly noticed at the time. He was finally killed jointly by the two Viking brothers. His horse must have been treated kindly by his master as he stayed there looking down at his corpse. 'Stay with us old girl, we might be able to feed you,' Ragnar said as he stroked the mare. 'Margit can ride you and she is far less of a weight than that fat old Norman.' From the ditch where she hid Margit was able to see part of the battle, which had lasted only six or seven minutes. As she prepared to climb out of the ditch she saw the surviving Norman gallop away northwards.

'Your God Odin must have been watching you, Bjorne the Red. You saved our lives, but why did you have to kill the horse?'

'Margit, it gave me great pain in my heart, certainly no pleasure, but I knew it was the only way to deal with the Normans' leader. First we must bury our Viking comrade Sven, killed in the fight, before we get on to Jorvik as fast as we can.'

After doing so they all sang a Christian hymn, Margit said a prayer, and a cross was stuck into the earth. Next to it was a split section of a bough on which Bjorne had crudely carved some Viking runes. 'Ragnar, you would have made a far neater job but I fear your right arm is not up to it. We will take strips out of this Norman's shirt and Margit you must bind Ragnar's wound to slow the bleeding.'

It was decided to put both Ragnar and Margit on the mare and make their way into the next village, regardless of who was there. For extra defence they each had a helmet now and a lance between them which was strapped to the side of the horse. Bjorne had the longer sword he took from the first Norman. As they entered Bulmer villagers either averted their eyes or gave that look that intimated they wanted to talk to them. A middle-age man whose dress suggested he was a freeman rather than a serf asked them 'Are you scouts for the Danish King?' adding, 'We are told that William has set fire to part of Jorvik and now departed. If you hurry up you can join the Vikings and their Saxon allies who are probably about to enter the city.'

'Thank you for that information sir,' Bjorne replied.'We are Danish and Saxons here, as this lady will confirm. The only enemies we have are the Normans, who attacked us down the road to Pickering. We are in need of some bread before we move on and perhaps we could trade you with this helmet which one Norman no longer requires.'

'That could have been one of the group of Normans who burnt several houses and killed sheep and cattle not far from here,' commented the freeman.'It seems that King William and his men are retreating for a while up the main north road to Thirsk or even beyond.'

Among the small crowd who had gathered, and obviously respected the views of the freeman, there was an elderly lady who was asking Ragnar if she could see the wound on his arm. It was still bleeding and the surrounding flesh was becoming more swollen and inflamed.

'I will be back in one minute, young man. I have a potion that we use on cuts to help stop them bleed and not go poisoned. Now you chew on some of that bread the Meister is getting for you and I will be back.'

On her return the old lady lifted off the blood-soaked bandage from Ragnar's arm and applied some sweet smelling ointment from a small stone pot.'What is it made of?' asked Margit.

'As you are a Saxon or Celtic girl I will tell you,' said the old lady.'It is a mixture of yarrow leaves and Lady's Mantle. My own grandmother told me it was a well used balm from the Celtic days.'

As they moved off, with Ragnar and Margit still on the mare, they noticed that not all the villagers looked upon them as friends. One or two looked at them in silent disapproval.

Bjorne said that perhaps they always had such miserable faces, but if they were supporters of the Normans there's not much they can do about it. From what the people who helped said, William could have taken all his men to the north for the present.

They moved as fast as they could and did not stop for rest until late afternoon near Strensall. Ragnar had made no complaints but all could see that he was in great pain and clinging on to the horse with only his left hand. Margit pulled back some of the new bandaging from an old shirt that the Meister had given him. 'That looks a nasty red, my love, and giving you pain,' she said. 'But the good news is that the bleeding is definitely slowing up.'

She applied some more of the balm that the old lady had given her, then reversed the bandage to hold it on to the wound.

They had only made another 500 yards when a dozen-strong mounted warriors came galloping towards them. As they pulled up Bjorne's diminished group could see that they were Danish Vikings and greeted them with smiles and a salute.

'Where are you from,' asked the leader. 'We came here with Harald Hadrada and survived the battle at Stamford Bridge,' Bjorne replied. 'This morning we were attacked by four Norman horsemen and we killed three of them. We lost one of our good Vikings and this one on the horse, my brother, is wounded. Is King Sweyn in control of Jorvik? If so, we will go there and rest up.'

'You could have difficulty in finding a good place to stay in Jorvik as the treacherous King William tried to burn the place down as we overpowered his forces. May Woden and Odin look after you good warriors, and your lady.' Bjorne repeated the story of how they had survived the attack by the Norman horsemen. He added: 'This Saxon lady is married to my wounded brother and we can stay with her parents, as long as William the Bastard did not burn their house down.'

'Go and see if Woden has looked after the needs of his good warriors,' said one of the guards. 'And may Jesus Christ give you his blessing,' said the other guard as they all passed through.

They stopped first at Edgar the Butcher, whose house had been spared the fires. He and his wife were overwhelmed to see Margit, who they thought had left them forever. They offered them their own bed so that Ragnar could recover from his wound. Since Margit's departure they had lost their eldest son, aged seventeen, in fighting against the Normans.

They then moved on to Cedric and Hild's more dilapidated

house, which had been partly burnt in the recent troubles. As Bjorne was standing there telling them what had happened, Brietta (who had heard his voice) came rushing in to be taken up in Bjorne's arms.'I am not leaving you again until I am killed or die in bed. I am now asking your father and mother for their permission for us to marry.'

The wedding was one of only two good things that happened that winter of near starvation. The other was Ragnar's eventual recovery from his poisoned wound. They all said it was down to the old Celtic lady's natural balm. Following King Sweyn's acceptance of William's bribe to go back to Danemark, King William began his 'Harrowing of the North' in earnest, reaching a peak from December 1069 to January 1070.

The people of Jorvik suffered less than those in the countryside west and north of the city probably because he needed a base that was more or less free from rebellion. General destruction of homes, stock and crops took place. Men, women and children were slaughtered as far North as the river Tees. Beyond this and up to the Tyne the 'Harrowing' was less general, although William the Bastard set an example of his ruthlessness by the almost complete destruction of the city of Durham.

* * *

'How strangely things grow, and die, and do not die! These are twigs of that great world-tree of Norse belief still curiously traceable'. Thomas Carlyle, 'Lectures on Heroes,' 1841

Chapter Three

The Wages of Stealing a Pig

As diminished rebellions continued in the North the by now obese King William decided to put his second son Rufus in charge of Northumbria. William returned to Normandy, where he died in 1087. Rufus decided that the best way to establish full control in the North was to partition Northumbria. In 1080 at the site of the almost completed castle he founded what was to become the city of Newcastle. From there up to the fluctuating border with Scotland the land was to be called Northumberland. South of the Tyne and down to the river Tees was the County of Durham. The land below and down to the Humber was now called Yorkshire, the biggest county in England.

At Appleton Roebuck it was harvest time in 1109. Just south of the village a small field of wheat had been cut and the sheaves were being stooked. The land workers were five in number, a white-haired older man, a young man and a boy, and two women – the eldest in her sixties. She called to the older man, who looked to be in charge.

'Walter Byrne, you can rest up a bit now, as we're nearly finished. You must look after your heart. The days of Bjorne the Red are long gone.' When she addressed him by two names, the first newly acquired, old Byrne knew that it meant that his wife Brietta was expecting him to obey her advice. Late teenager Gwenda smiled at her mother.

'Well lads,' replied Bjorne looking to his son, 'I've know women in Denmark and England with more clacking tongues than your mother.' Johannes, now twenty-eight, gave a laugh and said ' You wouldn't have it other ways. You worship our mother, like you do your grandson, my nephew Thomas here, because he don't explode with temper like his father did, but just gets on with the work as always.'

They had the tenancy of three small fields, one to lie fallow every third year. They paid rent as well as supplying half the crop to the Norman landlord. It was previously owned by a Saxon. He only took a quarter of the crop. A benefit of the rule of William Rufus, although it lasted only thirteen years, was that he kept the Norman Barons in check and prevented them from building more castles from which they might plunder the country and particularly the North East. Ten years previously this had helped Bjorne to acquire ownership of a two-acre piece of land which had been left derelict following the 'Harrowing' and was considered unproductive, even by the Church. At one time it had the tenancy from the King over considerable land areas and was not interested in holding on to the small property and sold it to Bjorne for forty shillings. He shared the use and upkeep of an ox with several other small land farmers. When asked what took him in old age to work so hard on the land, he replied:

'Idleness was painful after so many years of battles and bitter inter-clan feuds.'

It was in February 1070 when Bjorne and Brietta were married by Thomas of Bayeaux who was to remain the Bishop at Jorvik – or Yerk as some began to call it – until 1100. The old Saxon Church had been burnt down the previous late autumn and a Norman Cathedral was beginning to be built on its site and completed by 1100.

Four months after the wedding Ragnar and Margit had their baby boy christened by Bishop Thomas. They gave the boy two names: Edgar after Margit's father and Sven after Ragnar's Viking comrade killed in the fight with the Norman horsemen. Edgar was also the name of Margit's elder brother who had been killed by departing Normans when King Sweyn captured the city. The birth of the grandson gave much happiness to the elderly Edgar whose wife, also named Margit, had died of the consumption just two years previously. His surviving two sons came to run his butchery business, which had survived the two fires and the 'Harrowing'.

Much more damage had been done to the cloth weaving and dyeing establishment of Cedric and Hild. Following the wedding Harald and Einar helped Bjorne to repair the building, including Bjorne and Brietta's separate living and sleeping place.

To earn a living to keep his family Ragnar found a new place for his original smithy and took on Einar Hairfair to be an apprentice, at which he soon showed talent. Making and sharpening of tools was again the mainstay of their work. But for Ragnar job satisfaction came with fashioning ornaments with and without runes and, more popular, the long chain interlace patterning specialised in by his grandfather back in Danemark. Bjorne found that the smallholder tenant who let him work part of his land was pleased to see his return and within three years his advancing age meant he had given a half of the land for Bjorne to work. He said that within another year he would speak to the Norman Baron's bailiff to see if the strip could be transferred to Bjorne as the official tenant.

* * *

When Rufus became King, as William II , in 1087, Bjorne still had the tenancy of the acre strip just outside the city as well as the ownership of the two acres at Appelton which he had purchased that year. He had managed to save twenty-five shillings, approximately a shilling and six pence every year since his marriage to Brietta, and raised the forty shillings purchase price by a fifteen shilling loan from Ragnar. After a year trying to work both pieces of land by himself and his first son Alan, now sixteen, aided at sowing and harvest time by ten-year-old son Johannes, he put Alan in charge of farming the acre strip. At first this pleased Alan immensely: he was already one up from being a serf or a villein. He was a freeman. Although Bjorne had acquired a horse, which had the dual purpose of transporting him back and forth from the city and ploughing the two acres, he could see that this was uneconomic, apart from becoming progressively more tiring. In the autumn of 1090 he found a house, previously occupied by a Saxon widow lady who had passed on, which was to rent in Appleton. With three rooms this would be fine for him and Brietta , young Johannes and the two young daughters. Alan Byrne (as he called himself in order to sound more 'English') would stay lodging with Cedric and Hild in his parents old room.

Although dark haired, like his mother, Alan had several of the traits of his father. His lack of patience led him to cut corners in his work on the acre strip, resulting in smaller harvests which he could not put down to the weather. Bjorne had suffered these problems initially but age helped him to control natural impatience. Then there was the loss of a pig. His father would provide the money to purchase two or three piglets which he would fatten up, and manure the plot while doing so, until ready to be sold in the market. At night they would be shut in a rough but sturdy shed with the door held firmly closed with a padlock Alan had scrounged from Uncle Ragnar.

It was in his second year of pig keeping that Alan lost a pig almost ready for the market. He said that when he arrived one morning the door was open with no sign of the padlock and two pigs were still there. He added it could have been a wolf who had come down from the North Moors.' Wolves are not known to have the ability to unlock padlocks without a key,' snorted landlord Cedric.'In any case, where were the signs of blood?'

Alan flew into a rage saying 'I don't expect my Grandfather to call me a liar and suggest that I sold the missing pig.' With the ageing Hild looking on, Cedric quietly said, 'Alan, I never mentioned the pig being sold. To me that suggests that's just what you have done. I will have to report this to your father. I will also let him know that you have been over-indulging in drinking the ale I produce and then getting more down the taverns.'

'Yes,' added Hild, 'Your mother would be most upset at knowing what's going on.'

This hurt Alan and the colour drained from his face. He loved his mother, who he resembled in looks, more than his father.

'I'm going out, grandma. I do not want to upset you.'

He made his way to the Boar's Head, a tavern he occasionally visited where the customers were mainly young like himself and ready for banter. He ordered a tankard of ale, which cost a farthing. As he supped gently on his tankard he began to calm down and regret that he had indeed sold the missing pig and he would have to confess this to his father.

Two young well-built fair haired men who he knew came in and joined Alan after filling their tankards. He knew he was probably in for some leg pulling but was prepared to accept it.

'Alan, what's it like not to know when you get out of bed each day whether you are going to act like a good Celt , give people potions and do a bit of wizardry, or you're going to be a Viking berserker and take some poor bastard's head off.'

'Well, my good friends shall I say that it makes life interesting,' Alan replied with a smile.' Now if I was just a good old reliable Saxon pudding, like you two, life would get a bit boring.'

They all laughed. That's the way Alan wanted it to be that evening.

A tall older man who Alan had never seen before moved closely to Alan and his friends.

'Is this the lad who stole one of his father's pigs and tried to pretend it was eaten by a wolf who happened to be padding past his patch?'

'Ignore him Alan, ignore him,' said one of the Saxon lads.

For the second time that night Alan's face went white. Then as he just stood there glaring at the intruder it began to go red and he was breathing deeply. The stranger was about to move away when Alan launched himself upon him, bringing his tankard down upon his head, punching him and kicking him until he collapsed to the floor.

The landlord and his potman came rushing from behind the bar and grabbed hold of Alan.'Now young 'un we don't know what was said but you're going outside to cool off. You can come back tomorrow, but no more fighting.'

Alan leant facing the outside wall of the Tavern regaining his breathe and his composure. Suddenly he felt a terrible pain in his upper back. The stranger he had attacked had knifed him.

With the aid of some planking loaned by the landlord the two Saxon lads carried the dying Alan to his lodging. By the time Cedric and Hild saw him he was dead.

The elderly couple were heartbroken and embraced each other, weeping together.'Our only grandson is dead, because we entered into a pointless argument with him over the ownership of a damned pig,' sobbed Edgar.'If only we could put the time backwards our words would never have been uttered,' cried Hild, 'and our lovely grandson would still be with us. All he had was nineteen years of life, and just when we thought life in Jorvik was becoming more peaceful.'

The two young Saxons stood there with eyes watering at the loss of a friend and feeling they were intruders in the family grief. The bigger of the two – and slightly older – shuffled his feet and looking at Cedric said: 'Would you like me to go to Appleton Roebuck and tell his father and mother, who I believe is your daughter, of what has happened?'

'We would be most grateful if you would,' said Cedric.'My wife will write a note, as I'm not very good at the writing, to say who you are.'

'I am Edmund. Our family have started to use a second name now, and that is Thomson as my grandfather was called Thomas and my father is his son, if you see what I mean.' Getting over his confusion, Edmund added: 'I promise you I will set off walking to Appleton at the first light in the morning. I should be there by noon. I might be lucky and get a ride on a cart going part of the way.'

The other Saxon, known as John the Tanner, explained that his father counted on him as the only help in his tanning business, otherwise he would go.

In the middle of their sleepless night Hild suddenly exclaimed, 'Oh good Lord, what do we do about Frejya and the baby she is expecting?'

Hesitating for a minute, Cedric said, 'We have no choice we will have to let Brietta and Bjorne know.'

Almost a year previously one of Alan's friends from the Boar's Head had introduced him to his sister, Frejya. They were immediately attracted to each other. They talked of marriage but Frejya's father was opposed to his daughter marrying a tenant farmer's labouring son. Alan had tried to soften his view with the fact that they were both of Danish Viking origins, but to no avail. He decided that if he could save some money to put down as rent for some accommodation, either in the City or nearby, then both their parents would accept their marriage. This was Alan's reason for stealing and selling his father's pig. He felt it had become more necessary as Frejya's pregnancy had begun to show.

Like many young people (and those who wanted to relive the past) they had taken part in the May Day's celebrations that year with great enjoyment. They had joined in with a hundred or more who had danced their way out of the City into the country. On freshly greened common land and under trees whose summer leaves were about to break through, couples gave way to their lust for each other and some for their lasting love. With control abandoned as they lay entwined in the woodland, the love of Frejya and Alan for each other led to the creation of their son, Thomas Byrne.

* * *

It was not long after eleven that morning when Edmund Thomson arrived at the house of Bjorne and Brietta in Appleton. He had been fortunate in getting a lift for over two miles in a farmer's cart.

Brietta was in the house with her daughter Gwenda who was helping her mother in the weaving of hazel to form baskets. Edmund gave Brietta the note to read and in faltering words told her of the death of her eldest son Alan. She went white as the facts unfurled and fell back in her chair sobbing. Controlling herself she said to Gwenda:

'Run now to the field and tell your father and Johannes that I said they should come home immediately as Alan is dead.'

Within five minutes in the house listening to what Edmund could tell him Bjorne stood up and stared without moving, his face having gone red. Suddenly, he turned to Brietta:

'I am going into Jorvik on the horse and I shall not return until I find this man who killed our son. When I do, I shall take his life.'

Putting her arms around him, Brietta said quietly, 'My dear Bjorne your hands with the worsening of the little fingers, the curse of the Viking finger, do not enable you to grip a killing weapon any more. What we have here now, is an English life, not a Danish Viking life, as proud as all our family are of your origin.'

'No, father' Johannes interjected, 'Mother is right. I will go to Yorvik with Edmund here. He would find the man who did this if anyone could. I will then go to the steward of the local court and, with luck, we will see this man hanged.'

Bjorne, now slumped in a chair, had tears running down his face and looked even older than his sixty years. 'Go back to Jorvik with the good Edmund here and see if our old friends Cedric and Hild, even older than me, can give any further information. Also, let your uncle Ragnar and aunt Margit know what has happened.'

Johannes and Edmund found Ragnar in his smithy. Perhaps appropriately he and Einar were working on sharpening some tools and knives at the time, currently more in demand than their jewellery work. Neither of them suffered from the Viking finger to impede their work.

Expressing his sorrow at the death of his nephew Alan, he listened carefully at what they could tell him. Then he asked Edmund, 'Do you know who now has the knife that killed Alan?'

'I am certain that the landlord at the Boar's Head has it carefully wrapped up, just in case the court steward was even bothered to hold an inquiry.'

'I will come with you and see if he has it and let us take it away for examination. Einar and I could probably tell if it was made locally. If so, as we know the other three knife makers in Jorvik there would be a chance of finding this stranger.'

Ragnar had no problem in being given the knife, the landlord being glad to get rid of it.

About three weeks later the body of an unknown tall man aged around thirty was found outside the Boar's Head. His tongue had been cut out, his throat cut and he had been stabbed in the heart by someone who knew how to kill. A late drinker from the tavern, who had stopped to empty his bladder against the wall before going home, said he saw two middle-aged men dragging the body to the tavern. They were muttering something to each other and spoke with what were Danish accents, he believed. When Freyja gave birth to Thomas Byrne much was forgiven by her parents. Organised by Ragnar, a meeting was held in the city with Alan's parents where it was decided that Frejya and her baby would live with Bjorne and Brietta at Appleton Roebuck.

The months passed and within two years Bjorne and Brietta and the whole family regarded Frejya as well as Thomas as part of that family. Frejya helped in the house as well as on the small farm, which kept her mind away from periodic deep depressions, particularly as she noticed that her dear little boy was slowly looking more and more like his father. After another twelve years, in the late winter of 1109 Bjorne, now widely known as Walter Byrne, suffered a heavy cold that had gone to his chest. This turned to pneumonia and after fighting for his breathe for a week, the true Viking who loved being a farmer passed on. Whether it was to Heaven or Valhalla, only he would know. For all those who knew him the brilliance of his life would never be repeated.

* * *

Nine years before the death of Bjorne (Walter Byrne), closely followed by his brother Ragnar, Henry the First became King. Born in Selby, Yorkshire, he was the youngest son of William the Conqueror and married Matilda, the daughter of Malcolm King of Scots and Margaret, the sister of Edgar Atheling. This made him popular with the ordinary English folk. He also marched against several Norman Barons who did not show allegiance to their king. To please the English even more he learnt to read and speak the English tongue. Henry's son William, of whom his father had great faith in keeping the new peacefulness in the English and Normandy lands, drowned at sea when only eighteen. Henry's wife Matilda had died in 1118, so he set about securing the succession for Matilda his daughter. Henry died in 1135. He was a great king in that he did what was best for his people, who wanted nothing as much as to be safe from persecution by the great landowners.

Thus it was that in the towns and countryside of the North, and Yorkshire in particular, the people finally recovered from the great Harrowing and gained freedom from semi-starvation and the constant threat of death which had been the norm. The recovery was certainly the way in Appleton Roebuck. But that was about to change and much of the evil of the old days would return to afflict the ordinary folk. As yet no woman had ruled in England and the Norman barons broke their oath to Matilda as Queen and chose a king to rule over them. This was Stephen, the son of Adela, daughter of William the Conqueror.

The inexperienced Stephen allowed the Barons to build castles on their own land throughout England. He then realised he had to capture these castles and laid siege in order to capture them. This led to a number of battles and in his actions he began behaving more and more like his father, the Count of Blois. This led many Barons to declare their allegiance to Matilda in 1138. With the supporters of Matilda growing in strength, a state of civil war arose in England. Meanwhile, Matilda's uncle, David, King of the Scots, invaded the north of England to give her support. He marched to Northallerton where he was confronted by a 10,000 strong army of

Norman knights and English footmen who had been collected by the exertions of Thurston, Archbishop of York.

Even though he was over fifty, Thomas Byrne decided that Johannes and his sisters could run the farm at Appleton (which had recently acquired an extra meadow) while he joined the Archbishop's footman soldiers. Johannes said it was the blood of his father Bjorne the Viking running in Thomas's veins.

To encourage the soldiers the Archbishop allowed them to take with them the sacred banners of St. Peter, St. Wilfrid and St. John of Beverley, which were placed on a mast mounted on a cart. As the Scots attacked the English, who had closed up round the cart, Thomas found himself at the mercy of a Scot of much the same age as himself. Thomas had a small shield grasped in his left hand which could do little to defend him from the Scot's sword about to run through him. Suddenly the Scot said:

'I will nae kill ye. My kin also have the Northern Viking finger. Ye must be a Southern Viking, probably Danmark.'

'That's true, very true,' Thomas replied in what he hoped was a casual manner that did not show his fear.

The efforts of the English meant that the Scots could not break their ranks and the English 'victory' (really a stalemate) was called the 'Battle of the Standard'.

Afterwards Thomas looked at the hands on many of the bodies of the Scots who had been killed, but he could not see any with twisted little fingers. He hoped that the son of a Northern Viking had escaped.

Chapter Four
Langshanks Men

The Battle of Northallerton was but one of the battles fought all over England in the civil war that ensued between Stephen and Matilda. It was a terrible time of anarchy for the English people and agriculture and trade was ruined. Many of the barons locked themselves up in their castles and fed themselves by pillaging the lands of their neighbouring barons and the small holdings of freemen. Many barons committed terrible cruelties. This included pressing men to death in chests full of stones, or fasten a mass of iron to their necks so that they could not sit, nor lie, or sleep.

In Appleton Roebuck Thomas Byrne, grandson of Walter Byrne, and his wife Freda who was named after her mother, managed to survive as no battles or pillaging took place nearby. They had a ready market for their produce in Yerk. Thomas, who had managed to get out of further service in Archbishop Thurston's foot soldiers, drove their cart into the city where he and one of his two sons sold the produce for the best price they could get.

With Matilda finally giving up and living in obscurity in France and the death of Stephen in 1154, Henry II became King and immediately began to clear away the abuses which England and South Wales had endured. He was assisted in this by his Chancellor, Thomas Becket, who became Archbishop of Canterbury. In Yorkshire, as in many areas of England , the well established towns and cities such as Yerk again became involved in international trade. In agriculture more land, much of it at the expense of the royal forests, was brought into production to feed the growing population or to produce wool for export to Europe. Thomas Byrne and then his son William looked for extra land so that they could increase their flock of sheep which was producing wool equal to the quality of that produced down in Suffolk. However, because of the hard time of the Stephen and Matilda civil war they had spent all their money reserves. Following the death of his father, William Byrne decided to borrow money to purchase good sheep grazing land within a half mile of Appleton. As usury was banned by the Christian Church, he went to a Jewish money lender in Yerk who had been recommended to him by a distant cousin, Reginald Ragner. Ragner and his partner Ivor Fairhall were specialists in the design of Scandinavian style jewellery. They needed money to set up a prestige premises in Petergate and found Abraham Danziger, a courteous elderly Jew, offered lower interest rates over five years than many others in the city. Accompanied by Ragner, William Byrne met Danziger in his small business chamber at his home in a poorer part of Yerk. He was told that he would have the same special rate for five years as his relative. This was in 1187. Three years later, in the reign of Richard the Lionheart, a terrible thing happened.

Partly because of what appeared to be the strangeness of Jewish ways and partly because of some cases of clipping silver coins in money advanced in loans, the mob rose up and 150 Jews took refuge in the Royal castle, as they were officially supposed to be protected by the king. Reginald Ragner was one of the few citizens who protested at this persecution, but few other businesses followed his example as it could mean permanent damage to their own trade. Most of the local gentry did nothing because they had borrowed heavily from the Jews.

The Castle Keep they took refuge in (where Cliffords Tower was later built) was of wooden construction. Rather than accept offers to convert to Christianity, the Jews fired the Keep themselves and all perished in the flames.

* * *

Edward the First came to the throne in 1272 after the long reign of Henry III. Henry had been a weak king who gave way to the demands of many of his 'foreign friends' in France. Opposition from several barons, led by Simon de Montfort, saw more decisions given to Parliament, not that it led to any betterment for the ordinary people. Open war broke out between the king and the barons. As a rule the poorer districts, such as the North, were for Henry. The Midlands were divided and the South and London, the wealthier parts of England, warmly supported Simon de Montfort. Edward's father, Henry III, had handed over sufficient power to him that in 1270 he had legislation approved for the expulsion of Jews from England. They were not allowed back for nearly another 400 years.

Landowners in Yorkshire and the rest of the north, whether with large acreages or with less than ten, noticed immediate advantages in the stability that the reign of Edward Longshanks (or 'Langshanks' in the North) quickly showed. Cracks began to appear in the old demesne agricultural system where apart from small areas of common land most of it belonged to the Manor House in the area, much of it worked in the small strip system of an open field by villeins who paid the local lord for their cottages and land . In Appleton Roebuck, the acreage owned by the Byrne family freemen farmers had now grown to twelve acres. Some said that this growth had been helped considerably by the terrible death of the Jews in Yerk in 1190 in that the debts owed to the money lenders died with them. It was also an indication that the rights obtained by the barons from King John in 1215 under the Magna Carta were now beginning to spread down to the people, although not yet to abolish serfdom. For such people as the Byrnes to own land was still unusual. John Byrne, grandson of the William Byrne who had arranged the loan from the money lenders, now ran the farm with the help of his wife Freda and the eldest son John William Byrne. Their daughter Gwenda, aged twelve when Edward came to the throne, helped her mother in the home and on the farm at harvest time. The second son, Walter, started helping his father and elder brother on a part-timer basis as needed, such as at harvest time.

In Yerk, or 'York' as it was now being referred to in documents and even by some in speech, great interest was being shown in the rising of the great Gothic cathedral. Work started in 1220 on the site of the Norman church but it would not be completed until 1472.

King John had granted York its first charter back in 1212 for trading rights in England. By 1270 imports in wine were coming in to York from France and cloth, wax and canvas from the low countries. Timber and furs came into York from the Baltic. Exports included grain and wool, with a small amount of these coming from the Byrne's farm in Appleton.

The development of the economy in the north east, London and other parts of England was partially driven by the growth in the population. It was around 1.5 million when the Domesday Book was prepared in 1086 and rose to over 4 million in King Edward's time.

This time of growth in York was also the time when the first merchant companies were being formed that handled the import-export business. At an early age young Walter Byrne was learning to read and write by his mother. Freda herself had been taught by her mother who also taught other children in the area for a small payment from those parents who could afford it. Edgar Svenson, a distant relative in York, who the Byrnes had kept contact with, was working as a partner in the office of one of the new export-import merchants and told them that if Walter wanted a change from farm work he could find him a position as a clerk's helper in his office. Furthermore, if he wished he could stay at the home of Edgar Svenson and his wife Margaret as travelling from Appleton every day would not be practical.

At a meeting of the four adults and young Walter Byrne in the Svenson's house in York, the details were thrashed out and it was agreed that Walter would take the job for which he would receive a payment of sixpence a week but free board and lodging at Edgar and Margaret's home.

The liking that Edgar had for the young Walter Byrne was based on several reasons.

He knew that by stories passed down to him by his own father and grandfather that he and the Byrnes of Appleton Roebuck were related through their great-great-grandfathers being brothers from Denmark. A colouring feature was red or auburn hair which came out in some of the descendants with both Walter and himself having red hair, as did Gwenda Byrne. Whereas John Byrne had blond hair when younger and now that he was in his fifties he was beginning to suffer from the Viking finger that appeared now and again but not in all generations. This was in contrast to Walter and Edgar Svenson, who were practical, down-to-earth, people who must always be working, while John Byrne would spend any spare time playing his bone flute. As he was also knowledgeable on herbal remedies for various ailments, Edgar pointed out that in his side of the family there had been a distant Celtic lady who was believed to be a white witch.

Two years went past and Walter Byrne made great strides in his abilities to read all trading documents and write comprehensive reports on their legality and profitability, even if he was not always correct in his predictions. Edgar thought this was down to the character trait he had noticed of cutting corners on occasions. He had also noticed that unlike himself, Walter could become quite argumentative.

It was about this time that York received another stimulation to the economy. King Edward decided to make York a base for his war on Scotland, much to Walter's interest. This was after his subjugation of Wales. The annexation of much of Wales started when Llewelyn the Prince of Wales assumed greater importance than his predecessors during Henry III's reign and intimated that he would expect more under Edward Longshanks (so-called because of his great height). When Llewelyn proposed to marry the daughter of Simon de Montfort and repeatedly put off paying allegiance to the new English King, Edward invaded Wales in 1277. The Welsh made a vigorous resistance, but were hemmed in among the mountains of Snowdonia and forced to come to terms. Llewelyn was allowed to marry his intended bride, but only to keep Anglesey and the districts of Snowdon as his principality. Peace continued for three years when Llewelyn's brother David who had been on the English side suddenly attacked Haywarden Castle. Llewelyn sprung back into action in the south of Wales while David attempted to defend the north. The outcome was that Llewelyn was killed during a skirmish on the river Wye and David was captured and then condemned to a traitor's death, which means he was hung, drawn and quartered.

Edward then annexed the whole of Wales. As his son Edward had been born in Carnarvon he was the next Prince of Wales. Edward I then came to York where he was building up an army to invade Scotland with the objective of bringing about a union of the two countries.

Walter Byrne was twenty-two by then and began to wrestle with the desire to join the King's army or to look more to his future of becoming the manager, and perhaps even the owner of the prosperous export-import company. In fact the latter was a possible development as Edgar Svenson was now over fifty-five and not in very good health. Having lost a son and a daughter from diseases in their childhood in some way he regarded Walter as a son. His father and mother arrived from Appleton to persuade him not to join the army and be seriously wounded if not killed, but to stay with the company. Edgar was in tears as he pleaded with Walter.

After quietly listening to the advice that they were all offering, Walter made this announcement.'I do not know why I feel this urge to join the King in battle. However, I feel that it could lead to perhaps lasting peace between England and Scotland which would improve the prosperity of all the people, and not just the barons. Therefore, I will go with the King for this one battle but not for a long-term campaign. I am sure that this duty I feel I must carry out will then be completed. I will then return to our business here which I am sure my uncle Edgar will continue to run in his own efficient way.'

John Byrne glowered at his son: 'You've got it all worked out, my boy. Your mother and I let you come here to work for your uncle at a time when we just about had our heads above water on the little farm. It is true that you worked hard here, but now to satisfy a whim you leave your uncle in the lurch and think you will go off fighting for a little glory and just return after a year not realising that either you or the King, or both of you, could be killed or badly wounded. If the King is killed then the next one could be harmful for us the ordinary free people, let alone the poor serfs. We know where we are with Edward Langshanks.'

Walter's mother put his hand in hers and looking him in the eyes said:

'You will be here for at least a month training to be a useful soldier. Therefore, at the end of the training if you realise it might be best for you, and not just us, if you do not go off to fight the Scots, just sneak away and hide with us in Appleton until the King and his army have departed.'

'That, Mother, I will do if I change my mind.'

Walter Byrne did not change his mind. He made application to train in York for King Edward's army and found that the attack upon the Scots was not imminent. In consequence his training period was limited to one day a week, which meant he could keep working for Edgar Svenson, whose former partner had died, much as before. This continued for nearly a year, by which time Walter was in fact the manager in all but name for the still expanding merchant company.

To complicate things further the relationship he had with a girl friend Edwina had in time become a deeper affair than either had originally visualised. He knew that Edwina Rawlinson had come from Selby to live in York about two years ago when she was seventeen. He had met her when she came to the house to take reading and writing lessons from Edgar's wife Margaret. She was earning her keep working as a milliner's assistant and all that she would tell him as to why she had left Selby was, 'I had an argument with my parents and I do not wish to discuss it.'

It was a week or so after he had first done his one day a week army training that they had first exchanged kisses. A few weeks later Walter Byrne initially thought it might be a decisive occasion when Edwina had called for an English lesson while both Edgar and Margaret were out for at least two hours.

Having taken Edwina to his room their embraces became more passionate so he gently pulled her to him on his bed. As he kissed her bare breasts she suddenly pushed him away and leapt up.

'As much as I now love you, Walter, I am not prepared to end up in child outside of marriage. This is what I was faced with in Selby and why I left.'

'But there are ways we can use to release our full passion and love but will stop you being in child,' Walter said quietly.

Edwina began to cry.'Don't tell me about horrible ways such as soaking nettles in cow's pee and placing it in me before you insert your thing. I'm not going to do that and in any case a friend of mine did it and it didn't work. She had a baby which died in two days.'

Walter stood up and gently put his arms around her.'If that is so upsetting for you, it will not happen. When I have done the duty I feel I have to do and go off and fight for my King, we can talk of marriage if we are both of the same feeling.'

Edwina returned his hug and whispered to him, 'I will wait for you and you alone. Please try and keep from harm so you can return still as a whole.'

* * *

After thinking over what she had said William realised that the girl from Selby who had suffered the indignity of useless birth control was in fact Edwina herself. This was why the poor girl had left Selby. He loved her more for her courage.

Edward the First, about to win the title of the Hammer of the Scots, made great use of Parliament, which helped to maintain stability in the country. It also brought in regular sums of money which he needed for his oncoming war on Scotland.

In 1287 Alexander III, King of Scots, died suddenly leaving a succession crisis. His throne looked likely to pass to his infant granddaughter, Margaret, the Maid of Norway, who was the daughter of Norway's king. Edward had planned that his own son, who was to become King Edward II, should marry Margaret and thus control Scotland through this marriage. The plan was scuppered when Margaret died en route to Scotland.

As a recognised expert on legal matters of state Edward was chosen by the Guardians of Scotland to adjudicate the many claims to the Scottish crown, as England and Scotland had enjoyed a lengthy period of peaceful co-existence. The Guardians were in for a rude shock.

Edward insisted that he be recognised as feudal overlord of the Scots before a new king be appointed. Edward's initial role was to adjudicate over the two rival claimants, Robert Bruce and John Balliol. If there were more than two then, under medieval law, only a judge could pronounce a verdict. Edward demanded authority as a judge, which meant overlordship.

Edward's plan worked, with other claimants coming forward to swear allegiance and thereby becoming his vassals and it did not matter who became King, as Balliol found when he took the crown of Scotland, to help fight his wars. This led to the start of rebellion.

Walter Byrne's long wait was over. So it appeared was any further delay in the forthcoming marriage with Edwina, as long as he returned as a 'whole man'.

One person who would not be at the wedding, assuming Walter returned, was his father. At the age of fifty-two John Byrne had dropped dead of a heart attack.'This was because he worked from dawn to dusk every day of his life from the age of twelve,' said Freda his wife to the complete family who had gathered to pay their respects before his funeral. Turning to Walter, she said harshly, 'If you had done your duty to your father and stayed to help him, with your strength he would still be here. But your other callings had to come first. As it is I do not know what we would have done without the dedication of John William, our Gwenda and recently John William's son Richard who has helped out since he was ten.'

With tears in his eyes, Walter looked at his mother pleadingly and with the opening and closing of his mouth from which no words came. He knew that if he put his arm around her, as he wanted to, she would push him away. Four days later the funeral service for John Byrne was held at Appleton's small church, which was situated alongside the nunnery. It was attended by all the family, including Edgar Svenson and his equally elderly wife Margaret, and most of the local villagers known to the family. There was one stranger present. This was Edwina. Walter had persuaded her to attend as a signal to his mother and the rest of the family that his intention, following what he considered was his military duty, was to settle down as a married man maintaining his contact with the rest of the family. In this context he would help his mother when he could.

He had hardly returned to York when he was informed that as a trained foot soldier he must be ready the following day to depart from York with King Edward's army to pacify the rebellion in Scotland. He made an emotional farewell to Edwina and the Svensons who promised that they would send a message to Appleton to inform his mother. In the privacy of his room he promised Edwina that he would only do what was necessary in any fighting so he could return for their marriage.

It was mid-March when the bulk of Edward's army set off from York. The weather was still wintry with a north-east wind bringing in sleet showers. They pulled their cloaks over their knee-length tunics and pulled their hoods up. Few had any armour, perhaps one in twenty had just a breastplate or a helmet. Walter had a helmet which had been passed down the family. That first night the majority of the horsemen and the forward units of the foot soldiers made camp just south of Northallerton – where nearly 160 years earlier the English had defeated the Scottish invaders at the Battle of the Standard. With the temperature near freezing Walter Byrne was lucky to find that his unit had a barn to stay in for the night. In the barn were some broad beans, onions and turnips, which a farmer had left over from the late autumn crops hoping to use them for his family until the next harvest. These were boiled up for a vegetable stew and augmented the bread ration provided by the bakers of York working night and day to provide the army's basic rations for perhaps seven days. After that 'army rations' meant living off the land.

Marching from dawn to dusk, in another two days they reached Durham, with its classic Norman cathedral which had been completed nearly eighty years earlier on the site of an earlier part-Saxon and part-Norman church destroyed by William the Conqueror during his Harrowing of the North.

They crossed the Tyne going through the town of Newcastle that had been founded by the Normans to pacify the North. In a further two days they marched through the length of Northumbria, now living mainly off the land to the detriment of the Northumbrians. Then they came to Berwick.

Berwick-upon-Tweed in the late 13th century had a population larger than Edinburgh. At one time it was considered as the future capital of Scotland.

As the army crossed the Tweed at Coldstream on March 28th the few hundred Scottish soldiers either disappeared to the north or inside the mainly earthen defence walls of Berwick. King Edward made camp outside the walls and summoned the burgesses of Berwick to discuss surrender terms. He waited twenty-four hours but none came forth.

There were a number of his ships in the harbour and one of them discharged several cannon into the town. Whether this was done by intent or by accident, no one knew, but it was taken as the signal for Edward's soldiers to storm in and slaughter up to 5000 Scottish people as well as soldiers. These were violent times. If surrender was rejected, it was what happened in England, Scotland or anywhere in Europe.

Walter Byrne, who had been adjudged as a strong-willed and efficient swordsman in his training, was in the unit that first stormed the north wall. His thoughts on the long march up from York centred on how he would try to avoid the centre of the battles ahead so as to reduce the chance of being killed or badly injured. He had to get back to save the business with Edgar, help his mother with his earnings and to marry Edwina. As the order was given to climb over the walls and attack the enemy all these good intentions disappeared from his mind.

Two Yorkshire men who had trained with him were on each side of him as they got over the wall. Both were speared with pikes through the chest and fell to the ground vomiting blood with their last breath. More men came over the wall and took their place. Walter felt a violent rage possess him and he imagined that he was not really in the midst of the action but hovering above it. Putting his full strength behind his action he swung his sword at the neck of the first pikeman and took his head off. Within seconds he had swung round to plunge his sword point into the ribs of the second pikeman. Walter felt faint but staggering to the ground he slumped on to a step, while the rest of the men in his group stormed forward with the Scottish defenders now in retreat. 'Where is this blood coming from', he asked himself as he came back into the world of reality. It was his left arm above the elbow – fortunately not his sword arm. It had been pierced by a pike or a sword point and was bleeding profusely. He tore the undershirt off one of the dead defenders and used it to make a tourniquet above the wound and stem the blood flow.

Shouting and screaming had risen to a crescendo. Ordinary men, women and even some children of Berwick as well as the erstwhile defenders were now being butchered. He wanted no part of this barbarity of the time and staggered out of the nearest gate. He pretended that his wound was greater than it was in the hope that he could be allowed to join the other seriously wounded men of Edward's army. Little was done for them, other than to be given some bread and broth – if lucky – and allowed to rest up to see if there were some who could be made ready for action before the army resumed its march northwards to conquer Scotland. Those who did not improve by then were left to make their own way home, or die by the wayside.

A group of a dozen or so wounded men, several of them from York and also exaggerating the limitations they were suffering from their wounds, decided to get out of the town in the morning before the survivors took revenge upon them. This did indeed happen on some of the more immobile and seriously wounded.

Marching as fast as he could and leaving some of the more seriously wounded limping behind or being carried on poles as stretchers by their comrades, Walter stopped at the village of Haggerston, five miles south of Berwick. He stopped at a hut, where an old man sat outside looking warily at the group of injured soldiers but ready to sell some turnips or onions. He gave him two groats for some turnips and asked him if he knew where he could get some yarrow leaves or Lady's Mantle.'I know what you want that for,' the old man said quietly.'The ancients used to make it into an ointment to stop wounds bleeding and keep them clean. Go down the road and turn towards the castle and there's an old man in the only hut you see. You ask him.'

'Thank you, sir. Please take this for your help.' Walter Byrne gave him another two groats and hurried down the road but feeling some concern that he might be seen by any regular soldiers or knights in the castle. It would be hard to satisfy them that he was not a deserter.

After knocking on the hut door several times it was opened slightly. A black and white cat shot out, and an elderly ill-dressed peasant peered at him while he explained what he wanted. His reply was limited to, 'You stand there, and I will be right back.'

In two minutes he returned and handed him some ointment wrapped in a piece of linen.

'Now please go and don't let them see you from the castle. It will help your wound to heal young man.'

He thanked him profusely, gave him three pennies, and rejoined the road south to Newcastle.

It took them five days to reach Durham, with several detours to avoid groups of horse soldiers making their way north, presumably to join Edward Langshanks army now subduing Scotland. His Celtic ointment, as he and his four comrades from York called it, had stopped his wound from weeping and the red inflammation that had started to build up had now almost disappeared. All five of them used it on their wounds until it was used up. All five finally arrived in York in an early spring snow storm after nearly two weeks from the slaughter. Walter was pleased to find that his mother, although looking much older, was happy to see him return, as were his brother John William and sister Gwenda, who had got married while he was away. He gave his mother two pounds that he had built up in his savings. This was prompted by the fact that Uncle Edgar was now confined to his bed and he would now be manager of the merchant trading business.

The person who was the happiest at his return in one piece, even if permanently weak in his left arm, was Edwina.

The wedding was attended by Margaret Svenson, Walter's family from Appleton and Edwina's parents from Selby. Music at the reception was supplied by Gwenda playing her fiddle and John William on his bone flute, which was the first time since the death of his father.

Chapter Five

Victory For Yorkshire Rose

The Peasants Revolt of 1381 shook the feudal order and limited the levels of royal taxation for a century to come. Violence in the north of England was not as intense as in the south, although York, Yorkshire and Lancashire saw militant action. The main risings were in Essex, led by Jack Straw and in Kent led by Wat Tyler. The rebels appealed to King Richard II that the customary services by villeins and labourers to local lords should be abolished. Instead, the rent paid for the land should be four pence an acre instead of the former services and that all should have liberty to buy and sell in fairs and markets. These demands were originally granted by the King.

In Appleton Roebuck, as elsewhere throughout the country's predominantly rural villages and small towns, these developments were slowly applied and widely welcomed. The Byrne family were still freemen working their twelve acres and were now able to share two oxen for ploughing with other local freeman farmers.

The family was headed by Richard Byrne, the grandson of John William Byrne whose brother Walter had become a successful merchant in York and was distinguished in later life by his withered left arm.

Walter and his wife Edwina had eight children, with three of them dying before the age of five. The two eldest sons, Henry and Edward, took over the York merchant business in imports and exports after Walter's death at a ripe old age. Ten years after Walter's death the terrible pestilence of the Black Death, bubonic plague, hit Britain in 1349. Its outcome eventually led to the Peasants' Revolt. The ravages of the plague were nowhere worse than in York with its crowded and unhygienic conditions. The population of around 15,000 was almost halved. This included all but one of the dozen or more of the Byrne family living in the city of York . The survivor was ten-year-old Edwina (named after her paternal grandmother). She was taken to the nunnery, also affected by the plague, adjacent to York Cathedral to be looked after until they could find whether or not she had relatives in the area who would take her in. She told them, 'I have an uncle and aunt and family, all called Byrne, who live at Appleton. I have only seen them about twice in my life, once was last Christmas when we all went to the church there.'

Richard was only a young teenager at the time of the Black Death. His father, Alfred, was infected and came out with the large blisters but was one of the lucky ones who recovered. His youngest sister, Annie, who was five was not so lucky and was the only one in the immediate family taken by the Black Death. Elsewhere in Appleton about one in four had died, which was low compared with other villages nearby and in York and Selby. Alfred Byrne had a theory as to why the death rate was that much lower in Appleton.

'It's down to the water we drink and use,' he would say, 'It's either rainwater coming off the roof into our water barrel, or it's what we get from the spring down the road apiece. When I got struck that's all I drank. Young Richard here got the water for me every day and I got better.'

It would be about three weeks after the Black Death had spent itself in the area (although various plagues were to hit York five more times during the rest of that century) when a messenger arrived from York. Alfred and his wife Kathy could both read reasonably well, but asked the messenger to read it as well to make sure they had understood it properly. It had come from the York nunnery and said that they 'had Edwina Byrne, aged ten, in our care who had now fully recovered from the plague which had taken up to our Lord her loving parents Henry and Elizabeth Byrne. As all others of her family in York had also gone, could they take their young niece Edwina in to their home?'

'Oh the poor little mite!,' cried Kathy.'Now we know why we've had no message from your cousins Henry and Edward. If she has recovered like you then she won't get it again.'

'That's right,' said Alfred, butting in.'She can take the place of our dear little Annie.'

Turning to the messenger, he said, 'Tell the good Mother Superior that I will come tomorrow noon time with my horse and small cart to pick up the young girl, who is our kin.'

All went to plan and by the late afternoon of the following day Edwina arrived at the home of the Appleton Byrne family. All were there to greet her, with her aunt Kathy giving her a tight hug as she arrived. Then she was kissed on the cheek by Richard. His sister Elizabeth, who was two years older than Edwina, and John who was two years younger, also gave her a great hug.

* * *

In general the survivors of the Black Death were made more prosperous, with labourers' wages rising as landlords strived to get their fields cultivated. To keep wages down Parliament passed several laws forbidding labourers to receive higher wages than they had earned prior to the plague. Because of the rise in the cost of living it was found impossible to enforce these laws. The more scrupulous landowners then tried to make the labourers perform their old services associated with raising crops for local manors and reducing the payment in money.

It should be mentioned that in York the number of craftsmen and traders who were quickly made freemen of York quadrupled as new freemen replaced those who had died. This was also the case in the large cities such as London and Norwich. However, it can be seen why in 1381 the peasants had cause to rise up in revolt: the nation was predominantly given to agriculture.

The Hundred Years War with France had come to an end and French raiders were attacking towns all along the south coast of England. The Commons in Parliament voted a large sum for defence provided by a tax of 4p a head for the lowest paid. Unfortunately this was not enough and a poll tax of a shilling each for everybody over the age of fifteen was demanded, while the yearly pay for carters, ploughmen and shepherds was only 13s 4p.

When Wat Tyler and Jack Straw led their men to Clerkenwell Fields in London Richard II promised to meet the demands and asked Tyler to send the peasants home. One of the King's advisors mortally wounded Tyler. With no attempt by the King to save the Kentish peasant who he had earlier praised, Tyler was then beheaded and his head stuck on a stick. The peasants realised they had been trapped. Richard declared the promises he made to be null and void and stressed what their lot in life was to be:

'Serfs you have been and are; you shall remain in bondage, not such as you have hitherto been subjected to, but comparably viler.'

In Appleton Roebuck, as in the surrounding villages, the suffering of the common people was less than those in Kent and East Anglia, probably because serfs were now outnumbered by those who had become freemen.

Alfred Byrne had died three years before the Peasants' Revolt at the good age of sixty-five but his widow Kathy was still active in the home. With no signs of loss of her mental powers the advice she gave to the family was still listened to and mainly acted upon.

During the previous thirty years both Edwina and Elizabeth had got married and now had seven children between them. Elizabeth and her husband and four children lived in York. She had married John Fairhall who was the grandson of Ivor Fairhall (descended from Einar Hairfair) who had gone into business with Reginald Ragner making and selling Scandinavian style jewellery in Petergate in York. The business was still surviving with John Fairhall being the sole owner. Their eldest daughter, Margaret, served in the shop as did Elizabeth whenever running the family household allowed her to do so. Their eldest son, Ivor, worked with his father in the manufacture of jewellery and, when time permitted, the creation of new designs. Because of her bad memories of the Black Death, Edwina would not even visit York if she could help it, let alone live in it. So she and her husband Henry Johnson, who had a two acre strip he worked as a new Freeman in Appleton, lived with Kathy and Richard and his wife and children in the enlarged family home.

Richard persuaded Henry to consider their two separate agricultural units working as a combined farming business. Henry would concentrate on the rather more profitable root crops of parsnips, turnips and yellow carrots, as well as chick peas, broad beans, cabbages and onions. Richard, with the family's twelve acres, would devote five acres of this to grassland for sheep rearing as he could see that the English cloth industry was beginning to become well established. The remaining seven acres would entail two acres being left fallow in yearly rotation, and the remaining land devoted to wheat and barley.

Aided by a gift of £2 from his mother and a loan of £3 from Richard to be repaid at five shillings per annum, John Byrne, the youngest was able to buy a two and a half acre plot of land further out from York in Church Fenton – previously called Kirk Fenton. Later he confessed to Richard:

'I should have seen the land in February or March instead of last August when it was so dry. His Lordship at the Manor told his bailiff to say nothing about the flooding. The old scoundrel has sold me a swamp. He probably thought he would teach this cocksure serf a lesson.'

'Apart from the fact that we are not serfs, but freemen,' commented Richard, 'all is not lost because my lads and Edwina's boy can all come over when we are not so busy and help you build a drainage system at that top end of the land. Down the bottom swampy end you could keep a few sheep.'

'How can I pay you for their time, after you have already helped me?'

'Well, you and your good lady Catherine will have to feed them lads. They eat like horses.'

* * *

As the 14th century reached its final year the seeds were sown that the next fifty years would produce more death and destruction in the conflict between the houses of York and Lancaster, which became known rather euphemistically as the War of the Roses.

While Richard II was in Ireland causing havoc for the Irish, the new Duke of Lancaster came back to England and demanded the estates of his father. All those who were opposed to Richard's arbitrary government flocked to his standard. The Duke of York, who had been left as regent, offered no resistance and in consequence the whole country passed into the power of Lancaster.

Richard finally landed in Wales and was then tricked into surrendering himself into the hands of his cousin and a Parliament now under the influence of Lancaster deposed him. The throne was then claimed by Henry of Lancaster as the descendant of Henry 111. Thus in 1399 began the fourteen year rule of Henry IV. He died in 1413 to be succeeded by his son Henry V, who reopened the war against France by making a formal claim to the French crown.

An army was hired in the usual way, with an earl receiving 13s 4p a day and an archer 6p, so that as the ordinary wages of labourers was then only four pence, Henry had little difficulty in getting troops. He landed at Havre in the summer of 1415 with twenty-four thousand Welsh and English archers and six thousand men-at-arms. Dysentery swept through his camp and reduced his active force to only 900 men-at-arms and five thousand archers. Trying to evade the French force, said to outnumber the English by seven to one, in late October Henry V was forced into what became the historic battle of Agincourt.

Among the archers who achieved the outstanding victory was 19-year-old Alan Byrne, grandson of the late Richard Byrne of Appleton Roebuck. After Agincourt Alan returned to the family in Appleton. He was determined to settle down and work with his father, Rufus Byrne, and two older brothers on the family's twelve acres. One of the factors that persuaded Alan to give up his service in the King's army was the mutual affection between him and

Catherine Hood, whose father, formerly a serf, but now a freeman like so many agricultural as well as townspeople, worked a five acre plot rented from the local squire. A year after his return from Agincourt Alan and Catherine were married in Appleton church.

At the wedding reception Rufus Byrne and his wife Mary took their son to one side for a quick private talk.

'You don't have to be worried as to whether there is enough work to go round. That was an astute arrangement your grandfather Richard made with Henry Johnson and your great aunt Edwina to form a co-operation between our family's twelve acres and their two. Henry was a hard working man who loved aunt Edwina.'

'As we all did,' Mary interrupted.'She was as good natured as she was beautiful.'

'That's very true' said Rufus.'She was as good a woman as you are, Mary, and just as lovely, but I was about to add that Henry's only son John turned out to be a work-shy drunkard. He went off to live and drink in York and no one has heard any more of him for the last twenty years.'

'I don't suppose Henry Johnson's wife could still be alive, and did John have any sisters?' asked Alan.'No,' Rufus replied.'Therefore me and your mother think you should be in charge of that two acres and working in co-operation with us as normal. If a reformed John Johnson should turn up one day we will talk about it with him.'

'And now you also have this lovely girl Catherine,' Mary said giving her son a hug, 'you must give up all ideas of being a soldier again.'

Alan smiled and kissed his mother on the cheek. A tragedy, not unusual in those times, struck Alan and Catherine. Their first child lived but four days and died of congested lungs on the fifth night of her short life when she could not breathe. A year later Catherine gave birth to a stillborn son.

Eighteen months passed and Catherine found she was again pregnant. As with her pregnancy with her stillborn child she began to suffer from blinding headaches. Mother-in-law Mary, who loved her as she did her own children, told her to do her best to relax and she would go away for two days and try and get the advice of an elderly lady who was knowledgeable about birth problems and who could probably help her.

Mary got Rufus Byrne to take her in the cart to Sherburne in Elmet. This village was the site of the most easterly part of an ancient Celtic kingdom stretching to the modern West Riding of Yorkshire. In the early seventh century it resisted being taken over by the incoming Anglo-Saxons for at least a hundred years.

Mary's mission was to find an elderly medicine lady who had a reputation for being able to offer old Celtic remedies for treating illnesses, particularly those related to child-bearing. Her enquiries were met with caution initially until she stressed that the lady she was looking for was certainly not a witch but was helpful with ancient medicine remedies. On the third attempt she was directed to where she could find this elderly medicine lady. Mary explained to her why she had come.'Have you got willow trees growing near you?' asked the medicine lady.

'Yes, there are several willows near by us,' replied Mary.'

'Then peel off a few small sections of willow bark, making sure that it is not cut in a ring all round the trunk, which will kill the tree. Boil up some sections as you need them. Let it cool and then drink half a cup every three hours and you will find it will take your headache away for at least a day. Then do it again for a day or too and the headache won't return.'

The medicine lady continued: 'When your baby is born, directly you have cut the cord you must bathe it all over with cow's urine that is fresh that day. That will help keep the pox away that kills so many new bornes, especially in the towns. That's why milkmaids don't often get the smallpox. When the baby is dry, you should then rub it all over with this ointment. It is made from sheep wax, or Lanolin as some folk call it, mixed with herbs. Also use it yourself as it will keep the skin nice and fresh and keep most ills away.'

'One other thing I would ask,' she added.' When you attend church please do not mention to others what I have recommended.

Even though it is now the 15th century it will still conflict with the church's view of Divine Will.'

Mary and Rufus were impressed with the medicine lady's explanations, which contrasted with mystic witch talk they had heard at a York fair that summer. They were also impressed with the fact that the lady only wanted a shilling for her advice and the ointment.

Within ten days Catherine's headaches had settled down to being only minor periodical affairs.

After twelve months she gave birth to a healthy boy and followed all the advice of the Sherborn-in-Elmet lady to the letter, much to the amusement of some members of the family when it came to washing in cows 'piddle'.'Are you sure it's fresh enough, Catherine?,' or 'Make sure the old bull has not been at her'.

Alan told them to shut up. He was so pleased that his son Bryan was obviously a fit little boy and his wife Catherine had recovered her health. By the time Bryan Byrne was four years old he had become a well developed child, both physically and mentally, although he still had fits of bad temper that are usually confined to two-year olds. Then when he had just turned five a terrible event struck the family.

Alan, Catherine and young Bryan were now living in the small house (basically a hut unchanged in design since the coming of the Anglo-Saxons) originally rented by Henry Johnson next to the land he had worked. That day Catherine was helping her husband on the two acres to weed some autumn-sown beans. As was the custom in days like this Catherine's mother Mary was looking after Bryan, who was playing with a toy cart with its hand-carved horse which his father had made for him. Being cold for early April, Bryan was in the house pushing his cart and horse along the beaten mud floor. Intent with the game he was playing he backed into the fire in the centre of the hut and knocked a flaming log outwards, which immediately set light to a torn table cloth spread out on a frame to dry.

He yelled for his grandma Mary who had been dozing on her

stool. By the time she got up and was near enough to pick him up the flames were singeing his jacket and hair and were swept up by their own heat through the smoke extraction hole in the thatched roof. As she grabbed Bryan and beat down the flames on his jacket with her hands, flaming sections of the roof thatch began to fall down upon them. She could see that the one small window, which was nearer than the closed door, was the best way for a quick escape. She picked up Bryan and bundled him through the piece of deer hide that covered the window space. She knew he was safe when she heard him shrieking from outside, 'Grandma, come out now! Grandma, Grandma, come out!'

Grandma Mary never did get outside. The rest of the flaming thatch fell in and covered her. She was asphyxiated. Her body was consumed in the fire.

* * *

By the time Bryan Byrne became a young teenager his mother had taught him to read. Noting how quickly he picked it up, Catherine, fully supported by Alan, thought that it would be better for him if he could obtain an apprenticeship working for one of the businesses in York or Selby. In his case they thought it would be more rewarding for him than helping with the family's farming. He had been doing this in snatches since he was ten. He always showed outstanding strength for his age, but this was offset by his inconsistency and periods of daydreaming. At fourteen he was friendly most of the time with other boys and girls in the village. Then there would be the sudden outbreaks of rage when he terrorised his contemporaries and apologised to them when he had cooled down.

Catherine and most of the family said that this was a reaction to the trauma he suffered ever since he saw his grandmother's terrible death.

'I don't think that is all the answer' said his father. 'It's a trait that comes out, usually in boys, every so often in this family, but most learn how to control it. Having been a soldier, I think the best thing for Bryan is to join the King's army. He will like that and it will show him how to use discipline.'

Despite the opposition from Catherine to this decision, and her refusal to allow Alan to her bed for a week or more, in 1440 when Bryan Byrne was seventeen he enlisted to serve the Duke of York in what was to become the War of the Roses.

Richard of York, the 3rd Duke of York, was the grandson of Edward III's second son and his claim to the throne was through the female line. Although he never became king, he was the father of two kings of England, Edward IV and Richard III, who died at the Battle of Bosworth in 1485 as the last Plantagenet and Yorkist king.

The Lancastrian dynasty was descended through the male line of John of Gaunt, the 3rd son of Edward III, whose son Henry deposed the unpopular Richard II to become Henry IV. His son Henry V, after becoming the victor at Agincourt (1415) made an unsuccessful claim for the French throne. Bryan Byrne trained as an archer with the English longbow. He soon developed the ability to fire arrows as fast as his companions with much longer service. For close fighting he was equipped with a medium length sword. English archers only protection was a basic helmet giving full vision. The English bowmen had developed a reputation of being some of the roughest and coarse soldiery in Europe. On his first tour of duty with Richard of York in an unrewarding campaign trying to hold on to English possessions in France, he became the victim of several physical attacks by fellow archers. This mainly came from those who were jealous of the speed at which he became so efficient in the use of his weapons. A certain arrogance he displayed did not endear him to some of his tormentors.

By the time they were transferred to Ireland in 1445 Bryan's bravery in the limited actions they had in France and his ability to defend himself from any personal attacks meant that he was now accepted by his fellow bowmen. His satisfaction with the life he had chosen also meant that his rages now were rare and mainly confined to the battlefield.

Dissatisfaction was centred on the early death of his father Alan in 1447. Bryan's captain gave him time and a travel document to attend the funeral and comfort his mother and his younger brother and sister, both of whom he found he could now relate to as they were in their mid-teens. Following the funeral he was introduced to a mourner who was a close friend of his sister. Called Elizabeth, she had also been helped by his mother in dealing with the problems of life that so often face late teenage girls. He and Elizabeth had made a noticeable impression on each other. There were many nights when alone in his Dublin barracks he considered the fact that next time he was home in Appleton he would find that Elizabeth was married – but not to him. This was another source of dissatisfaction.

Although the Duke of York had provided over £38,000 of his own money to maintain English interests in France, he was replaced as Lieutenant of France by the Duke of Somerset, a strong supporter of the House of Lancaster as a cousin of Henry VI. Creating the Duke of York as

Lieutenant of Ireland was in reality exile by office.

Richard of York, to the surprise of his opponents, was effective in his control of Ireland. He soon became well liked because of his relative honesty for the period and his efficiency. He kept the peace between the Anglo-Irish Earls of Kildare, Desmond and Ormonde, who between them controlled most of the whole of southern Ireland, with the exception of the area around Dublin, known as the Pale. Here the Duke of York was the Lord Deputy, maintaining English rule and law over the mix of people of Irish, English and Norse Viking origin. Whatever Bryan was asked to do he did efficiently. Apart from being part of his nature, as the situation in the Pale was peaceful he was planning to ask his captain if he could take three months leave and assure him he would willingly return. His mind was being dominated by Elizabeth. He knew that he had to see her before she decided to marry someone else. They needed to talk to each other far more than the few sentences they had exchanged at his mother's funeral. Would she accept him as a soldier for the next few years? Would she be prepared to be the mother of his children?

The Captain granted him a meeting, which was promising in itself, and Bryan stated honestly the purpose of his request for three months absence. The captain listened and replied:

'This is something we would not agree to normally, for how can we be sure that after all your training you would not return and thereby dishonour your allegiance to Richard, Duke of York, hopefully our future King. However, I feel sure you are a man of your word and return to your duty when you have resolved your problems. If you do not return, I will personally see that you are hunted down, taken to the gateway to York Castle and in front of your family given two hundred lashes on your bare back.'

'Yes sir,' Bryan replied.'I fully understand and I thank you for your trust. I will return three months to the day, sir.'

* * *

It was early September in 1445 and Catherine Byrne was busy preparing an evening meal for seven family members who had all been working on the harvest and would be coming in dog-tired in about half an hour. She looked up as the door creaked and slowly opened. It was her first-born, Bryan standing there smiling.

'Oh Bryan,' she cried, giving him a hug and a kiss on his forehead.'What are you doing here? Have you left being a soldier for the Duke?'

'I talked to my captain and told him I urgently needed three months leave of absence to sort out a serious problem.'

'What ever is the problem my dear boy? '

'The problem, Mother, is that I want to marry Elizabeth Turner, unless I have left it too late. I just can't stop thinking about her.'

His mother pursed her lips and looked at him for half a minute or so.'Well, I do know that she is walking out with a young man, but I don't know how serious it is.

Your sister Johanna will know as she and Elizabeth are still good friends.'

No more than ten minutes passed by when voices could be heard approaching the house.

They came tumbling through the door, eager to get a stool or bench and rest themselves after ten hours work. As they did they spotted Bryan. Johanna led the rush to give him a hug of welcome. His brother Richard turned round to mother and excitedly asked her:

'Mother, I know you have some ale left. Let's get it out to welcome Bryan's return, hoping it's still drinkable that is! Catherine beckoned Johanna and whispered to her:

'Come and help me get the food in. I want to ask you something important about your friend Elizabeth Turner.'

'Why's that, Mother?'

'Because your brother Bryan says he wants to marry her.'

'Oh mother, I think that is good news. From what she says to me I think she would say yes if he asked her. She likes Edgar Carpenter, whose father is the blacksmith, as you know, and she sometimes goes for a walk with him and they often sit next to each other in church. But she told me only last week that she does not really love him.'

'Well, Johanna, directly you get the chance to talk to Bryan more or less in private tell him what you've told me and then you can arrange a meeting between him and Elizabeth.'

The meeting was arranged with great success. Within a week the church issued the banns and five weeks later Bryan Byrne and Elizabeth Turner were married in Appleton Roebuck church.

A three week honeymoon was spent in their own room at the back of her father's smithy. Using the last remaining money he had saved from a year's wages as a bowman, plus a donation from his parents as a wedding gift, Bryan returned to Dublin barracks the way he had come.

The quickest way to get to Bristowe – later called Bristol – for a ship to Dublin would be on horseback. The much cheaper but slower alternative he was forced to choose was by cargo carts. On very poor roads, mainly following the old Roman Roads and without springs in the carts, long journeys could be painful. Bryan's was as he went mainly via the old Fosse Way.

At Bristowe he only had to wait six hours before sailing to Dublin where he arrived four days before his three months had expired.

It was almost a year to the day since Bryan Byrne had left his bride when he received a month-old message from his mother that he was now the father of twins, a boy and a girl and that they and Elizabeth were all in good health. If he agreed, they were to be called Bryan John and Edwina. He would not see them, nor his wife, for nearly four years.

Mainly due to the inept handling of the campaigns in France by the Lancastrian Duke of Somerset, by June 1451 England had lost nearly all its possessions in France bar Calais. The Duke of York decided to risk all and attempt to wrest control from King Henry VI by force. By 1453 England was plunged into a series of minor wars between the land's most powerful lords which the Duke of York as protector was able to handle to his advantage.

Bryan Byrne distinguished himself in these minor wars and skirmishes, particularly with his ruthlessness in the midst of battle, so much so that his captain, looking to retirement, consulted the Duke and had Bryan appointed as a captain. This enabled Bryan to make several visits to see his wife and children. Initially the children hid behind their mother's skirts at this strange man. On his third visit they had got round to happily accepting this man who they now knew as 'funny daddy'.

Richard, Duke of York was slain at the battle of Wakefield in late 1460 and his army defeated, with Bryan Byrne narrowly escaping capture. The Wars of the Roses were well under way.

For the second time during his reign Henry VI was judged to be insane and he was deposed.

Edward IV, the son of the late Duke of York, beat the

Lancastrians in a race to become King. He did not waste time over his coronation, for the moment was ripe for a decisive blow.

Previously the people took little interest in the war and the battles were fought by the noblemen and their retainers, such as Byrne. The men of the rich counties of Essex and Kent had now joined the Yorkist ranks. With a powerful army Edward took the northern road in the spring of 1461 to meet the Lancastrians. At Ferrybridge he drove Lord Clifford from the banks of the Aire and made his way into the plain of York. At Towton, between Pontefract and York, he thoroughly beat the Lancastrians in a pitched battle, which gave Edward the complete command of the great plain of York, which secured his powers in the north.

It is said that this was the bloodiest battle ever fought in England. Thirty-eight thousand men were killed that day. Among the corpses, surrounded by a ring of dead Lancastrians, was Bryan Byrne, with his sword still clutched in his hand.

Chapter Six

Love and Survival under Henry Tudor

As the church bells at Appleton Roebuck began to ring in the New Year of 1528 Bryan John Byrne and his sister Edwina knew they were lucky, and unusual, in that if they lived another three months they would be celebrating their seventy-ninth birthday. Both had limited movement due to crippling arthritis. Both wheezed with chest infections. Both had claws rather than what were once hands. Most of their fingers were permanently bent inwards, as the inherited Viking Hand disease progressed.

Both had outlived their spouses – Edwina by more than twenty years. But surrounded by several generations of the family this was an occasion to be joyful and not to dwell on the physical and sometimes mental pain for having lived so long. As with many people of North European descent they were greatly troubled by osteoarthritis.

Sons and wives, with grandchildren and several great grandchildren were all excitedly trying to guess what the actual time would be on the church clock when the New Year began, because there would be different times shown on every church tower in Yorkshire. When the general consensus was that it must be midnight the New Year was greeted with cheering. Then songs accompanied by bone flutes and a young lady playing a fiddle.

'Look at our Jane's eldest boy, William, who does that remind you of?' whispered Edwina to her brother.'You must cast your mind back, Bryan, to when we were about nine or ten.'

Bryan John stared at his grandson William, a tall blond youth of around nineteen who was laughing at some joke.

'By God,' he replied, 'Our father the last time we ever saw him.'

His eyes began to well up as he grasped his sister's hand and whispered:

'To think he was killed not five miles from here and grandmother Catherine could never find his body. What she saw that day brought on her early death. Grandfather was wiser and would not go.'

The young man who had told William the joke that gave him much laughter was Abraham Carpenter. He was the great grandson of Edgar Carpenter who had married Elizabeth Byrne three years after she was widowed. He had always loved Elizabeth and he knew that she could never love him, or at least not as she had loved Bryan Byrne. And so it was until he died.

When they married they had thought it best for both families if they moved away to start life anew.

Fortunately Edgar's father, still the blacksmith at Appleton, knew of a blacksmith at Sherburn in Elmet (only ten miles from Appleton) who was retiring. Edgar and Elizabeth were able to move into the three-roomed house that stood behind the smithy within a fortnight. It was there that Elizabeth gave birth to three children, one of whom died when only a month old.

With Henry VIII having been on the throne for nearly twenty years life for a skilled tradesman had improved. England was becoming a more commercial country and mining of coal, tin and lead flourished, as did iron manufacturing. This was helpful to Edgar Carpenter who looked more to manufacturing iron utensils as much as to horseshoeing and mending traditional agricultural tools.

In York and most other towns throughout England, and to a lesser extent Wales and Scotland, towns were growing larger, with as many wandering around penniless as those in work and living a better life than their forebears. Upper class and middle class people benefited from the growing wealth of the country. For the poor in

Tudor times life did not improve. For them life was hard and rough and usually short-lived.

In the small villages serfdom was long gone but the wage labourers' life was very hard and they earned just enough for basic food, clothes and shelter to survive. As with the poor and unemployed in the towns, most were illiterate. Slightly better off were the tenant farmers who leased their land from the rich. This included that section of the Byrne family who were still working some five acres of land by now in Kirk Fenton. With such a small acreage, some of the sons and even daughters had to move into York or Selby where most, particularly those who were fully literate, were fortunate to obtain work with trades people. Those in the Byrne family who remained in Appleton to work the fiftyacres they now owned were recognised as yeomen farmers. This meant they belonged to the second highest social group, the highest being the gentlemen landowners – the gentry. Above them, of course, were the nobility, as of today. Some yeomen could be as wealthy as the gentry but the difference was that the yeomen worked alongside their farm labourers.

On the land iron plough shears were replacing wood, although oxen could still be seen to pull some ploughs. Even in Eastern England, where the soil and climate is more suited to arable farming, mixed farming was still carried out everywhere. The animal dung was necessary to keep the soil productive and enabling fields to be left fallow only one year in three instead of one in two.

A main crop was long straw wheat for bread making for the growing population and oats in the North. Barley was essential, as it is today, for beer making.

The variety of vegetables had hardly changed from the early medieval period: cabbages, turnips, broad beans, peas, parsnips and carrots (which were usually white). Following autumn ploughing and harrowing, all seeds were sown as early as possible and not left to the spring. With more people having money to purchase alternative richer tasting vegetables, farmers started growing skirret. This also had a sweeter taste and was said to be a favourite of Henry VIII The problem for the farmer, which caused the higher price, was its relatively low yield and its difficulty to harvest.

* * *

To return to the New Year's eve party of 1528, young William Byrne was the son of Thomas Byrne, who had died of typhus the Year that HenryVIII was crowned king. Thomas himself was the son of Bryan John, the twin who together with his sister Edwina was wondering whether they would see their seventy-ninth birthdays.

Edwina, who still showed one of the family characteristics of auburn tinges in her greying hair had originally married a young man, Oswald Blake, from a neighbouring village whose family were yeoman farmers. She had two sons who decided to work for export-import trading companies in York. One of them departed for London to make his fame and fortune. That was forty years ago and she never heard further from him. She had a daughter, but after a mere two years of life she was taken by consumption. As for the younger son, Stephen Edward Blake, whose work started with such promise at the York trading company, he began to give more of his time and energies to the social life that the big towns could offer and small villages could not. Although boys kicked footballs – two were flogged for kicking a football in the minster itself – there were no organised sports as such, unless you included cock-fighting, bear-baiting and bull-baiting. At first Stephen attended the lot until he realised that he did not really enjoy the cruelty.

His enjoyment and eventual downfall switched to the pleasures of the alehouse. What was a pleasure slowly became a necessity. After twelve years with the trading company his employers realised how incompetent he had become when they found that a twelve-year-old boy they had recently taken on was secretly correcting his figures. Then came the day when at only eight in the morning they caught him drinking gin and water from a bottle.

Stephen Blake made great efforts to give up drinking and on several occasions he was dry for a month or more. In these periods he managed to get work with various companies who had reached busy periods and needed extra temporary bookkeepers. Again his particular demons gained control and he had to resort to begging to live. He had long given up the occasional visit to his mother, Edwina.

Between extended drinking bouts somehow he survived another six years, mainly by the luck he had in placing small bets on horse racing which had started in a small way just outside York. Struck down by a feverish illness he passed away just one year before the first officially recorded horse race took place in York. This was between William Mallory and Oswald Wolsthrope in 1530. The winner received a silver bell which he undertook to return a year later when his horse should compete for it against any challenger.

* * *

It was early spring in 1529 when Bryan John Byrne gave up his struggle against pain and died of pneumonia. In early June his twin sister Edwina lost the will to live. On her deathbed, holding her eldest daughter Jane's hand, she said,

'It was only the pleasure of sharing the joys of all the children, and helping them to deal with the woes, that's kept me going.'

The family gathered, including those from Kirk Fenton and Sherburn in Elmet, in even greater numbers than at the earlier funeral of her brother. William Byrne had often secretly toyed with the idea of moving to York and trying to get a job with prospects in one of the new companies organising coal and lead mining or iron making. But here at grandmother's wake the conversation showed that he could not talk of leaving the farm to somebody else to run. When asked to address them on this matter he said carefully:

'You can count on me for the present time to manage our farm, with my brother Arthur being my deputy. As it is I could not manage without him, or the hard work of those others working for us.'

Those present clapped him.

Before he could move away to where he had left a glass of parsnip wine, his aunt Jane grabbed his arm.

'Are we to give up the two acres that the drunken John Johnson left us now that a grandson of his has suddenly appeared and claims it is his?'

'We have approached a lawyer in Selby,' William replied, 'who is looking into this and thinks that this grandson has little substance for his claim.'

William decided not to say that even if they lost the two acres, they still had forty-eight acres left. Therefore, it was not worth building up extensive lawyer's fees which would never be recovered on crops from two acres. Later he did let Arthur know his view, which the younger brother agreed with.

With the family business out of the way, the next subject of keen discussion – as it was all over England – was Parliament's agreement with King Henry that England's church could break away from Rome.

One of the younger ladies present got the support of all the other ladies and most of the men when she said: 'After all these years he has been married to Queen Catherine of Aragon, King Henry wants to throw her away like an old shoe that won't fit his fat foot so he can have his legal way with Anne Boleyn.'

'There's some truth in that,' said William Byrne after the laughter had died down.'But in over twenty years of marriage she wasn't able to produce one boy child that didn't die within a year.'

The same lady, who was one of William's cousins, gave him a fierce look.

'We all know, William, that you will defend King Henry no matter what. You have even grown a spade beard just like him and his courtiers. Perhaps the poor little children died because of his seed. What about that!'

To quieten things down at what was originally a family funeral wake, William just smiled and said, 'You also have a point there, Charlotte. Oh, and by the way spade beards are now all the fashion.'

Waiting for the laughter to die down, Charlotte's husband

shouted out: 'There can't be much wrong with our seed. We've only been married for two and a half years and we have three little bairns. All seem healthy so far, praise the Lord.'

As was the custom, almost all present regularly went to church on a Sunday and other holy days. The mention of the Lord led to a discussion on whether Henry VIII would become a Protestant if the break with Rome went fully ahead. This seemed to worry them. The Father at the local church who had conducted both of the twins' funeral services had spoken to a few of his parishioners, but generally he kept a low profile at the family gathering. Gently raising his voice so that all could hear, he said:

'Although our King has unfortunately broken away from the Holy Father in Rome, I can assure all you good souls that he will always remain a Catholic. Whatever some people may do in Denmark, Sweden and some of the German states our King Henry will ever remain a Catholic.'

The priest turned out to be right. But when Henry died the reformation was to come to Britain.

In 1533 there were two marriages of significance. Henry VIII married Anne Boleyn and William Byrne married Ellinor Burton in York. Henry had Anne Boleyn (mother of Queen Elizabeth I) executed only three years later, allegedly for her infidelity. Two days later he married Jane Seymour.

Even allowing for the harshness of royal rule of the time, Henry VIII had an unsurpassed record in the executions he carried out on those who roused his anger. Apart from the occasional wife, these ranged from Sir Thomas More, his Chancellor, to several abbots who were to criticise his dissolution of the monasteries.

During the four years that had passed since William Byrne told the family at the funeral of the twins that he would continue to manage the farming of the fifty acres, his brother Arthur had virtually taken over the role. The difference was that Arthur lived for his work and how he could utilise nature's whims to produce the best crops or feed for his stock. William enjoyed the fact that as a yeoman he was in charge of an agricultural business but his inner restlessness meant he wanted to try management away from farming.

Arthur's dogged reliability seemed to match his appearance. His dark eyes, brown hair and barrel-chested physique contrasted with the mainly light-eyed and fair to red hair of many of the Byrnes, including William.

The management change really began when Arthur decided to get married to a local girl, Freda.

He and William were hoeing, when suddenly Arthur stopped.

'William, can you come with me to York and help me chose a ring for my engagement to Freda?'

'Save some money Arthur and give her a curtain ring. Tell the dear girl she will have a better wedding ring.'

Arthur hoped William was joking, but he wasn't sure.

'Of course I will come, Arthur. We could go Friday in the horse and trap. I know a good place in York who will have something good at a reasonable price.'

Come Friday they first set the two labourers their work for the day and left cousin Francis in charge. Arriving in York they stabled the horse and trap and went to Fairhall & Sons, now run by brothers Eric and John Fairhall.

'Can I help you gentlemen?'

Arthur looked at William waiting for him to reply. But William just kept staring at the young lady who had greeted them. He was so mesmerised by her dark-haired beauty and the musical note of her voice that what she was saying was not registering.

Arthur coughed and poked his brother gently in the ribs. The young lady no longer smiled. She began to worry whether these two strange men were planning to rob the shop. Trying not to tremble, she calmly said:

'Oh, I will call one of the managers to deal with you gentlemen.'

William smiled at her.'I am so sorry we appeared to be a pair of idiots. We were waiting for each other to answer you. We would like to see some engagement rings. Attractively made but not too expensive.'

Ellinor Burton thought, 'What a nice man with a nice voice. Pity he has auburn hair.'

Still addressing William, she said, 'Are you getting married, sir, or is it for your colleague?'

She hoped he would say it was for his colleague.

'No it is for my brother here, Arthur Byrne, who is to wed a lovely girl in our village, Appleton Roebuck. I am still waiting to meet the girl I would wed.'

Arthur smiled at Ellinor as she showed him a tray of rings. She thought, 'He's the shy one of the two, but a gentleman like his brother. And to think I thought they might be robbers.'

Arthur made his choice, while William did his best not to keep looking at Ellinor.

As Arthur went to pay her the two pounds and three shillings for the silver ring with a runic design and its small ruby stone in the centre a tall fair man came in from the rear office.

Did I hear you say you are of the Byrne family in Appleton Roebuck?

'Yes we are' replied William and Arthur almost in unison.

'I am Eric Fairhall and with my brother John we run the company and make a considerable part of the jewellery ourselves. Miss Ellinor Burton does all the hard work in trying to sell our products.'

'And very efficiently and charming with it' interrupted William, smiling at Ellinor who blushed.

'The point I was about to make,' said Eric Fairhall, 'About six months ago my brother and I decided to sort out some old order documents going back nearly three hundred years. Some were almost undecipherable because the ink used had faded, but we could see the names of John Byrne and his father or grandfather also named William Byrne. Our ancestor who founded the business in these very premises was called Ivor Fairhall. Our grandfather told us well before he died that the real founder of the jewellery design and manufacture, working in an 11th century hut in York, was in fact a Danish Viking.'

The brothers had listened in silence to this account of distant business between the Byrnes and the Fairhalls.

'This is amazing,' commented William. 'There has long been a belief in the family that we might have come from Danish origins. If it is true then it is even possible that your ancestors and ours may have come over to England with King Harald Hadrada. But who can prove it and does it really matter five hundred years later?'

Ellinor Burton had listened to the conversation with fascination. 'If I may say something,' she said, 'my parents, who look like most people in York, say my dark hair and eyes could be down to Jewish blood inherited from one of the poor souls who were murdered here three hundred years ago. But as they rarely mixed with our people it could be from a Norse Viking, a number of whom were dark eyed with dark hair, unlike the Danish.'

'Whatever the reason for your comely looks may be,' said William as he turned round to her, 'I hope I will see you both again. Arthur and I must be on our way back to Appleton.'

Eric Fairhall smiled as he said, 'Both of us and my brother John will be pleased to see you.'

Ellinor looked down at her feet, not wishing to look at William as he and his brother departed. She wondered whether she had said too much.

* * *

As the brothers drove the trap back to Appleton, Arthur, who had hold of the reins, grinned as he turned to William.

'You've fallen for that girl and I think she's fallen for you.'

'That's true,' William replied, 'but I do not know what to do next.'

'Well, I will tell thee. You must come to York and work in one of the businesses as you really want to do. I will be quite happy to run the farm and you can see by now that I can do it.'

'That's true, Arthur. And mother won't be really worried when she knows that I am going to get married – assuming that Ellinor agrees to it.'

Five days later William called at Fairhall & Sons shop in York. Much to his pleasure Ellinor Burton was at the counter. She greeted him with a smile.

'Good morning, Mr Byrne, have you come to purchase another ring?'

'No Miss Burton, although I find it a pleasure to talk to you, on this occasion I wanted to talk to Mr Eric or Mr John Fairhall if one of them could spare me just ten minutes.'

She rang a small handbell on the end of her counter nearest to the door leading to the back office. Almost immediately Eric Fairhall appeared.

'Ah, good morning, Mr Byrne. Can I help you with something? If it is a personal matter, William, if I may call you so, then you can come into the office.'

William stated that he had no objection to Ellinor Burton hearing what he had to say. Eric Fairhall quickly glanced at them with a slight smile. William explained that after his six years of experience in managing and running the family farm he was handing this over to his brother Arthur, 'who may well be coming into the shop for a wedding ring.' He was now proposing to take up residence in York city and see if he could find employment with one of the expanding number of commercial companies involved in industries such as mining or iron manufacture, where he thought his organisational experience and a talent for mathematics could be useful.

'Come into the office and repeat to my brother John what you are intending to do. We may be able to put you on to such a company.'

The two brothers signed a note of recommendation and suggested that he made an appointment to see the manager of a company that was operating new coal mines now working in Selby and also in Ingleton in North Yorkshire (the main collieries had recently started in south Yorkshire). The recently opened

York office was concerned with control of production costs and arranging shipments of coal down the Humber to markets as far down as London.

William was successful in obtaining employment with the mine operating company on a six month's trial basis. If he proved to be competent he would be paid eight shillings a week. He also found respectable lodgings nearby. Also important to him, within two weeks he received an acceptance from Ellinor to accompany him to a concert of mainly non-sectarian music.

In July that year he attended brother Arthur's wedding in Appleton, with Ellinor being one of the guests. In September William and Ellinor were married in York Minster with a full contingent of the Byrne family in attendance, plus Eric and John Fairhall and their wives. William soon found that the eight shillings a week was not the princely sum he thought it would be and for the time being he and Ellinor, who still kept her job, moved into her parents house, where they had a room to themselves. With this arrangement they managed to save a little each week for the future. Although moralists preached the virtues of hard work and parsimony, wages in a Tudor city were not really adjusted to the constant inflationary process. A typical journeyman worked in the winter from dawn to sunset, in the summer from 5am to 7 or 8pm, with only two half-hours for breakfast, dinner or drinking. This would often be for 5 shillings a week, or less.

At this time there were throughout England more than six hundred monastic houses run by monks and nuns. With the help of his chief advisor, Thomas Cromwell, Henry looked upon them as a potential source of income. By an Act of Parliament in 1536 the smaller monasteries were dissolved. Their fate frightened many of the greater ones into voluntary submission. Those who acted too slowly for King Henry, such as the abbots of Glastonbury, Colchester and Reading, were indicted for treason and executed.

By 1538 in York city, St. Mary's Abbey and St. Leonard's Hospital were the largest monasteries to be dissolved. Nearby in the countryside the remains of Fountains Abbey and Rievaulx Abbey are on the modern day tourists check list.

In 1536 the northern counties, where the monks were more popular than in the south, rose up in rebellion against the suppression of the lesser monasteries. This movement was called the Pilgrimage of Grace. Its leaders and four abbots were executed, but the common people were treated with leniency. One result of this rebellion was the formation of the Council of the North, a committee of the Privy Council which from there on sat for four months of the year at York, Hull, Newcastle and Durham.

In 1547 Henry VIII died. His sixth wife, Katherine Parr, survived him, unlike Anne Boleyn and Katherine Howard who lost their heads. Catherine of Aragon, Jane Seymour and Anne of Cleves, all of whom he divorced, also survived him. Meanwhile William Byrne and Ellinor celebrated their sixteen years of marriage. They had two surviving children, Jane and Abraham, twelve and ten years old. Mainly down to the lack of proper hygiene conditions in York (as in all of Britain's cities at that time) the first borne, a girl, died of diphtheria at six months and the second, a boy, just stopped breathing after two weeks of life.

William had recently been made manager of the mining company and although they had moved to their own Tudor built house in the city with its over-hanging first floor, sewage still flowed through the streets. In 1549 York began to be hit once more by a succession of death-bringing diseases, including forms of the plague, typhus and a mysterious 'swetting sickness' which was similar in some ways to the plague. William and Ellinor decided that the best chance of survival for their children Jane and Abraham was to send them to stay with the family in Appleton. They would visit them on Sundays as long as they were still in good health themselves.

A great advantage was that the Byrne family home had been extended and the lavatory situated fifty feet from the house. The contents were regularly emptied into a slurry pit and the solids mixed with compost and then ploughed into the land. Coupled with regular hand washing at least once a day it seemed to lessen the chances of picking up the serious illnesses. William paid for the children to go to a small school in the village so as to continue with the lessons that he and Ellinor had been giving them.

This arrangement seemed to be working quite well, although Ellinor was depressed much more than William by the parting from her children for six days a week. Suddenly after two years tragedy again struck the Byrne family. Ellinor caught the swetting sickness and in three days she was dead.

William was so distraught at losing the only love of his life that he told the owners of the company that he must take three months off work without pay. He told his brother Arthur and his mother, who was still alive, that he would work on the farm without pay, other than his meals with his children.

His daughter Jane was now seventeen. He felt some escape from his loss every time he looked at her. She was so much like her mother. Just as beautiful and as caring for the others in her family.

Chapter Seven

Escape From Marston Moor

'*You would think it strange if I should tell you there was a time in England when brothers killed brothers, cousins cousins, and friends their friends.*' Sir John Ogler, a Royalist

With his small, pointed Van Dyke beard there was no mistaking that Richard Byrne was a supporter of the Stuart King Charles the First. Aged forty-six he had been a harquebusier (horse soldier) ever since King Charles took the throne. Like many yeomen they were sought after for both the Royalist cavalry and the Parliamentary forces when the English Civil War commenced with the battle of Edgehill in October 1642.

At Selby in the spring of 1644 a Royalist force was defeated by a Scottish Covenanters army, paid for by the Parliamentarians, and driven into York and held there under siege. Much destruction was caused in Appleton Roebuck as the Scots forced the Royalists back to the city. Perhaps because of its size the main house of the Byrne family was first commandeered by the Scots, then pillaged and burnt down. Probably because the family was known as being mainly Royalist. Richard Byrne's father Cedric, grandson of William Byrne of Tudor times, was killed trying to fight the blaze. Most of the survivors, including Richard's wife Mary, managed to make their way south to Church Fenton, where nearly three hundred years earlier John Byrne had purchased a little over two acres of swampy farm land. This had since been expanded with new drainage work making the land more profitable.

Not all of the locals were Royalists. Some, including a few older members of the Byrne family, were Puritan Parliamentarians. Others, who had no strong allegiances either way, joined them in shaving off beards and head hair as in the manner of Cromwell's 'round heads'.

As an experienced yeoman, Richard Byrne had risen to the rank of captain and headed one of the many troops of one-hundred cavaliers that rode with the charismatic Prince Rupert of the Rhine. Part German he was a nephew of Charles I. For protection Richard wore a 'three-barred pott' helmet, breastplate and backplate. He also wore a leather jacket and thick riding boots. This armour would have cost twenty shillings – a servant girl's wage for a year. Soldiers usually had to pay for their equipment, though sometimes the regiment supplied the armour. He was armed with a short-barrelled musket, heavy sword and a pistol. In June King Charles ordered Prince Rupert to raise the siege of York. Gathering support in Cheshire and Lancashire he crossed the Pennines reaching Knaresborough on the Nidd. The Parliamentarians and Scots raised the siege of York and drew up to join battle with Rupert on Marston Moor opposite where he had crossed the Nidd. However, Rupert eluded them by marching north then coming down the left bank of the Ouse and relieved York. The Parliamentarians retreated to the line of the Wharfe in order to hold it against Rupert's return. The Royalists marched out of York, but did not attack their opponents who instead launched an attack upon them led by Cromwell's Ironsides cavalry. Prince Rupert's cavaliers were generally routed at the first charge and it was not long before the Royalists were forced to retire in disarray.

Richard Byrne's cavalry troop was on the right of the line and therefore missed the full charge of the Ironsides. As the attackers wheeled away Richard's troop fired their pre-loaded muskets causing a number of casualties. Prince Rupert's men on their left were now unable to hold their section of the line and were subsequently faced by three lines of Roundhead infantry: the first line kneeling, the second line crouching and the third standing and all firing at the same time. One further charge by the Ironsides and there was no alternative to retreat for Rupert's men. This was the first major engagement of Cromwell's finely trained Ironsides, who became one of the finest bodies of horsemen the world had seen. They carried the day at Marston Moor, which was the beginning of the end for King Charles' support in the North. Losses in Byrne's troop were light compared with the rest of the Royalist army, with only ten deaths and twenty-five wounded. But the low quality of medical care in the period meant many wounded men would soon die.

Richard Byrne had to make a lasting decision. He had heard from one of the local Royalists who had been in York during the siege that Appleton Roebuck had suffered considerably and he believed that most of the Byrne family had gone to a village further south. That could well be Church Fenton, he thought. He must try and get there and see if Mary and his children were still alive and well. Against his will he must be a deserter. That night under cover of darkness he broke away from the remnants of Rupert's cavaliers and headed east. After an hour's riding he stopped by a stream, watered his horse – named Boudicca – and then cold shaved off his beard with the razor he always carried to trim it and cut his hair so it was just above his ears. He turned his leather jacket inside out so that its crimson band indicating he was a follower of Prince Rupert could not be seen. Underneath he still wore his breastplate and backplate. He had lost his helmet by a blow from a Parliamentarian's pike as they retreated from Marston Moor. Fortunately it did not wound him, other than giving him a headache. He resisted the urge to stay where he was and sleep for an hour or two. As a military man Richard knew that Cromwell would not be sparing many of his men to hunt down individual Royalists. His army was driving Rupert's followers ever southward and the more miles that Richard could gain by riding east the safer he became.

Two hours after sunrise, which being early July would be around six am, he came to Church Fenton.

A cock crowed and a dog barked but all seemed still asleep. Then round the corner came a farm worker of middle age.

'Good morning,' said Richard, trying to look completely at ease.'Can you tell me where the Byrne family, recently of Appleton, are now living. I am one of their family.'

'I work for them and you must be the elder son who is a horse soldier. Go down this road and when you get to the church the family live first house just past it.'

'Thank you,' Richard replied, still smiling.'I will tell them that you helped me. What are you called?'

'I am Henry Bygod,' was the quietly said reply, 'but I would be obliged if you do not mention my name to anyone else. Some folks here are Royalists and some are Cromwell Puritans. And some will spill each other's blood to show it. It will blow over soon and how will they feel then?'

Keeping his voice low, Richard bade him goodbye and added, ' I agree with you, my good man, but I fear this discord between us English will last longer than we think.'

Richard decided to walk through the village leading Boudicca. He thought this was less likely to raise too much notice of his arrival. As he approached the church he noticed two men standing at the door of a small thatched house. They stopped their conversation and stared at him in a cautious manner. He decided that if they spoke to him he would reply courteously, whatever they said. They did not speak, nor did he.

There was just one modern-looking house past the church. He thought that this must be the Byrne house. As the two men were still watching him, without showing any hesitation he walked down the side hoping he had not picked the wrong house and be liable for a musket to be discharged at him – and his horse. Seeing a post by a grassy patch some ten feet from the door he tied his horse to it. As he did so he was aware that a woman was looking out at him as she removed the night shutter.

She pushed open the back door and came running at him. It was his sister Katherine.

'Oh Richard!, she cried.'We thought you might be dead in the battle. Did the Royalists drive away those Roundheads?'

'No, dear Kathy, they drove us away at Marston Moor. Although Prince Rupert lost a lot of good men he lives to fight again for our rightful King. And I shall rejoin his cavaliers when I know you are all safe here. Where is my wife Mary and my children? Is our dear mother still with us?'

Katherine grabbed his hand.'Quick, come inside. We cannot stay here discussing our lives.'

He followed her through the door to be faced by seven or eight people. He immediately recognised his younger brother Cedric and his wife Ellen and gave them both a hug. Smiling at him was a young boy of around eight or even nine. It was his son Bryan who with his dark wavy hair and brown eyes stood out from most of his cousins, some younger and some older, who were gathered in the room. As Richard picked him up, to Bryan's embarrassment in front of his male cousins, he asked him, 'Where's your sister, little Emily, and your mother?'

Bryan made not a sound, but tears began to flow down his cheeks.

Katherine caught hold of Richard's arm.

'Richard, Mary is alive and well. But it's best if you follow me upstairs where mother has taken to her bed. She will love to see you are safe now our father has gone, dying so nobly to save us. As she is now deaf I can then explain in private what has happened.'

He put Bryan down among his cousins and told him he was just going upstairs to see Grandma. He found her in a tiny box room, which emphasised how packed the house was now that over half the family from Appleton was taking refuge. His mother's first response was to stare at him and then burst into tears and hold out her arms. In a loud voice that deaf people often develop she called him to come close.

'We all need you here now that your dear father has gone,' she said, hugging him.'There are plenty of folk who want to go fighting. They don't need you. Whether they are Catholics like me, or Protestants or even Puritan Roundheads, they will learn to tolerate each other, not to go fighting again.'

'You may well be right, mother. I am staying around here for a while and will come and see you most days.'

Richard turned round to his sister and dropping his voice, he said, 'Well, where has Mary gone? I take it that little Emily is with her?'

Kathy took in a deep breath.'I am so sad to tell you, Richard, that she died of diphtheria. She is buried in the family plot at Appleton Roebuck. It was just after her third birthday. Mary and I nursed her and tried some of the old family medicines, but the Lord took her.'

Richard grasped both of Kathy's hands and stood there motionless. Tears slowly rolled down his cheeks, a rare reaction from a King's captain of cavaliers.

Controlling his emotions Richard said quietly.'I loved that little maid. She could be so cheeky, just like her mother. I only saw her about four, perhaps five times. I was looking after King Charles.'

'That was what you were trained to do', said Kathy, giving him a hug.'You could not have saved her if you had been there.'

'And I don't think I can save the King either', he said quietly.'He has to make some compromises with the Parliament.'

'Now tell me, where is Mary and what is going on.'

'She is in Sherburn in Elmet.'

'Whatever for?', he almost shouted.

'Most of us now in this house have our views on the troubles that are going on,' replied Kathy, 'but we are not going to fight about it. Perhaps because of the death of Emily, Mary has become a firm Puritan, as with a few others and they have gone to the house of a cousin of ours, James Byrne, in Sherburn. That's the only active group of Puritan Parliamentarians we know round here. Most folk in the Yorkshire villages are Cavaliers, or indifferent to both.'

It must have been a full minute that Richard stood there motionless, his face becoming ever more red. Kathy felt frightened, because she knew from an event when he was just an early teenager, what he was about to say.

'He is a sly dog who does not have the right to bear our family name. I will go to get him and he will bear our name no longer.'

Kathy grabbed his arms. 'Richard, you are a disciplined man of forty-six, no longer a wild youth who can't control that occasional old Saxon or Viking outburst of violence. Sleep on it and I promise I will take you to see Mary in the morning. Just remember that if you strike James Byrne down with your sword the patched up arguments in our family and our neighbours on whether to support the King or Parliament will break out again.'

'Kathy, I will sleep on it and give you my view in the morning.'

* * *

Richard did not sleep well that night as he kept turning over in his mind what action he should take over his wife's departure. Voices in conversation and banging of doors as the fit members of the family departed to work the land had awoken him around seven. He went down the stairs quietly to find Katherine and one of the elderly aunts giving some bread and jam slices with cups of milk to the younger children. He asked where his son Bryan was.

'He has gone to muck out the pigs,' Kathy told him. 'I know he is young, but he's very strong for his age and anyway he asked to do it. He just works until noon and then might lay down for an hour.'

'Some might think that is a bit hard for a young boy, but I think you are doing the right thing, Kathy.'

Richard cut off a piece of bread from the crusty end of half a loaf and with his knife that always hung from his waistband sliced off a piece of cold pork. He said nothing further until he had breakfasted. 'Kathy, I want to go to Sherburn in Elmet as soon as possible and want you to come with me. I can promise you that no one will be killed through my making, whatever the outcome. I will leave my sword and musket here and just keep my pistol and this knife in case they are needed for our protection on the journey.'

'I can't do it today,' Kathy replied, 'but we will go tomorrow and start off early so we can be back here by nightfall. I can arrange with Ellen, your brother's wife, to look after the young 'uns here. Today, she is over at her mother's who is a little unwell.'

'I appreciate that. If there is not a horse you can borrow, you will have to sit up back with me. After all it's only about five miles away, if that.'

He added in the manner of an afterthought: 'We could do with two horses, then you and Mary can come back together on one.'

When his brother Cedric came in around six that evening Richard asked him if he and Kathy could borrow a horse as they planned to go to Sherburn in the morning to pick up Mary.

'Borrow mine,' he said, quickly glancing at Kathy and raising his eyebrows.

'That's fine Cedric, said Kathy butting in.' I've explained the situation to Richard as we know it.'

The following morning the brother and sister set off for Sherburn in Elmet. He was somewhat surprised when Kathy told him that she understood that Mary was living in a small house next to the Puritan's chapel. This had been the smallest of Sherburn's two churches and in keeping with the Puritan belief had been stripped of much of the Christian display that still existed within the larger Anglican church.

Coming to the small house next to the chapel where they believed James Byrne lived, they dismounted and Richard knocked on the door.

It was soon opened by a middle-aged woman. When they told her that they were looking for Richard's wife, Mary Byrne, and her cousin James Byrne they were amazed at her reply.'They left here some three weeks ago now. Twelve of them, all God-fearing Puritans, have gone to one of the colonies in the New World, New Plymouth I think they said, where they can practice the religion without interference.

Richard turned pale.'You must be mistaken, my good lady, this is unlike my wife to do such a thing, and leave our young son behind. Did James Byrne go as well?'

'Yes,' was the reply.'He went with his wife Margaret, who I have known for years. That's how I have got this house now.'

On the woman's advice they went into the chapel and spoke to the pastor who was there preparing for evening service. He confirmed everything the woman had told them, adding that he felt sure that the ship they were sailing on had picked them up at King's Lynn in Norfolk.

For the next twenty minutes they rode back in silence. Suddenly Richard said, 'Kathy, in spite of what you say this tragic business is mainly my fault. I should have taken more time off from the Cavaliers. The Duke valued my experience so he would have granted any request I made.'

'There is still a chance that the ship has not yet sailed from King's Lynn so I will leave at first light in the morning and find out. If the ship is still there, held up for some reason, I will ask Mary to come back with me. If not, I will ask to go with them to the New World. I have a little money put aside to pay the fare.'

'Richard, I understand that you feel you must do that, Kathy replied.' 'Even though you are not a Puritan they would probably value your presence in that New World.'

Insisting on making a payment for forage to take with him for the horse and some food for himself, Richard bade farewell to Cedric and Kathy. He told them not to say anything to their mother or others in the family as to where he was going, unless he did not return within ten days. He set off for Doncaster where he picked up the old Roman Ermine Street to Lincoln, then making his way across country on minor roads and lanes to Boston, where he caught a ferry across to King's Lynn.

The harbour master assured him that the party of Puritans from Yorkshire had joined others and sailed on the *Speedwell* direct to New Plymouth almost two weeks earlier. When Richard asked if it would stop at Rotherhithe near London first the harbour master said it would not. This was because the drinking water loaded in barrels at King's Lynn was clean, he claimed, and not contaminated with plague, cholera and other illnesses as with

London or Southampton drinking water. This was why so many people died on the *Mayflower* nearly forty years previously.

* * *

Richard had heard that it was not unusual for ships taking people to the New World colonies to make a final stop at Falmouth to top up their fresh water supplies. It was only twenty miles before entering the Atlantic. He soon dismissed the idea as it meant a 350 miles ride across the breadth of England and then Cornwall and it was likely that this would kill his mare who was beginning to show her age, even if he could find her enough forage en route. More important, if he did try to reach Falmouth there was no evidence that the *Speedwell* would stop there, and if it did it would be half way across the Atlantic before he got there.

He decided to return to Church Fenton but at a more leisurely pace than the outward ride. Partly to save the fee on the ferry from King's Lynn to Boston he decide to go through the fens, which had recently started being drained in schemes backed by King Charles I and the Duke of Bedford. Nevertheless, as he rode through Holbeach, Spalding and eventually Sleaford to strike north to Lincoln he found that the people were overwhelmingly for the Parliament and Oliver Cromwell – born in Huntingdon – in particular. In any conversation where he stopped for food and forage he said he was a Lincolnshire farmer and expressed sympathy for the Parliament. Heroics in this situation would achieve nothing, he thought.

After ten days he arrived back at Church Fenton. He asked his sister, brother and sister-in-law Ellen if they would look after his son Bryan in his absence. He told them that he was going to try and make contact with Sir Thomas Glenham who was left as Governor in York immediately after the battle of Marston Moor. If Sir Thomas was no longer the Governor then he would find whoever was in charge in order to serve as a cavalier horse soldier again, even if he was demoted from his captaincy. He said that he would gloss over his desertion after the battle but if his subsequent actions were questioned he would ask for his absence after Marston Moor to be excused saying that as he was cut off he went to check on his family and found his wife and daughter had died. He would say that he did not intend to be a deserter but to make all the necessary funeral arrangements for his family.

The family listened quietly at what Richard had to say and all assured him that whatever happened they would look after Bryan and see that he had a basic education.

'I will give you this advice,' said Cedric.'From what we hear nobody seems to be in charge in York, although the mayor, whoever he is, still turns up at his office, as do a couple of councillors. It seems that a third of the people in the city are still for the King, a third for Cromwell and Parliament and a third are trying to stay neutral and keep alive. Just be cautious brother, and don't let your temper rise up.'

The following morning he rode off to York, again not displaying any weapons. As he started he said to Boudicca his mare.'Well old Boudi it will not be a long ride this time. Then you can rest awhile.'

He added, 'I want you to stay with me so that we can make our last charge together. It must happen within the next twelve months.'

Once inside the walls, which were partially broken away in several places as a result of cannon and mortar fire, he soon found the council offices. An armed door-keeper asked him his business.

Doing his best to look at ease he replied, 'Good afternoon, I am Captain Richard Byrne and would like to offer my services to whoever is now in charge of our city.'

The reply was much as his brother had prophesied.

'At the moment, sir, you could say that the mayor is in charge, but he is not here today. But one of our Councillors is, he is Mr Arthur Winterton and you can see him if you like.'

'Yes, I would appreciate that'.

In ten minutes the door-keeper returned and asked Richard to follow him.

Richard explained his background as a Captain in the cavalier horse soldiers and emphasised his fictitious story of arranging funeral services for his wife and daughter. He then offered his services if they required them at any time for peace-keeping duties in York.

'I can fully sympathise with you for the steps you had to take at the time of your bereavement,' said Councillor Winterton in a friendly manner.

'As for your offer of services, we will bear that in mind for any forthcoming developments in these troubled times. You have to appreciate Captain that the population of this city is more or less evenly divided between Royalists and Cromwell's Parliamentarians. It is like living alongside an opened powder keg waiting for some idiot to drop a lighted torch in it. Therefore, I certainly will not write down your offer of services at this stage in case one of my fellow Councillors who strongly supports the Parliamentarians should read it.'

'I must now end this meeting, Captain Byrne,' said Councillor Winterton extending his hand, 'but should there be an occasion when you wish to rejoin your cavaliers you should contact Lord Digby at this address.'

The Councillor wrote down an address not far from York on a piece of plain paper and handed it to Richard.

As he departed Richard said, 'I am honoured to have met you sir and will treat in confidence all that you have told me.'

By the time he reached Church Fenton he was completely unsure of what action he should take. He told Cedric:

' I suppose I should forget the Civil War, particularly as the King's cause is probably lost because of his failure to compromise. I understand that some Royalists are also leaving this country for the New World. If I did take that option it would not be to try and join Mary. The severity of her departure from me tells me it is over. An alternative is to find myself a small house here and as I am still fit for my age I could work with you and the others in the village on developing the drainage system.'

Cedric had listened carefully to what his brother had to say. After a pause he said, 'I am sure we can find you your own house here and there is certainly work, starting as a labourer, on the drainage of the Fen. But everything will be so different to what you have been trained for, as a fighting horse soldier. You might regret it later if first you did not contact this Lord Digby.'

'Perhaps you are right, Cedric, in regard to first contacting Lord Digby. Let me sleep on it and I will decide in the morning.'

As the following day was a Sunday and he felt the need to go to the village Church of England in the hope that it might settle his mind, he decided he would try and contact Lord Digby on the Monday.

The hall where Lord Digby was said to be living was near Pocklington which was a good twenty-five miles from Church Fenton. Richard had decided that he would go via York and stay the night at a tavern which was said to be not unduly rowdy in view of the current crisis. He would make an early start the following morning and hope to arrive at Pocklington an hour or so before noon, which he thought would be good time to catch his Lordship, if he was there.

He checked in at the Black Bear tavern and told the tavern keeper he would have an early start and would like to leave with his horse around 6. 30am in the morning. He paid his bill in advance to include his dinner and a small breakfast and stabling and forage for the mare. His dinner was half a chicken, which Richard thought probably died of old age, with some bread and a bowl of bean and onion soup. He washed it down with a tankard of ale.

Also eating were three other men, one of them accompanied by a middle-age lady. They all looked at him on various occasions but nobody said a word to him or to each other, apart from the man with the lady, probably his wife. This was indeed a classic of the times.

Was that one a spy for the Puritan Parliamentarians who would try and find out if you were a Royalist, and if so were you part of a hidden army?

That man sipping on onion soup looks like a cavalier with a haircut he did himself. Was he the one who blew my brother's head off at Marston Moor?

Just to see what the response, if any, would be the former Captain of Cavalier horse soldiers ordered a brandy. 'It's a night cap,' he said, smiling at the bar man. 'Yes,' came the reply, 'It's a great help to get you off.'

The bar man moved away to polish some glasses that did not look as if they needed it. In former days he would start telling you his life story, whether you were interested or not. The woman whispered something to her partner but no comment was made by any of the other guests.

Finishing his brandy Richard walked towards the stairs leading up to the bedrooms. As he reached the staircase he stopped with one hand on the banister. Turning round he bid them all good night. Without exception they all quietly responded.

He had no difficulty getting off to sleep although it had only just got dark. About two hours later he was awakened by hearing raised voices below, then some banging as stools or benches were knocked over. Further argument and the sound of doors slamming with the arguing sounding quieter as it continued in the street. This was followed by a loud bang. As a soldier he knew that was a firearm; almost certainly a pistol.

He lay awake for an hour or more, but all remained quiet.

* * *

The next morning as he chewed on some over-salted bacon and the end of a three-day old loaf he said to the bleary-eyed landlord, 'Was that a bit of trouble I heard last night as the drink loosened the tongues of Royalist and Cromwell supporters?'

'No sir, mainly young lads who get carried away after too much ale. My barman and me had to chuck 'em out.'

'Is that so,' said Richard with a half smile 'One of them must have fired a pistol. Hope it did not hurt anybody.'

'Look sir', said the Landlord quietly and looking over his shoulder.'I gathered you are, or had been, a Cavalier soldier. Personally I respect you for that, but to keep earning a living I must not take sides. I hope you won't be taking what you heard further.'

'I give you my word, landlord, that I heard nothing untoward last night. What is more I thank you for good stabling and a decent nose bag you have given my horse this morning.'

The weather had kept good, as September days often were. It was about half eleven by the time he found the hall near Pocklington. It was not really a hall as such but a large house that had the style of those built in the early days of Queen Elizabeth.

He thought of going to the side door but changed his mind and, making sure he was standing upright and not bent through five hours riding, went straight to the main door and knocked. After a few minutes that seemed much longer, the door opened and a man of about his own age and in a partial uniform appeared.

'What do you want sir?,' he demanded.

Richard Byrne explained who he was, then added that Councillor Arthur Winterton at York had told him that he might find Lord Digby here so that he could offer his military services again to fight for King Charles. Relaxing, the man invited Richard to step inside and explained that he was one of Lord Digby's military aides and that his Lordship was rarely here and at present was down at Oxford supporting the King. He added that among the next messages sent to Lord Digby Captain Richard Byrne's offer would be included.

The aide, Colonel John Baxter, then added: 'There are currently no situations in Yorkshire that the King's army needs cavalier horsemen. However, we are about to lay siege once more to Hull, where men and materials are constantly landed by the Parliamentarian forces. Then Scarborough, another crucial supply port for action in the North, has already changed hands five times to my knowledge. I am sure you would fit in a static action at either location.'

Richard thanked him for the offer but thought that as

his military experience was based solely on cavalry actions, particularly those recently upgraded by Prince Rupert, he would prefer to wait for a call to support any future actions of this nature. He wrote down his name and address at Church Fenton for Colonel Baxter and bid him farewell. As he stepped out from the hall he turned to the Colonel and said, 'May I water my horse, sir, at your stables before I depart? She is named after Boudicca the ancient British queen and is getting rather old. Colonel Baxter replied, 'Certainly, you will find my groom in the stables and he will give your mare some fodder as well to help her on her way.'

As Richard and his horse turned towards the stables the Colonel muttered to himself, 'If that man is a Cromwell spy then he has certainly got impudence. Can I water my horse, indeed! But he may well be genuine, which we will find out in a few days. If not, I have only told him something the Parliamentarians already know.'

Richard returned to Church Fenton on the direct route using lanes and byways without incident. It was dusk by the time he and his old mare reached his brother's house.

* * *

He got up early the following morning so that he could have a few words with Cedric before he went off to the farm. He told him that as a result of his meeting with one of Lord Digby's men it was unlikely that the Royalists would be calling for him to come back for cavalier horseman service. In consequence, said Richard, he would be grateful if he would talk to the spokesman for the group working on the expansion of the drainage of the Fen (from which the original Kirk Fenton derived its name) to tell them he was keen to start as a labourer.

Cedric returned about seven that evening and told Richard, 'It's all arranged and you can start in the morning at two shillings a week. Don't get drawn into conversation about the King and

Parliament as there are two Puritans working there who know who you are and were opposed to you starting.'

Grabbing his brother's hand Richard told him, 'Rest assured, my temper is kept well under way nowadays and I will not respond to any name-calling or abuse from a couple of Puritans.'

By October Richard was well immersed in his drainage work and had become accepted by all, including the two Puritans. Initially he found it was physically hard work but as he had always kept fit for a man of his age he soon became accustomed to it.

Cedric had found him a small house to live in until he could afford or arrange something better. In reality 'hovel' would be a better description of the building than 'house'. It was a 12th century style timber framed construction with wattle and daub walls and a thatched roof and had just two rooms. At one end two thirds of the wall was brick built to enable an open fire to be used, with the smoke passing up through a hole in the thatch. His son Bryan thought it was a fine place to live and came to see his father regularly, particularly every Sunday after church.

As winter came in he found he needed that fire, even when first lit it meant that the room became full of smoke until the fire generated enough heat to drive it up through the thatch hole. The cold of that winter became the main subject of conversation, more than the occasional news of skirmishes rather than battles between the supporters of the King's army and that of Cromwell's. From 1350 onwards warm summers had stopped being dependable in Northern Europe with ever increasing snowfall and ice formation in the winters. The first frost fair had been held in London in 1607 when the Thames froze almost solid. The effect of the cool summers had for several years by now led to lower harvest yields. The subsequent higher prices, not matched by higher wages, led to an increased death rate throughout Britain.

It was in that winter that although he was not a heavy drinker Richard started occasional visits to the local tavern, which had not been the habit of the Byrne family. He found it relaxing to talk to the bar maid, a young Irish woman called Maryanne. By late

January 1645 when her work was done she joined Richard in his little house for a bowel of soup he had earlier prepared and warmed up on the fire. They then kept the icy cold at bay by snuggling up in his rather restricted bed. When Cedric told Richard that his relationship with the barmaid had become the subject of village gossip he informed him, 'There's no need for the family to worry. I am not going to marry the poor girl, we just keep each other warm and reduce our bills for kindling wood.'

Cedric saw no reason to laugh so he advised his brother, 'I suppose it is one way of handling a man's normal sexual urges, but please make it not so obvious. And remember, she is also a Catholic which could introduce more problems, and you are probably still married to Mary, wherever she may be.'

Richard smiled as he put his hand on his brother's shoulder and told him, 'I will be careful and as I live apart from the family the gossips can see that what I do does not necessarily meet the Byrne family's approval.'

The seasons of that year passed through, with plenty of rain but not enough sunshine for that summer. Richard had been given an extra four pence a week to mark the satisfaction that the drainage organisers had for his work. After her bar work Maryanne would still come and join Richard for a bowl of soup two or three nights a month, as the nights were still a little chilly.

* * *

It was October 8th that a rather agitated Cedric told Richard at his work site that Councillor Arthur Winterton was at the Byrne home and wanted to see Captain Byrne urgently.

Richard went to his own house first, washed and dressed in his best non-military clothes. He then went to the main house where his sister Kathy let him in and, adopting the manner of a servant maid, led him to Councillor Winterton. Shaking his hand, the councillor told him,

'Parliamentary troops are gathering near Sherburn in Elmet , almost on your doorstep , probably to attack York. Lord Digby is raising a cavalier force as well as troops to beat them to the punch and asks you to join him in your rank as a Cavalier Captain. Have you still got a horse and weapons?'

'Yes I have,' replied Richard.'Where shall I report and when?'

'Come to Heslington, which is near the Osboldwick gate to arrive early morning of October 12th. Travel by night so that it lessens the chance of you being seen by the enemy.'

Richard told his brother and sister Kathy of his actions and to say nothing to his son. He was going to tell Bryan that he had to go away on business for a few days. He asked Cedric to tell the drainage organisers much the same story and give them his apologies.

It was just after dawn as Richard arrived at Heslington. Seeing the other horses gathered there Boudicca's ears pricked up and she raised her head and whinnied. She knew that she was going to be in a great race again with many other horses and lots of noise with men shouting, screaming, all to a cacophony of explosions and bugles blowing.

He pulled her up and as he patted her on the side of her chest he was sure her heart was racing.

'Calm down my old Boudi. It's not the big race today. Only practising.'

The 'practising' went on for another two days, during which he met up with some of his former Cavaliers who survived the battle of Marston Moor. Although Lord Digby had hoped for more men, particularly horse soldiers that had turned up over the three days, he gave the order mid-morning on October 15th for the foot soldiers to set off towards Sherburn in Elmet. Two hours later, the Cavaliers set off with Captain Richard Byrne in charge of a forty-strong troop protecting Lord Digby.

They were about to fight a battle only three miles from the site of the battle of Towton where in 1461 Edward IV established the supremacy of the House of York over Lancaster at the cost of 38,000 lives.

It was just after passing through Appleton Roebuck when the horsemen caught up with the foot soldiers. They told them that they had seen several Roundhead mounted scouts. The hope of carrying out a surprise attack was now gone.

It was mid-afternoon when the Royalists approached the outskirts of Sherburn. The Parliamentarians foot soldiers had manned a barricade and were supported by what appeared to be less than a hundred mounted Ironsides. Still some 400 yards out from the barricade Lord Digby gave the order for the Cavaliers to charge and the foot soldiers to load muskets and follow up. First away was Richard Byrne on Boudicca. They had gone less than one-hundred yards when Boudicca reared up then fell to the ground and lay motionless. The rest of his troupe went round them as Richard looked in vain for any signs of blood on his horse.'Oh God, my dear old Boudi your heart just gave up,' he cried.' You knew this was going to be your last charge.'

Two foot soldiers eagerly accepted his request to help him move the horse close to a hedge alongside a ditch so as to give free movement for returning horsemen. Richard stayed there, nearly in tears, hoping that when the Cavaliers returned there may be a rider-less horse he could capture and so rejoin his men. Digby's quickly taken charge was initially successful and they took control of all the village. But with only half an hour of daylight left the Parliamentarians led by Colonel Copley counter-attacked and routed the Royalists, taking around 400 prisoners.

Quickly seeing that it was highly likely that Digby's forces were now incapable of a further attack, Richard threw himself into the ditch hoping that the nettles he had fallen into and the bulk of Boudicca's corpse above would hide him from any Roundheads looking for prisoners. Before doing so he had also removed his saddle from Boudicca and used that as further cover in his hiding place.

He remained there for what he imagined must be not far from midnight. With his saddle strapped to his back he moved through fields and along ditches around Sherburn. Again without using the lane connecting directly with Church Fenton, he made his way across country for five miles or so before reaching the comparative safety of his wattle and daub cottage.

After six hours deep unbroken sleep he got up, ate a piece of stale bread and drank some milk that had still not gone completely sour. He went to the Byrne family house to let them know he had survived.

The men, and his son Bryan, were at work, but Kathy and Ellen were there looking after the children and Mother, who now had serious dementia. They both hugged him. Sister Kathy said:

'Richard, you are indestructible. But it is such a shame for that poor old horse who you worked to death.'

Looking serious, Kathy added.'A message arrived for you. It was from James Byrne and took nine months to get here from New Plymouth in the New World. Your Mary died of pneumonia just before last Christmas as a result of the intense cold they get there in wintertime.'

Richard stood immobile and said not a word in reply as his eyes welled up with tears. After two or three minutes he just said, 'Oh, my poor Mary, I should never have left her for so long.'

Ellen, who was never diplomatic, quietly cut off some fresh bread and a piece of bacon.'Here you are, Richard, we imagine you have not had much to eat since your escape. What is the past must now be forgotten. You can marry the lovely Irish girl Maryanne now, particularly as she is expecting a baby.'

Chapter Eight
Laki Brings Destruction

Apart from the argument she had had with her cousin Ellen, Maryanne Byrne was very pleased with herself. Having worked for a doctor in York as an unrecognised nurse, due to his influence she had just been appointed as an official nurse in the York County hospital opened in 1740.

The argument with Ellen that took place at the Byrne family home in Church Fenton was catalysed by the treatment that Ellen had insisted on giving to her year-old daughter Molly who had contracted smallpox. There was another outbreak of the disease in York itself and two children in the village were now showing the symptoms.

Ellen's remedy was an ancient one handed down by her mother. It consisted of mixing sheep dung in white wine and rosewater, to which was added fennel, coriander and cinnamon. The little child then had to take a teaspoon of this mixture every four hours.

In some ways it was unfortunate that Maryanne should be visiting her elderly parents, Seamus and Beatrice Byrne at the time. When she was told of the composition of the so-called anti-smallpox medicine she could hardly believe it and flew into a rage.

'What disgusting medieval witch's brew is that you are giving to a baby?' she screamed at Ellen.

'This is the middle of the eighteenth century and you are going to poison her with some sheep shit because a thousand years ago some wizened Celt or a Viking too old for raping and pillaging said it worked!'

'Just because you now work in the new Hospital you think you are already a clever doctor,' said Ellen in an almost calm voice.'The doctors' answer to everything is to bleed you to let the nasty blood out, so the idiots have been saying ever since the ancient Greeks thought of it.' Warming to her argument, Ellen added,

'The best medicines they depend upon are still ancient ones like bark from the birch tree. Chew it, or brew it, and it will cure your headaches. Common chalk ground up and mixed with milk will always cure your acid stomach.'

Seamus suddenly interrupted them.' Now girls, calm down. We don't want to see cousins falling out because of different views. Ellen, you have to understand that Maryanne's great-grandmother, with the same name, came from Dublin in Ireland, which was founded by the Vikings. That's where she gets the red hair and the quick temper. It seems to have passed me by. Mark you, she may also have some of her great-grandfather's blood. He was a captain in King Charles the First's horse cavaliers and fought like a demon but mainly, it is said, controlled his vile temper. His first wife left him and went off to America. Then he met Maryanne from Dublin. They say that she would throw things at him in his old age, but he would just laugh.'

Maryanne looked at her father then walked over and kissed him on his forehead. Smiling sheepishly she went over to Ellen and said,

'Do forgive me, Ellen, my dear cousin. You are entitled to your views, although I do not agree with this particular one.'

Ellen smiled at her.'You might be right, Maryanne. All that it has done so far for poor little Molly is to make her sick.'

Within a week Molly seemed to have recovered, whether or not it was down to the sheep's dung medicine cocktail. The small blisters she had disappeared without leaving the pock marks of small pox. Seamus's wife Beatrice said that what the baby had caught was cow pox, which made the victim feel ill, but did not last long. More important, she said, was that once you have had cow pox you will never catch small pox.

Following the argument with Ellen, Maryanne had to leave to

get back to York Hospital by prior arrangement with the owner of a pony and trap who was also taking another lady to York. This meant she missed seeing her brother Thomas and her cousin Richard Byrne who was married to Ellen.

Beatrice was the first to tell them of the fun they had missed as a result of this latest outbreak of Maryanne's famous temper. Thomas, who was three years older than Richard, laughed as much as everybody else. The episode prompted him to tell the others a few more details about their common great-grandfather Richard.

'Did you know that when Cromwell's people chopped off King Charles' head in 1649, one of the staunch Puritans working on the land drainage said that it was a job well done. Our great-grandfather apparently grabbed him by the throat and raised his knife threatening to give him the same treatment. That was the only time apparently that they had seen him unable to control his temper. He was docked a week's wages, but was promoted to foreman two years later. My grandfather, the first Seamus, told me that great-grandfather Richard was the hardest working man on the drainage system, even when his little fingers began to bend over, and just dropped down dead one winter morning when he was sixty.'

Because of the Byrne's nearly two hundred years of work in helping to drain the fen land between Sherburn and Church Fenton each generation had been able to purchase another acre or two at discounted prices so that their holding was now over fifty acres. The other branch of the family still at Appleton Roebuck held a similar amount. The more populous parishes in the area in the mid-18th century retained the open fields and common pastures for their animals, but elsewhere the local squire enclosed all available land.

The Vale of York area was a district of mixed farming paying equal attention to livestock and arable crops. As a result of the gentry in the York area beginning to add potatoes to their menus, the Byrnes decided that as the soil at Church Fenton was said to be very suitable they would try growing some.

Although Sir Walter Raleigh had first brought back potatoes

from the New World in Elizabethan times, they had not become popular. The peasantry in particular disliked them for their lack of flavour and because they really did not know what to do with them. They had a bulk about them which could fill you up, but the only way to make them taste was to tip some gravy over them. There was similar resistance to eating potatoes in the rest of the British Isles, and on the Continent. In Prussia, followed by the rest of the German states, the breakthrough came through the dedication of Frederick the Great in making them acceptable. Not only did he campaign amongst the ordinary people in stressing that they were 'good for you and are nutritious', but he regularly made a big show of eating them at state dinners, smacking his lips enthusiastically.

The winter and summer temperatures had only risen slightly from the lowest of 1650 in Britain's mini ice age, which meant that English farmers were accustomed to lower crop yields than in late Tudor times. The Byrnes cousins were surprised – and pleased – to see that the potatoes grew quite well. From 1741 demand very gradually increased for their potatoes, until 1783 when nothing would grow.

* * *

By 1745 England had become used to the Hanoverian kings and having grown more prosperous they had no desire to go back to the rule of the Stuarts. Charles Stuart – Bonny Prince Charlie – thought otherwise and a large number of Scots gave him their support, but very few English Jacobites. Having crossed into England and got as far down as Finchley, just north of London, Charles' army was driven back to the Scottish Highlands. In the early spring of 1746 although the Highlanders fought bravely they were massacred by the mainly Hanoverian troops of the Duke of Cumberland.

The Jacobite rebellions largely had no affect on York. When the Scots were defeated the city sent congratulations to the King and invited 'the Butcher' Duke of Cumberland to accept the freedom of the city. Twenty-two Jacobite rebels were beheaded at York and two of the heads were placed on Micklegate Bar in 1745. They stayed there until 1754, despite some protests of 'barbarity'.

A leader of the protests for the first few months was Maryanne Byrne. She was spoken to by her former Doctor employer who suggested:

'You can be far more useful in helping civilisation to advance in York by making sure you hold down your nursing job in the County Hospital. I can assure you there are some people with influence who would have you thrown out of your work and imprisoned as an active Jacobite.'

Following her initial characteristic response of waving her clenched fists and shouting, 'How dare they! I will give them a piece of my mind!', Maryanne saw the logic in the doctor's sound advice and assured him she would now keep quiet on the question of the severed heads. She avoided Micklegate Bar until someone stole the heads.

She knew that as elsewhere in the British Isles most citizens enjoyed the spectacle of public executions and the subsequent display of rebels' heads. In York they flocked to Knavesmire for such executions, including that of the highwayman Dick Turpin in 1739. Life in York then was no rougher, dirtier or more brutal than in other towns of a comparable size. It had remained as a market town, with many craftsmen but no industry. It had lost most of its textile manufacturing trade to the West Riding towns, which like the formerly small towns in the North and North East of England were now overtaking York in size of population.

Maryanne was certainly not content with the Hospital's work in making slight improvements in the area's public health. Some said that much of the improvement was down to the installation of water supply through wooden pipes – for those who could afford it. At least half of young children were still dying from the diseases that engulfed foul-smelling cities such as York, although this death rate was slightly lower in the villages. Smallpox, measles and even outbreaks of 'plague ague' were still taking their toll. To this was added typhus from 1770 onwards.

An Act was obtained by 1763 to light and clean the streets of York and regulate the hackney carriages. Later, a man called a scavenger cleaned the streets of animal dung and other rubbish. This further contributed to the city's confidence in claiming that it was 'the capital city of the northern parts of England and a place of great resort and much frequented by persons of distinction and fortune'. This may have smacked of exaggeration but at least by 1744 the first theatre on the site of the present Theatre Royal was built. As well as shops, the number of coffee houses expanded. Some of the attraction of the coffee houses lay in the opportunities they gave for gambling. The less 'refined' people, i. e. the majority, still found their pleasures in the ale houses, which like London saw the 'Rise of Mother Gin', or in cock-fighting. The Cockpit lay in Bootham at its junction with the modern street of St. Mary's. Some elements of all classes looked for their pleasures in the brothels, usually found in thieves' kitchen areas, and provided additional patients for the overworked York County Hospital. It was just after Maryanne's clash with authority over her objection to the display of the Jacobite heads that she fell in love with a young trainee doctor straight from Durham University. Such was the pressure of their work that their courtship was sporadic. Finally a date was set for their wedding in June 1748. In May he died slowly from the effects of smallpox, which he had contracted as a result of his work at the County Hospital.

For the next decade Maryanne dedicated herself to improving the success rate of the hospital and always supported trials on new medicines and medical procedures that were being developed all over Europe. Her outbursts of temper became legendary, but were directed only at doctors and nurses and never at patients. If she had been a man at that time she would have been appointed as a doctor, but she had to be content at being made the head nurse in 1757. Mainly through the persuasion of her elder brother Thomas she would visit the Byrne family at Church Fenton perhaps twice a year.

As a result of testing some new medicine for curing cholera,

Maryanne died in the early winter of 1760, with her auburn hair just beginning to fade. Her brother Thomas organised her funeral at St. Mary's in York. It was attended by most of the hospital doctors and nursing staff (leaving a minimum to look after patients) as well as family. Also present were at least a dozen patients who she had helped to recover from some of the serious diseases. 1770 brought a major outbreak in York of typhus, the new disease which had just come to English cities. The harvest in most parts of the country was particularly bad mainly due to another cool summer. At least Church Fenton managed to raise some crops, which was put down to the richness of the drained soil. Hired labour on the Byrnes' land in Appleton Roebuck as well as Church Fenton had to be dispensed with for the first time in living memory, leaving only Byrne family members now working on their land. A bonus from the wet summer was that the potato crop did well and as it was at last beginning to be looked upon as part of working family's diets, it was likely to be completely sold by mid-winter.

In September that year the marriage took place in Church Fenton of Arthur Byrne to local girl Joan Pryke. Arthur was the son of the late Thomas Byrne, the brother of Maryanne, and had a brother and a sister who had died before the age of three. A reflection of the sombre times they lived in was that although the Byrnes had always been known to enjoy making music on festive occasions, at the reception for Arthur and Joan following their marriage in the church celebration was subdued. The harpsichord remained covered and fiddles and flutes were left at home.

A week later a conference was called to discuss ways of overcoming the downturn in their farm harvests and whether or not they were concentrating on the right crops, or should they expand the areas down to pasture so they could increase the raising of livestock. Present as chairman was Richard Byrne, now fifty-four, his son Bryan and wife Anne, Richard's youngest son Cedric (now eighteen), Arthur, the son of the late Thomas Byrne, John Byrne, another fit fifty-year-old, representing the smaller farm land at

Appleton. Also present was Ivor Fairhall a cousin who lived nearby at Sherborn. His grandparents had left York when their jewellery business went bankrupt following a robbery. On the days when Ivor did not come over to help on the land, he worked as a part-time ironsmith specialising in making decorative ironwork and even basic jewellery.

It was decided without any real dissent that there was little they could do to improve profitability with any new crops, other than supporting any promotions in York for people to eat more potatoes, even where it meant a discount on price.

The four youngest – Bryan, Anne, Arthur and Cedric – were keen on increasing production of livestock. Bryan and Anne handed out a number of leaflets showing the views of Robert Bakewell who was fast making a name for himself all over Britain with revolutionary new breeding techniques. These called for grassland irrigation and flooding (in both of which the Byrnes had gained considerable experience) and fertilising the pasture lands to improve grazing. Soon, all of them were interested, particularly with the idea of cross-breeding sheep from native stocks to give a meaty body with long wool.

Robert Bakewell was the first to breed cattle to be used primarily for beef. Previously cattle were first and foremost kept for pulling ploughs – as oxen were. He crossed long-horned heifers and a Westmoreland bull to eventually create the Dishley Longhorn. In 1700 the average weight of a bull sold for slaughter was 370 pounds. By 1786 that weight had more than doubled to 840 pounds.

Within five years the Byrnes were beginning to see a better living as a result of applying Bakewell's techniques to the raising of improved sheep stock and some cattle. The original scepticism of Richard and John Byrne had been won over. What is more the potato crops in Church Fenton were doing well in most years and more and more ordinary people throughout England were now eating them. The acreage formerly devoted to wheat, barley and beans was now reduced and most of the crop was for animal feed.

Bryan and Anne were also happy with their immediate family. Their first child, a girl, had only lived for three months. The next child, Matilda had got through the childhood diseases that took so many and was now a healthy girl of ten, her eight-year-old brother William was tall and strong for his age, but on occasions afflicted the family with outbursts of temper.

More than once when the two children were playing together Anne had said to Bryan, 'Look at those two. You can see they love each other but are so different. Matilda looks like a gypsy girl with those lovely dark eyes and that black wavy hair. And William is so fair with his strong blue eyes. He may look like an angel but too often acts more like the devil. That's what some of you Byrnes are like.'

Bryan smiled at what Anne had said.'I remember my father and grandfather saying something about there being dark Norwegian and definitely Irish blood somewhere back in the family which results in these beautiful gypsy-looking girls appearing every so often. As for William, he may look a bit like me, but I never had his temper. My father Richard has it still but now he's reached the good old age of seventy he has learned to control it. Have you seen his fingers all bent up? Now I will tell you who really had the temper and was more like a Viking lady warrior than a nurse ...'

'I know who you are thinking of,' cried Anne butting in.'Your great aunt Maryanne with the flaming red hair!'

* * *

By the spring of 1783 the Byrne family had survived another bad harvest – which not all farms in Yorkshire and the North East had been able to do – and contemplated what this summer would bring.

William, now sixteen, and sister Matilda, both worked on the Church Fenton farm. As was the custom of the Byrnes for nearly two hundred years, from the age of twelve they would have two mornings off each week to attend the small private school in the village. This ended when they reached seventeen. Thus Matilda was wondering whether or not to remain with the farm or become a nurse like her great aunt.

Then in June that year the minds of Matilda, William and countless thousands of others throughout northern Europe were dominated by the cataclysmic eruption of Iceland's Laki volcano. By June 22nd the ash arrived in Northern Europe, being particularly heavy in Scotland and Northern England. An estimated 120,000,000 tons of sulphur dioxide was emitted. This caused a thick haze to spread across western Europe with record high temperatures. Inhaling the poisonous gas caused victims to choke as their internal soft tissues swelled.

Parish records for the Vale of York, as well as most parts of Britain showed a startling increase in the number of deaths. In Britain overall it was around an extra 30,000 above normal. It was particularly high among farm workers. In Church Fenton one of the first to go was Richard Byrne, quickly followed by Arthur's wife Joan.

Gilbert White, a clergyman in Hampshire noted that the vegetation was yellow and looked 'as if scorched with frost'. For those farmers rearing animals, such as the Byrnes, this was a major feed problem. Describing the effect on the animals Gilbert White again writes:

'All the time the heat was so intense that butcher's meat could hardly be eaten the day after it was killed; and the flies swarmed so in the lanes and hedges that they rendered horses half frantic. The country people began to look with awe at the red, louring aspect of the sun. There were alarming meteors and tremendous thunder storms.'

By June 23rd the fog was so thick that boats stayed in port, unable to navigate, and the sun was described as being 'blood coloured'. Crops were withering and dying in the fields and in Church Fenton the potato crop was completely ruined.

One report says that in some parts of Eastern England from Lincolnshire to Eastern Yorkshire 'entire families of farm workers were virtually wiped out.' By late July, elderly Thomas Byrne, father of Arthur, and Ellen the wife of Richard had died together with several young children of the family and among neighbours, including the four-year-old sister of Matilda and William. Then in August Arthur, with a wet towel around his mouth and fastened at the neck, was digging in the field to see if any carrots and turnips had survived. Gasping for breath he collapsed to the ground. In ten minutes his body was carried from the field. All over England and Scotland farmers had not enough hands to gather whatever harvest there was as the sight of grown men dying in the field became commonplace. Small towns and villages used to burying only a handful of people each year, suddenly had to deal with four or five times the usual number. When the winter arrived the deadly haze of sulphur dioxide had slowly dissipated. In its place was the most severe winter ever recorded, to be repeated in the following year. In his report Gilbert White said even down in warmer Hampshire there were twenty-eight days and nights of continuous frost. Following the damage done to their lungs in the summer the intense cold in Yorkshire added John Byrne at Appleton Roebuck and Cedric, Bryan's younger brother, to the Byrne family's death list.

Ivor Fairhall and his wife and small son had now moved in at the Church Fenton home primarily so that he would eliminate travelling and have more time to work the farm as best they could. It also meant that they could pool living and the important heating costs.

In early March Bryan suggested they should decide what was the best deployment of their labour as so few crops had survived. He told them:

'When the wind comes down from the north west we are still getting some of the poisonous clouds from that volcano up in Iceland and who knows when it will stop. What is more, the winters have been getting colder for some years now. So as it is, not only do we not need to hire labourers for the fields, but if only for one year it might be best if two younger ones amongst us look for work in York or Selby.'

Addressing his father, William said, 'As much as I love my parents and the rest of the family, what is happening makes me want to try some other work.'

Before he could develop his theme Ivor interrupted, 'I have often thought I should concentrate on making jewellery. After all, it's in my blood. But I need to be in York where my customers would be but it's where I have a higher risk of getting one of the death-dealing diseases.'

There was silence for a few seconds before Bryan offered his advice.

'Ivor, I think you ought to stay here at least until the latest typhus outbreak in York fades away.'

'Yes, cousin Ivor,' added William, 'There is no need for you to leave. Matilda and I have decided that we shall go to see if we can find new jobs elsewhere. She would have no difficulty as a teacher for the children of more prosperous families.'

His mother Anne staggered to her feet coughing and grasped his arm.

'You may be as big and as strong as a man, but you are still a boy. I won't let you and my Matilda leave us on a wild goose chase to London.'

'Let me speak, dear Mother,' said Matilda in a quiet but firm voice.'We are not going to London. Disease, robbery and violence down there is said to be worse than in York. Until the volcano eruption brought its death clouds Londoners were leaving in droves to come North and find work.'

'Well, that's true,' said her father butting in.

Matilda continued.'We aim to go to Newcastle, which is now a key centre for new industry particularly iron goods, toolmaking and the new pumping engines. Not only is William strong and hard working, remember he can read and write and do his sums. That's the difference between him and general labourers.'

'Mother, please don't cry,' said William.'Matilda has explained our plans exactly and when we have made a bit of money we will catch the stagecoach from Newcastle to York and come and see you.'

'How will you get there?' his father asked.

'We can't ask you for a horse, because there is only one left now in our stable. So we will walk and hopefully beg a lift from passing carters here and there.'

Now the outline of the proposed adventure of the young pair had been thought over by the family, they all went into an excited discussion.

'When do you propose to go?' asked Bryan.

'April 2nd,' William replied.'It should be a little warmer by then, and it's not April Fools Day'.

Chapter Nine

The Long Walk

It was April Fools day 1784 and Anne Byrne was shedding tears again.

'My good Lord, look at my Matilda's beautiful curls lying there on the floor. I hope they grow again by the time you come back to see me.'

'Don't fret mother. It's just to help me look like a boy when we're travelling. If any villains try to give us bother they will find I can fight as well as William.'

'Mother, stop worrying,' said William, 'I will be seventeen in a few weeks and at six foot I am bigger than most men already. Matilda will be dressed in my smock and breeches I grew out of last year. We will have to make out she, or he rather, is a bit fat so as to hide her bosom.'

Matilda pulled her brother's ear and grimaced at him. The remainder of the family laughed. Only his father knew that he would also be carrying a dirk for protection.

Over the previous months William and Matilda had saved £1 and 2 shillings to help on night accommodation if it was too wet or cold and for some basic food. Their parents stocked up their backpacks with some bread, pork and salt beef from their own reserves and gave them another £1 and 5 shillings. Through contact with another surviving local farmer Bryan Byrne had negotiated a good price for his two offspring to be given a lift by a carter who was going to York to pick up a load of glass bottles and take them to a brewery in Northallerton. It was half past six when the carrier stopped outside the house that April morning, but there was still frost upon the ground. Anne hugged and kissed her children and wiping her eyes said, 'Pass word on with carriers that you have arrived safely in Newcastle. And do come back soon.'

Bryan hugged his son and kissed and hugged his daughter more gently. He went indoors quickly. He did not want them to see his tears. He knew and his children knew that it was unlikely they would ever see each other again.

As they made their way to York they could see that there was no let up in the desolation of the countryside and no visible signs of the return of spring normally expected in early April.

No cattle could be seen so they assumed survivors must be in barns as it was still so cold. The hardy sheep would normally be out in the fields, but fewer than normal were to be seen.

When they arrived in York to load up the bottles the two young Byrnes did not dismount, other than to briefly stretch their legs, in order to make less contact with the people and thereby reduce the chances of typhus infection. They ate some of the bread and pork they had brought with them as well as a drink of water from a flask filled up at home.

Leaving York, the countryside looked as desolate as it was when they left home. For the first time for at least a month a slight smell of the sulphurous fumes was in the air. This could be due to the fact that the wind was now in the north and again bringing the reduced discharge down from the Icelandic volcano. They resorted to applying dampened handkerchiefs around their mouth and nostrils.

They reached Thirsk around 3. 00pm. On the right loomed the western edge of the North York Moors, still with a covering of snow. The people here looked less disconsolate than those they saw in York. Perhaps it was just their imagination that things might get better the further north they went. More likely it could be because the wind had dropped down considerably and was veering to the east, and they could no longer smell the sulphurous fumes.

Running parallel to the Hambleton Hills that form the western edge of the North York Moors they reached Northallerton just as dusk was falling. The carrier stopped at an inn called the Rising Sun.

'This is where I'm having my supper and staying the night,' he told them.'If you want to make your money last then he will give you a bowl of stew and let you sleep in the barn, all for two pence each.'

'Thank you for that information,' William replied.'That is just what we will do.'

The carrier grinned at them both and looking at Matilda he said, 'Keep in the dark as much as possible because though you might be wearing your brother's old clothes you haven't really got the shape of a boy, you know.' She blushed but made no comment.'Just be careful,' the carrier advised.'It's Friday and Saturday night's you have to avoid, when some of them wild Northallerton boys have been paid and have a drink or two and start to chase any women who might be strangers. You should be OK on a Tuesday night though.'

This time it was Matilda who, with a smile, thanked him for his advice.

Taking a seat at the back of the main bar where the stew was served they found it better than they expected. With so many animals being killed by the destruction of Laki they found several pieces of mutton in amongst the vegetables.'Look,' said William, 'father would be pleased. There's some potatoes in this.'

As they were eating they saw the carrier come in, sit at the bar and order a tankard of ale. After the carrier talked to the innkeeper for a while William noticed that both suddenly looked in their direction. Half an hour later William went up to him to pay and told him the two of them were now going to the barn.

In a friendly manner the innkeeper told him, 'You and your partner go up the ladder to the loft because it will be warmer up there from the heat of the horses. There will be two or three men at the bottom who are looking after the horses. I know them as they pass this way regularly. They will not give you any problems.'

William felt a little awkward that the innkeeper obviously knew his sister was not a boy.'Thanks for telling me that' he muttered and smiled.

As they went into the barn there were two men not far from the door and near to three horses. They were shaking out their blankets and placing them over two straw beds they had prepared. 'Good night,' young 'uns,' they said. 'Good night,' they both replied, with Matilda putting on the deepest voice she could raise.

So that the horsemen could not see the form of her body, William told her to go up the ladder first and he would be as close behind as he could. Their eyes soon adjusted to the semi-darkness, with a little light coming from the men down below. They each had a rather thin blanket rolled up in their backpacks and laid down together on a good thickness of straw and managed to get some on top of the blankets as well.

Richard faced outwards, his back to his sister and his left hand on the dirk.

Awakened by a cock crowing, they realised that they had slept solidly all night until dawn. After about ten minutes they could hear the men below talking, followed by the horses neighing. They decided they would wait up to half an hour to see if the horsemen would be off on their way. Meanwhile they had some more cold beef and bread from their rations for breakfast and washed it down with the last of the water from home. As they finished breakfast and packed their backpacks, they heard the men departing and the horses hooves clattering on the cobbles. 'Ideal,' said Matilda, 'and I am the first one in the privy. I saw one at the back of the inn.'

Having washed their hands and faces from a pump they filled up their water flask, hoping that being pumped up from below ground it was unlikely to be carrying infections. It was a fine April morning and the slight night frost was fast disappearing. The air was different to what it had been for nearly a year: pure and fresh. As they stepped on to the street the innkeeper was standing at his door and waved them goodbye.

Thus they set out on their long walk along the Great North Road that runs from Edinburgh to London, and in those days via Northallerton before reaching York. It would take them through Darlington, Durham, Newcastle and on into Northumberland

– if they so required. The Great North Road was a highway that slowly evolved since Viking times. It was carved and rutted by feet, hooves and wagon wheels. After heavy rain it became a swamp and walkers had to take to the sides, sometimes a hundred yards from the true road. Fortunately by the late 17th century it was all on common land. By this time turnpikes were now in operation along the whole length of the Great North Road in England. The fees charged were supposed to cover the cost of road maintenance in the area covered by each turnpike, but only in the approaches to London was this really effective.

Half an hour after leaving Northallerton William and Matilda came to the monument at Cowton Moor which marks the site of the Battle of the Standards, also known as the Battle of Northallerton, where an English army eventually drove back an army of Scottish invaders. The section of the Great North Road from here to Darlington was the scene of many battles between the two nations over four hundred years. As the two young Byrnes stopped to read the plaque on the monument they were unaware that one of their ancestors, Alan Byrne, had narrowly escaped death at the battle. Being over fifty he had developed the bent little fingers in both hands. At the peak of the battle an equally elderly Scot had him by the throat and suddenly said, ' I will nae kill ye. All my kin have the Viking finger. You must be a southern Viking, perhaps Danish origin.'

The two pressed on with the target of reaching Darlington, a further eighteen miles, before dusk. There were stretches where the muddy, rutted road extended to adjacent farm hedges and fences, which slowed their progress. Apart from when they passed through villages, nobody overtook them nor did they come up to anybody else. Twice they met foot travellers coming the other way. On the first occasion it was two men who shouted out, 'If you're looking for work, friends, there's nothing in Darlington.'

They then crossed over and asked, 'What's it like in York, any labouring jobs there?'

William told them there were a few jobs but they had better

beware of typhus which was still around when they left. Putting on her deep voice, Matilda muttered, 'Yes, that's true.'

Further on two men and a woman came level with them on the other side, then stopped. One of the men mumbled something in an accent they could not quite follow. Perhaps it was the effect of drink. The woman just glared. By then William was carrying his dirk on his belt outside of his smock. As he and Matilda passed them he put his hand on the hilt and made sure they saw it. It had the required affect.

Any police in that period were only to be found in towns, where local improvement acts had often included providing for paid watchmen or constables to patrol towns at night.

Outside the village of Great Smeaton they reached a Turnpike where there were two carriages, one going north and the other south. Some of the occupants looked at the pair of walkers with curiosity. They probably thought they belonged to the nearby village.

It was not long after this that they lost their route and ended up on a country lane leading to the banks of the upper river Tees at a hamlet called Eryholme. A local lady told them that it was the last village in Yorkshire and when they had gone over the stepping stone bridge they would be only five miles from Darlington and in the county of Durham. Matilda's hair was beginning to grow again and formed tight little curls. The lady asked if she was a Spanish girl.'No, I'm Yorkshire born and bred,' she replied with a smile. They decided to stop at this idyllic spot and have a late lunch and early tea. This led them to see how fast their rations were being diminished. They also took their boots off and dangled their tired feet in the water of the Tees, cold that it was, and filled up the water flask.

They crossed the stepping stone bridge with caution seeing that the water was deeper and faster flowing than they thought. They stood on the bank and looked back at the only county of England they had ever known. They said not a word, but both wondered whether they would see Yorkshire again?

As they walked into Darlington in the early evening they could see that it was another country town rather like Northallerton but somewhat smaller. They passed two or three alehouses then came to two coaching inns within fifty yards of each other. The innkeeper of the first one told them that as Darlington was a favourite overnight stop for coaches going both north and south all rooms were full up, but they could sleep on a straw palliasse on the kitchen floor for two shillings each. Dinner would be an extra shilling each.

William told him, 'I will have to discuss this outside with my brother.'

Moving outside he said to Matilda, 'Well brother, I read in that newspaper from York just before we left that the cost of everything since the volcano went off has gone up by over fifteen per cent. His charges would take too much from our funds at this early stage. I think we should do as last night and sleep in the barn of one of the alehouses we passed.'

'Yes, we would be paying six shillings to sleep on a floor, with people coming and going all night after probably being fed pigswill,' Matilda replied in her affected deep voice. With Matilda still practising the manner of walking with bigger steps like a man, they walked back to the area where they saw the alehouses.

'Before we go in,' said William, 'Don't over do the big steps. It makes you look more like the village idiot.' She punched him in the ribs and they went into the first alehouse.

The innkeeper told them they could have a bowl of stew and sleep in the barn above the horses for three shillings for the two of them. William asked him what time would the stew start being served and was told, 'Anytime after seven. The earlier you come the more bits of pork you might find.'

'Right, sir, we will see you just after seven,' William told him.

They walked down the street to the other alehouse and found that it already seemed to have more drunks than the first one and the barn looked as if a good wind might blow it down. So they returned to where they had made a provisional booking and handed over three shillings to the innkeeper.

Again they sat at the back of the bar where the light from the candles and a modern oil lamp left them in the shadows. The few pieces of pork were already rather sparse so they ate with relish as they wondered how many pieces would be left by eight o'clock. With plenty of beans, turnips and some potatoes to bulk it up, the meal was edible and filled them up.

Halfway through their meal they noticed that two men in their late twenties to early thirties and poorly dressed had sat on a bench near them. In between slurping their stew Richard and Matilda noticed they were paying considerable attention to them and their conversation.

'I hope that couple of vagabonds are not sleeping in the barn,' Richard whispered. 'We will go now and as I get near them I will make out we are off to our home nearby.'

As they got level he said in a normal conversational voice, 'All right, brother, we ought to go home now as old grandma will think we will come home drunk.'

They went to the barn where two men were already making up their beds on the straw near the horses.

'Good night lads,' they said, to which William and Matilda – in her deep voice – responded. As before, Matilda went up the ladder first with Richard closely behind.

They prepared their straw bed in the same way as the previous night and kept all their clothes on. Again there was some light from the lamps belonging to the men below. Although it was only a little after nine they both felt tired after the full day walking and got into their straw beds, with William facing outwards and holding the hilt of his dirk in his left hand.

They had been in a deep sleep for at least four hours when William was awakened by muffled cries from Matilda and felt the pressure of someone's hands around his neck. He kicked away the blanket and straw and thrust his left hand, grasping the dirk, above his head. He felt it sink in to part of a body which released a scream of abuse from whoever was there. It was followed by a shout of pain from another male voice, followed by him shrieking, 'You've nearly bit my nose off, you gypsy slut.' The horsemen below were now shouting , 'What's going on up there?' Then some light appeared on the scene as two of the men from below came up the ladder.

When they surveyed the scene they burst out laughing. Matilda, who had bit halfway through the nose of her would-be rapist was sitting on his chest and punching him. He had no breeches on, nor drawers. The horseman with the lamp held it over him, saying, 'He couldn't do much with that little winkle, my dear! Perhaps you've killed his ardour.'

With blood pouring from his arm, William's assailant moaned and turning to the horsemen, said,' 'He tried to kill me.'

William grabbed him by his waistcoat top.'You were trying to strangle me whilst your fellow scum was trying to rape my sister. I am right-handed and if my dirk had been in it, and not in my left, you would be dead. I suppose you were planning this when you two kept looking at us when we had our stew? '

The wounded man turned to the elder horseman and whined, 'It's all lies. I want the innkeeper, Josiah Wilton, to hold these two here until the magistrate comes down from Durham city next week. He will probably have them hanged in Durham jail.'

The elder horseman whispered something to his partner, then said to the would-be rapist, 'Your friend has a point. Now just stay here you two until I come back and I will hand these young 'uns over to Mr Wilton – if I can wake him up.'

William was now red-faced and clenching his hands and his teeth. Turning to the horsemen he shouted 'You must be mad...' He stopped in his tracks as Matilda grabbed his arm and staring at him said, 'No more, William. We will go down with these two gentlemen and then wait for the innkeeper and explain what has happened.'

Without saying another word William picked up their backpacks and putting the blankets inside went down the ladder with the two horsemen. Turning to Matilda the senior man said, 'Unlike your brother, courageous as he may be, you put your brain before your brawn. Those two up there are local ne're-do-wells.

Despite that, as they will still have wounds to show next week, the magistrate might well rule against you. Therefore, you should both be on your way as fast as you can. If they get tired of waiting up there I will tell them I have shut you up in the kitchen.'

Matilda and William thanked them profusely. The horsemen asked them which way they were going and when they told them it was north to Durham, they said they would tell the villains that they were going south to York. The senior man then gave them some useful advice.'There's a good moon at present so keep on the Great North Road as you can move faster unless you see anybody, particularly on horseback or with a cart or coach, coming from this direction. Then get off the road and move behind hedges or into a copse or wood. In about six miles, where it starts to be a little hilly, at the end of a wood there's a meadow with a cow barn in it a couple of hundred yards from the road. The barn's empty because the poor old farmer lost nearly all his cattle last year from the great smog from that volcano in Iceland. You can catch up on your sleep there.'

Matilda kissed each man on the cheek and William grabbed each one by the hand and muttered, 'Thank you dearly'.

With the aid of the moonlight, even when a few clouds scudded across it, they were able to walk almost as fast as they could in daylight. It was probably nearly two miles before William could breathe normally and recover his normal calm and awareness. Matilda had calmed down as soon as they had left Darlington. Nobody had passed them coming from the south whether on foot, horseback or carriage. After another two miles they heard, then saw, a coach coming from the north. Quickly, they managed to get behind a hedge before it was near them.

They had been walking for at least an hour and a half and their tiredness had begun to slow their pace. There were now more clouds to reduce the light from the moon which had started to sink behind the tops of some hills.'These must be the hills the horsemen mentioned,' said William.'With your dark eyes you can see better than me. Keep staring for a woods and then a meadow.'

'If my eyes see better than yours it's only because you damage them with a burst blood vessel when you get in a rage.' William laughed and said, 'You've got an answer for everything.'

There must have been a gap in the hills, for suddenly the moon reappeared without cloud cover.

'Look!' cried Matilda, 'There's the edge of the woods and the meadow.' They heard the screech of a barn owl, a sign that they might be near a barn or ruined building.

The next ten minutes were spent going further back in the meadow, slowly moving right and left as they went. Then they found the cow barn. It was built from stone with a thin slated roof and the door was unlocked and held shut with a movable wooden bar anchored at one end. As far as they could see there was no sign of fresh manure on the earth floor and only one hole in the roof where they could see the moonlight. They chose the furthest corner, covered themselves up with the two blankets, and slept like logs.

* * *

They had no real idea of the time when they woke up, but agreed they must have been asleep for around six hours. It was the cold that woke them up. William opened the door cautiously to see it was drizzling. Nevertheless, as the cloud cover must have been thin he could see a lighter area to the south which he believed to be the position of the sun. As it was now entering the second week of April he reckoned this suggested it was about ten o'clock. He walked round the cow barn and saw a water butt at one of the corners which collected rain from the slated roof. Cupping his hands he sipped some and found it drinkable.'We must push on after we have had something to eat, so we can get as many miles between us and Darlington by tonight.'

'I agree,' said Matilda, 'but I must have a wash from that water butt after we've topped up our flask. It's no good you giving me that disapproving look, it will only take me five minutes.'

She took her wash, even though there was a thin film of ice on the top of the butt. She knew that William had expected her to mention the ice on the top of the water butt, so she said nothing.

They cut off some more pork and as the bread they had left had become quite hard they dipped it in water for about ten seconds to soften it up. As they walked down to the road they could see that the 'meadow' they had found would not be called a 'meadow' in the Vale of York. It was in fact moorland from which cattle or sheep might get some sustenance. Nearer to the road it became quite marshy. They had only been walking for fifteen minutes when they entered the village of Aycliffe. Here, they were suddenly passed by a stage coach coming from the south. No interest was shown in them by the passengers inside or on top. They apparently assumed they were local villagers, three or four of whom were around at that time of morning.

It was much the same in the village of Bradbury, which they reached just after midday. The only welcome difference was that there were two stalls open on the crossroads of this village, and one sold bread. The other sold turnips and kale, which had stood up to the extreme winter and was in high demand. They could see and smell that the bread was fresh so they bought three loaves for two pence. They sat on a low wall near the gate of the village church and ate one loaf between them, with some pieces of dried apple that had been preserved by their mother. As they were finishing an elderly gentleman stopped and asked them, 'As you are strangers to our village, are you looking for work? If so, there is work if you want to be a coal miner and there are several large new mines at Cornforth five miles on up the great road.'

They thanked him for his advice but explained that they were from a farming family, more than half of whom had died, together with much of their livestock as a result of the great smog that struck the North in particular last summer and early winter. They politely let it be known that as they were both literate William would like to try his hand in engineering work on Tyneside and Matilda would like to be a teacher of the young children of the managers and other executives in the new growth industry.

The gentleman could not help them, but they thought it was invaluable practice for when they got nearer to Newcastle and seeking their jobs.

As they set off again the drizzle, which had turned to light rain when they had reached Aycliffe, had now stopped and the sun came out in intermittent bursts. Matilda said that this made her realise two things. One was that even though the wind had swung round to the northwest there was no longer any trace of the sulphurous fumes. Secondly, it seemed very unlikely that the two 'horrible vagabonds' got anybody to try and catch us. William replied, 'It seems that both Laki the volcano and the innkeeper of the alehouse have decided to go back to sleep.'

Black coal dust lay thick on the ground in Cornforth and smoke was in the air. William thought he would be very desperate if he took a job as a miner. No wonder they were said to die at the age of thirty with terrible lung diseases. Yet even women worked down the mines when no other work was available, as did small boys as young as ten. They were usually dead by twenty.

Although their legs were aching and their feet were sore they decided to try and reach Durham City outskirts by nightfall. A fellow walker who they caught up with told them that a good and safe place to stop the night was at a refuge centre run by the church at Gilesgate Moor, just outside the city. In his late forties he had been a farm worker near Darlington and was one of those who had lost their job due to the effects of the Icelandic volcano eruption. He was going to try for work in one of the iron foundries on Tyneside and hopefully send some of his wages back to his wife and the one child who had survived the great smog. His name was Tom Shepherd. As he could not really keep up with their pace they thanked him for the information and added that if there were places available for the night at the church refuge they would ask them to keep a place for him.

They arrived at Gilesgate Moor around eight o'clock just as dusk was falling and soon found the church. The refuge was a recently built annex to the church. Three church men, one of whom they took to be the vicar, stood behind a desk at the door and asked them if they wanted to stay there for one night and how old they were. They both confirmed they would like to stay and hopefully have supper. Matilda explained they were sister and brother, gave her true age of nineteen, and William added an extra year and told them he was eighteen. One of the other men asked them why they were on the road and, looking at Matilda, were they and their parents of the Protestant Christian faith, which they affirmed was so. They explained how being farmers exposed to the effects of the volcano eruption, many of their family had been killed as well as most of their livestock, and as a result they had decided to look for work in industry on Tyneside or on farms in Northumberland.

The vicar and his colleagues had satisfied themselves that Matilda and William Byrne were genuine in their search for work. They were told that there were only four beds available that night but two of these were next to each other and would be theirs. William thanked them and told them that an older man called Tom Shepherd was about twenty minutes behind them as he was not walking at their speed. The answer was, 'If he turns up before the last two places go and is as genuine as you two appear to be, we will let him stay with us for the night.'

When William asked how much the supper and bed would be he was pleasantly surprised to be told that as they were a church charity there was no charge.'However, if you wish to make a small donation one shilling for you and your sister would be gratefully received.'

Tom Shepherd had made it just in time and sat down with them for supper at a long table which stretched the length of the hall. As on the previous two nights the meal was a stew, but a much superior one. It contained a considerable amount of chicken, with turnips, kale and a few potatoes, plus a sizeable hunk of bread. William whispered to his sister that it was the best value for money since they had left home.

After they had both given a hand in the washing up, the vicar announced that although it was not obligatory, those who wanted to would be welcomed at a short evening service before retiring.

They had regularly attended Sunday service at Church Fenton and in accepting the invitation they did so willingly. It was not just the feeling they had of thanking God for looking after them on their journey, but it cemented the spiritual attachment to their parents and the remainder of the family. The dormitory ran parallel to the eating hall and was between it and the side of the church, which meant that outside walls and heat loss was reduced to a minimum. At the end furthest from the entrance and the road there was an area for women screened off from the rest by some heavy curtains. This had six basic bed frames with palliasse-style straw mattresses, a sheet and a blanket. That night four other women were sleeping in that area. The men's area had much the same facilities except that, with one exception, there were no bed frames so their mattresses laid flat on the floor. The exception was a spring framed bed resting in isolation between the men and the curtains dividing off the women's area. This was occupied by one of the church men, more as a symbol of the church's desire that there should be no crossing of the ways rather than an effective barrier.

William and Matilda slept well. They were awakened by the churchman proclaiming in a loud voice that bread and cheese and a mug of hot tea was now ready for breakfast. Drinking hot tea had by now become more popular among all classes and exceeded the amount of English ale that was drunk. As the water was boiled it also helped to control the spread of diseases. The churchman also asked everyone to fold their sheet and blanket and place it on the foot of the mattress.

William first went to the men's washroom, where he joined the queue to use the foul smelling latrines.

After washing his face and hands in the cold water with the aid of a bar of home-made soap, he went into the eating hall where Matilda was already seated drinking her tea. She pointed to the back of the hall where he obtained his mug of hot tea and a pewter plate on which was a hunk of fresh bread, still warm, and a piece of cheese.

'Good morning my dear brother,' he said as he sat down next

to his sister.'Did you sleep well without me being close enough to hug?'

'Much better, thank you, as I did not have you snoring in my ear and an arm being thrown across my face periodically,' Matilda replied with a smile. After waiting for William to finish his bread and cheese and his tea, Matilda whispered, 'Although we want to get off quick to get to Newcastle, shall we first go into the church and offer a short prayer of thanks for our wonderful bed and breakfast, and perhaps put a penny each into the collection box?' William agreed. Just as they got up they saw Tom Shepherd come in just in time for his breakfast, looking rather weary. The three said good bye to each other and wishing success in finding work. This seemed to cheer Tom up.

Having made their prayer of thanks in the church they managed to get away before the morning service was delivered and resumed their walk to Newcastle. In typical April showers weather they passed through the ancient large village of Chester-le-Street, still set in the original Durham countryside. They moved on towards Washington. The rural surroundings that had been with them ever since York were rapidly disappearing with every step they took.

It seemed that the Washington area was taken over by coal mines, although they were told by a passer-by that there was a large iron foundry that had just opened up. William had no desire to go to the foundry and ask for a job. His enthusiasm to quit farming and get into the new heavy industry was beginning to fade. Matilda did her best to support him in his original objective, pointing out that it would appear to be dirtier than it was after being brought up in green fields. Nevertheless, she admitted that even if she was offered a teaching job in Washington she doubted if she would accept it, regardless of what the salary might be.

It was not long before they came to an oasis of green; a small public park with three or four bench seats. They managed to find room among locals who were eating a midday meal much the same as their own. They finished all their food reserves, which was the last of the beef and the dried apple pieces and some bread left over from yesterday. They washed it down with water as opposed to the cold tea favoured by the locals.

It was about five o'clock when they left Gateshead and went over the new Tyne bridge. Stone built, it had only been opened three years earlier after the bridge that had been there for 500 years was swept away by a great flood in 1771.

In the centre of the city the old buildings were being replaced by new, the larger ones being in the impressive Georgian style. This was fitting for what had become Britain's fourth largest city and was soon to be a power house of the industrial revolution, specialising in ship building and heavy engineering. They had already passed a luxurious public house (some of which were now being referred to as 'hotels') with doormen standing outside. A minute later they came to a smaller one, built in the same new Georgian style but not shouting 'expensive'.

They went round the corner and William took his sister's hand and said: 'I don't think this city centre is where we should look for the cheapest inn accommodation. We have been very careful with our money and there is still one pound and eleven shillings left. If we could get a room here and a supper for that eleven shilling that would still leave us a pound in reserve. Then perhaps we could talk over what exactly we should do next.'

'We must not let ourselves be carried away,' Matilda replied, 'Eleven shillings must really be our maximum expense. I fully agree that we should then talk over what we are going to do. If we can't come to a decision then we must return home and do what work we can until things get back to what they were.'

Prominently displayed on a board directly inside the door was a notice reading: 'Single room with double bed or two singles plus evening dinner and light breakfast, six shillings for one person or ten shillings for two.' They walked to the barman and told him they wanted a room for the night. He shouted across to a man sitting at a desk in the corner, 'A booking sir!' The response was to beckon them over. He was the manager who asked them where they had come from and where they were going.

So as to make themselves appear as lower gentry, William

replied, 'My sister and I own a farm at Church Fenton near York and we aim to continue our coach journey to Berwick-on-Tweed in the morning.'

'That is fine sir' replied the manager, 'A slight problem is that we are rather full tonight so would you object to sharing your dinner table with a respectable gentleman and his wife?'

Handing over ten shillings William said that that would be quite all right.

As they went up the stairs Matilda said it was a pity they had to share a table as it meant they could not discuss their plans in front of others, no matter how nice they may turn out to be.

Although Matilda could hardly carry a bustle in her back pack, she did have a frock. She shook it out vigorously and said most of the creases would drop out from the heat of her body. William put on his waistcoat he had carried with him, together with a clean under-shirt which only really showed at the neck.

The middle-aged couple sharing their table readily took to the young Byrnes. It was not long before they heard the full story of the crisis that had hit the family at Church Fenton and the quest for a new working life they were now undertaking. Mr and Mrs Palmer had a home in Morpeth, but frequently came to Newcastle where James Palmer had a directorship in a ship building company. Turning to Matilda, Rose Palmer said, 'This is amazing, you are looking for a teaching post and I am looking for someone to live in and teach our two children and also my sister's two. If you could stop off the day after tomorrow we could both come to a decision.' Before Matilda could say 'Yes', James Palmer turned to William and said, 'In Northumberland we have, of course, had the same problems on the land as you had last year in Yorkshire. But I could put you in touch with a farmer near Morpeth who is looking for a farm manager.'

And so the Byrne family established its roots in Northumberland and greater Newcastle.

Chapter Ten

John Byrne the Miller

Two days after William and Matilda's fortunate meeting in Newcastle with the Palmers, they spent five shillings to ride outside on a coach to Morpeth. They were given directions to the Palmers' house on the northern outskirts of town and arrived in the mid-afternoon. William detected that although James Palmer was obviously as pleased as his wife was to see Matilda, he looked rather embarrassed at seeing William.

Rose, leading Matilda out of the room by her hand, said 'I will introduce you to the children and get you to read to them from one of their books and we will see how you all get on together.'

Matilda smiled and thought that it was a delicate way for Rose Palmer to see if she really was a fluent reader and was likely to gain the respect of her children as a teacher.

As the women left the room, James Palmer turned to William.'Look young fellow, you have rather caught me on the hop here. I have not had the time to talk to Mr Michael Robson who farms over at Mitford and it is possible that he has filled the post of manager for his local farm. What I will do is write him a note now and you should go over to see him at the farmhouse there and present the note as soon as possible. Let me know how you get on.'

Rose Palmer could detect within a few minutes that Matilda was a fluent reader with a pleasant voice and within ten minutes her two young children were asking her questions. The girl, aged eight was Catherine and her six-year-old brother had been given the Christian name of Frederick, which was rising in popularity in England. Following a private word with her husband, Rose

Palmer offered Matilda the post of live-in teacher cum governess on a three-month trial basis. The salary was to be £70 per annum. Sensing that Matilda had not booked where to stay that night, she said:

'You can start living here tonight if you wish. This will not only enable you to see your accommodation but will mean that I can take you to Mrs Bell, the milliners in Morpeth in the morning where you can choose your dress that is best befitting for a teacher.'

Matilda decided to try and curtail the intense delight that swept over her on hearing what Mrs Rose Palmer had offered her and which would solve all immediate problems. She wanted to leap forward and hug her. Instead she said:

'I am so very pleased to accept your offer of this post to do my best to give your delightful children the basis of education. I will assure you I will not let you down.'

As they moved back into the drawing room William and James Palmer were talking about the improvements that had taken place with animal stock since the work of Robert Bakewell on selective breeding of animals. William could see by his sister's expression that her interview with Mrs Palmer must have gone well, which was confirmed by both ladies.

'Thank you for your help to both of us and your hospitality' he said, still clutching the note that James Palmer had given him.'I hope to see Mr Robson at Mitford tomorrow, and Matilda I will let you know how I get on.'

He shook hands with James Palmer, bowed to Rose Palmer and kissed his sister on the cheek.

* * *

The milliners shop in Morpeth was unusual for its time in that it was a meeting place for ladies of all classes. Farmers and farm workers wives, housekeepers, shop girls and whoever else who had saved some money for a new dress or other haberdashery items knew that it was likely that they might even exchange a few polite words with the wives of the landed gentry. The millinery shop in Newgate Street was run by Francis Bell and her eldest daughter Ellinor. Assisted by two younger daughters, dresses and blouses were made in the back room in order to supplement the range of more fashionable clothing that came from Newcastle, York and even London.

Before her marriage Francis's maiden name was Saint. She was proud of the fact that they could trace their family back to a great grandfather, Joseph Saint, who made baskets in Morpeth and was baptised in 1695, according to the local church records. The name was of French origin and it was believed that they could have been Huguenot Protestant refugees.

Henry Bell had originally been trained by his father as a blacksmith at nearby Woodhorn. Morpeth stands on the Great North Road and the proprietor of the Black Bull coaching inn saw some extra business in setting up a service for changing wheels and providing temporary repairs to coaches. It was fifteen years previously that Henry Bell came to be the coach services 'wheelright and coach engineer'. In many cases the name Bell is derived from Middle English occupational name for bell ringer. It is also a Border name for English and Scots meaning 'handsome'. It was also a habitations name for a farmstead in Norway.

If asked where his ancestors came from, Henry always said it was somewhere up near the border 'and we have been fighting the Scots ever since they stole our cattle'. He never acknowledged the occasions when Bells among the Border Reivers stole Scottish cattle.

From the middle of April onwards the people of Northumberland, and elsewhere in England, were remarking on how fine the weather was in comparison to the disastrous climate of the previous year.

In the back room of the milliners shop Francis told her young daughters, 'It is warmer than any April day I can recall and more like the temperatures we used to get in June or July.'

She could hear Ellinor greeting a customer in the shop. Francis

Bell looked through and could see that it was Mrs Rose Palmer, a regular customer, with a young woman with the striking good looks that sometimes goes with Irish or even Spanish girls.

'Good morning Mrs Bell, this is Matilda Byrne from York who has recently been appointed as the governess for my children and also my sister's children. I have just been telling Ellinor that I would like you to fit her out in some nice summer weight clothes which still retain the appearance suitable for a teacher or governess.'

'Good morning to you Mrs Palmer', replied Francis Bell, 'May I suggest that as my daughter Ellinor and Miss Byrne are of the same age group they can discuss the clothing required that is both fashionable as well as being suitable for a governess. You can then give it your approval.'

'What an excellent idea!' exclaimed Rose Palmer. Whether this was astuteness on Rose Palmer's part or pure chance, Ellinor and Matilda discovered an immediate rapport which went beyond the choice of fashionable clothes. Ellinor suggested that the fashion was to move away from hoops and chose a sack-back gown, although she would recommend one they had in stock which was of a lighter-weight material. From this first meeting a life-long friendship was established – which was to be extended to William Byrne.

When William left the Palmers' home (still clutching the note for Michael Robson) he realised that he could not sleep in a ditch that night, pleasant though the weather had remained. He would have to take a bed in the Black Bull tavern that night, with a cheap supper, so he could make himself look as presentable as possible for his interview in the morning. He was down to his last ten shillings, leaving Matilda with five until she reached her first pay day. He was pleasantly surprised when the innkeeper told him he could have a bed in a small attic the size of a large cupboard with a lamb stew that night and tea and porridge in the morning for three shillings and sixpence.

Having paid the innkeeper to ensure that he would be returning at supper time, William thought he would take the opportunity to look around the town and also not be tempted to stay and buy a pint of ale, which could lead to several more. His tour took in Bridge Street, Newgate Street and Old Bakehouse Yard before he made his way up to the castle that stands just above the town. Coming down to Bridge Street he found a welcome seat that overlooked the river Wansbeck. As he sat there in silence and the tranquillity of his surroundings he wondered whether he had done the right thing. He and his sister had left home to better themselves. But their mother was ageing fast and their father was getting rather forgetful.

Well, he thought, *if I do not get the farm manager's job tomorrow I will return home to help them. Matilda has got an excellent post which she must stay for. If I do get the job the first thing we must do is to send a letter home.* As a result of the increase in coaches and turnpikes a letter would only cost seven or eight pence and be delivered at Church Fenton in three or four days.

Possibly because of his hunger the lamb stew at the Black Bull was very satisfying. Resisting the temptation of a penny's worth of ale, he went up to his attic bedroom and cleaned his clothes the best he could with a brush stored in his backpack.

Having slept well, William had his breakfast and set off for the four mile walk to Michael Robson's Home Farm, at Mitford. The weather was colder than it had been of late and there were occasional light showers. He decided that if he walked at a good pace the heat of his body would dry the rain spots off before he looked as if he was dressed in a wet sack.

He knocked on the main door of the large house at Home Farm and told the servant girl who opened it, 'I have an important letter for Mr Robson from Mr Palmer of Morpeth and I will wait for a reply'.

After waiting on the doorstep for five minutes that seemed like twenty, the girl reappeared .

'The master said would you please come in and take a seat in the hall and he will see you directly.'

Following another six or seven minutes the girl came back again and said, 'Would you please follow me, sir. My master, Mr Robson, wishes to talk to you.'

Michael Robson was a grey-haired man of about sixty, who sat very upright in his study chair. Looking at William with his fading blue eyes he offered his hand, which William shook, but made sure his grip was neither too hard nor too weak.

'Take a seat young Byrne. You obviously made an impression on my friend James Palmer who tells me that you are from a long line of freemen farmers down in Yorkshire. Yes, I believe you suffered more than we did from the effects of that damn Icelandic volcano. Now, Mr Palmer tells me that you are interested in the ideas for selective breeding of farm animals put forward by Bakewell. Tell me why it might be of benefit to our livestock in general, including our dairy cattle?'

The discussion, which moved to general farming practice, lasted for a good half hour. It ended with Michael Robson raising himself from his chair by his arms and saying, 'As you will see I am not very mobile as a result of a riding accident two years ago. In consequence I need someone who can think beyond the basics of farming which will enable me to check over what's happening on our 500 acres only once a week or so, instead of daily as now. I want to be able to go round with a manager weekly who can tell and show me exactly what's happening. You are rather young for this post, and you have no experience of the use of collies for sheep-herding, but you are well informed. I am going to offer it to you on a six-month trial basis. You will live here on the farm, of course, and have your own room and be fed the same meals as the rest of the house staff. Your salary for this trial period will be £35 per annum, paid monthly. Other than during harvest times you shall have every Sunday off for church and your leisure. What do you say young Byrne?'

'I say thank you, sir, for the confidence you have shown me and I am determined that by my work you will have no cause to regret making this offer.'

Michael Robson had gathered by now that William had no fixed abode as yet in Northumberland so he told him that employment at Mitford could start that day. He sent a messenger out to bring in his senior labourer, Abraham Marshall, who would take William round the farm and show him as much as possible of the mixed farming being undertaken at Home Farm. He could then discuss what he saw with Mr Robson at tea – this being the main meal time of the day. He was also informed that a message had been sent to James Palmer informing him that William was now in his employ and he should pass this information on to his sister.

Three days quickly passed as William immersed himself in the farm and it was Sunday – his day off.

By previous arrangement he skipped going to church and walked into Morpeth and called at the Palmers where he met his sister. He also met Matilda's new friend Ellinor Bell. During the rest of the day they both found that they were much at ease in each other's company. Matilda told him that Mr and Mrs Palmer had invited the three of them to join them for lunch and afterwards they had planned to go for a walk down Bridge Street to the river, if the weather stayed dry.

She also told William she had written a letter to their mother and father, sent three days ago by coach mail for seven pence, telling them they were both well and had found good employment. On the Thursday of the new week Matilda received a letter from her uncle Arthur and aunt Joan with the tragic news that Matilda and William's mother, Anne Byrne, had died a fortnight earlier. Although Anne had been ill with suspected consumption for a good twelve months her death was put down to the effects on her troubled lungs of the sulphurous haze that beset the land the previous summer. To make things worse, probably because of the shock of the death of his wife their father, Bryan, whose memory had been fading for the last six months or more, did not – or would not – recognise anybody other than the vision in his mind of his departed wife who he kept calling for. Five acres of the Church Fenton farmland had to be sold to cover outstanding debts and

Arthur and Ivor Fairhall were running the farm assisted by Arthur's twelve-year-old son David Byrne and another young nephew.

Matilda burst into tears on reading this devastating news. Hearing her sobbing, Rose Palmer ran up the stairs to her room. When Matilda had managed to tell her what had happened to her family she said that as James Palmer was down in Newcastle dealing with his business, she would drive Matilda in their pony and trap over to Home Farm at Mitford to inform her brother what had happened.

On hearing the tragic news William's self-assurance disappeared. For a moment he acted as though his sister, just eighteen months older than him, was his mother. As he hung on to her he cried,

'What shall I do Matilda? It's all my fault. I thought I would like to be an engineer. But I left our farm and came all this way to be on another one. If I had stayed our mother would still be with us and Dad would know who we are.'

'William, there's nothing we can do to return the old days,' said Matilda, doing her best to control her own emotions.'It's God's will. Mother would have died whether we were there to comfort her or not. The truth is that the old family farm was going down hill and you have a better future here, as I do as a teacher to the two lovely children. We have to stay until we have earned the money and the time to take a week off to go down to our Yorkshire by mail coach and see our family survivors.'

* * *

Two years had passed and they had still not visited the surviving relatives down in Church Fenton. William said that this was because he could not be spared the time off from Home Farm. This was partly true. Michael Robson's son Frederick had great respect for his father but saw a limited future in tying himself down to farming. He was adamant in his belief that the future for the North East was to push forward the industrial revolution which was leading the western world. For the past five years he had worked for James Palmer and was fast becoming the company's main design engineer in the ship-building sector of the business.

Matilda salved her conscience by making the coach journey down to Church Fenton and found that the Byrnes and Ivor Fairhall were at last getting the farm back into operation, aided by two good summers. However, she was saddened to see that her father did not even recognise her. He did not utter one word to her or anyone else during the three days she was there. His actions suggested that he considered everyone to be strangers and he saw no reason to communicate with them.

When William said that he did not have the time to spare to visit the remainder of the Byrne family down in Yorkshire, this was only partly true. For the last eighteen months he spent every possible moment of time off from Home Farm in the company of Ellinor Bell. In fact on May Day that year they had become engaged. This took place at a special church service with the only additional attendants being his sister Matilda, Francis and Henry Bell and James and Rose Palmer.

The special church service, arranged at short notice, had been insisted upon by Francis and Henry Bell because their daughter was pregnant. Matilda and James and Rose Palmer, together with the potential father of the unborn child, readily accepted this decision. As much as they loved each other, almost from the day they first walked down Bridge Street to the river, William and Ellinor's original plan was to delay an engagement and subsequent wedding for at least another year. William had received an increase in his wages as promised by Michael Robson but needed to save more to meet the rent of a small house near Home Farm. On an occasion when Michael Robson was away and Ellinor joined William in his bed, their passion for each other looked like raising difficulties in implementing their plan.

Ellinor had initially tried to abort her pregnancy by taking old Celtic and Saxon folklore remedies, which were unsuccessful. Her subsequent morning sickness periods could not be hidden from her mother who decided that Ellinor and William's engagement should be arranged, followed by the wedding as soon as possible. They were not married in the Bell's and Palmer's favoured church in Morpeth but by special licence in the church of St. Mary The Virgin in Woodhorn in front of seven witnesses. William was only nineteen and the consent of parents or guardians was required then for those under twenty-one. Due to the need for an early marriage it was decided that he would put his age in the register as twenty-one, which was Ellinor's true age.

A robust boy was born in November 1786. They christened him John Byrne.

New Year's eve had only three minutes to go before James Palmer put down his trusty pocket watch and struck the dinner gong to welcome in the new century. It would be 1800 and in February he would be sixty, a year older than his wife Rose. After James and Rose welcomed their fifteen guests from family and close friends to join with them in bringing in 'the new age of the new century' he said that he thought it was the right time to give up the chairmanship of the company.'This,' he said, 'will start the process of letting the younger blood within the company run it as necessary for it to remain profitable and forward looking in this new century, where the rest of Europe is looking to us in order to spread our industrial revolution. That was, of course, until France had its bloody revolution and Napoleon even tried to invade Ireland.'

More applause followed when he announced that 'The new manager of the ship building sector will now be Frederick Robson, whose father Michael, my dear friend, sadly passed away six months ago.'

Fredrick Robson was not the only Frederick present that night. Thirteen-year-old John Byrne's middle name was Frederick. The name existed in Saxon England but was not in common usage until the Hanoverians became Kings of England with the popular son Friedrich of George II gathering a liking for the English form of the name. Another factor was the admiration that many in Britain had at that time for the Prussian King, Frederick the Great.

William and his ever loving wife Ellinor were also at the New Year party, with son John's younger sister Elizabeth. Following the birth of John Frederick they had another boy child who died after three months of an unknown infection. Then there was a little girl, Charlotte, who made the age of three before falling victim to diphtheria. In consequence the auburn-haired and good natured Elizabeth was much loved by the family, including John.

Three years before his death Michael Robson became virtually bed-ridden. As his son Frederick lived mainly in Newcastle to be near his work and had no desire to run the farm, both were happy that William, Ellinor and their two children should move into the large farmhouse, and that William should continue to run the 500 acre farm in an efficient manner. He thus had good accommodation and a salary considerably in excess of the income he would have received for running the less than 200 acres at Church Fenton. He was disappointed that John Frederick had said that directly he was fourteen he would start an engineering apprenticeship at Morpeth's wagonways terminal. Remembering his own desire to quit farming and become an engineer he decided to give his son his support. He knew that this meant that his son would not stay long at Morpeth and would go down to Newcastle. Morpeth's only 'industry' as such was tanning and cloth manufacture. As for the wagonways terminal at Morpeth this was a result of the development of nearby coal and iron industries that had just begun to change the area rapidly.

Starting with Bedlington as a larger settlement, it acted as a focus for many smaller colliery settlements. This led to iron working in Bedlington becoming a significant industry in the late 18th and early 19th centuries on the banks of the River Blyth. The network of horse-drawn wagonways (soon to be replaced by stationary steam engines) carried coal to Morpeth and to Staithes on the Blyth.

Also present at the New Year party was the woman young John

Byrne loved as much as he did his mother. It was his aunt Matilda, with her fascinating dark wavy hair, who had done her best to teach him to read and write at her small school since he was five. Matilda was there with her husband, Arthur Dodd from a long established Northumbrian family, and their two children. The five-year-old girl was a mini Matilda in her looks and her character, even at that early age. The boy was only three and had the traditional fair to auburn hair and blue eyes of many of the Byrnes (and also his own father). He also showed a common trait of not appearing to listen to what was being said but to be living in another world.

Once the serious speeches were over and the guests started to celebrate the New Year, Matilda sat down at the piano and was joined by Ellinor as the singer. Within five minutes William joined them with a flute that had appeared from somewhere in the Palmer's household. For six years Matilda had remained as the teacher-governess to the Palmer's son and daughter. The son went into the business in Newcastle, reporting directly to Frederick Robson. The daughter, Catherine, took Ellinor's place, working for Francis Bell in the millinery shop.

Due once again to the help from Rose Palmer in letting Matilda have use (at a peppercorn rent) of a small house she and her husband owned, she was able to set up a school where she taught the basics of education for those who could afford the fee of two shillings a week.

* * *

By 1810 John Byrne, now a married man of twenty-four with his wife Margaret expecting her first child, was working at an iron foundry in Newcastle. Because of its limitations he had realised earlier after two years that he was in a dead end with his apprenticeship at Morpeth. He was attracted to work in the foundry when old Henry Bell told him that he had heard that the foundry was looking for some youngster with a little foundry experience who was prepared to become an apprentice in their tooling development section. One of the first Boulton and Watt steam engines was used here to give power to other areas of the foundry. Several were now used in the nearby pits for pumping out water.

As an apprentice his earnings were only £20 a year. His father subsidised him for the remaining five years of apprenticeship in order that he could pay the rent for his accommodation and eat meat twice a week. And then he met Margaret Bevis.

It was six months or so after completing his apprenticeship that John Byrne found that one of the privileges it gave was the opportunity to go through the foundry gates at noon and buy a hot snack (or 'bait' as they called it) from a nearby stall. Among the women and children who were often standing at the gates to hand over some home produced bait to their fathers or brothers working in the foundry, he spotted an attractive blonde girl of around eighteen. He noticed that she was there only around three days a week.

Moving on from exchanging 'good mornings' with her, after a week he asked her why she seemed to come on alternate days. She replied:

'I am doing washing and ironing for several customers on the other days. Then one of my young brothers, usually Mick with the dark hair, brings in our Dad's dinner bait.'

One day he had gone to the gates and saw her father taking his dinner bait away. He had seen him a couple of times working in the smelting plant, which was hot and hard work and no doubt had contributed to his elderly appearance. In fact he was only thirty-nine. John Byrne decided that he would play it safe, even if it was becoming less important, to ask Arthur Bevis's permission to take his daughter out. He walked back with him to the smelting plant and struck up their first conversation by asking him what the family used to work at. Not surprisingly he, like his forefathers were farm workers who lived and worked on a farm near Morpeth for many generations.

'My father,' said Arthur, 'was a master ploughman, as his father before him, and became the foreman on the farm. Hard work, particularly the 14-hour days at harvest time killed them both off before they were fifty. That's why I left the land and now I'm in this devil's kitchen being roasted to death. At least it pays better. Certainly better than down the pit where some of our folk are, including lads and lassies.'

'Our family worked on the land for centuries,' said John, conveniently not mentioning they were farmers, not labourers.'My father and his sister walked all the way from near York to get work. That was twenty-six years ago and he's still working. Don't you find that now the war could soon be over with old Napoleon our cost of living has gone up but wages stay the same?'

'Bloody right,' said Arthur.'When the war with the French is finally over our unwanted soldiers will soon be competing with us for jobs. As for problems for farm workers, a new one is that these new winnowing machines and now the threshing machine have led to men losing work. It's not only at harvest time but over the winter when we used to have work threshing corn by hand flails.'

'Agree, Arthur. They will be using steam to drive ploughs and more machines in the future. That's why I did not follow my dear old father but have gone into engineering. Still long hours and hard work, but more pay.'

Having established a work-time friendship with the father, John took every opportunity to talk to Margaret Bevis. She did not rebuff him, but greeted him with a smile on every occasion. These meetings did not go unnoticed by Arthur. After a week or more he came up to them as they were talking.

'You two seem to have a lot to talk about.' Arthur Bevis's voice sounded rather cold.

John smiled at him.'Well, Arthur, I was going to ask your daughter if she would care to come out for a walk with me one Sunday. If she said yes I would then speak to you for your permission.'

Arthur looked at him without saying a word for ten seconds or more. Then he said, 'When a young man asks to take a girl out it is usually because at the back of his mind he thinks it could be his chance to sew some wild oats.'

Margaret blushed and looking at her feet, said, 'Fancy saying that Dad. If John Byrne or anyone else asked me to go out for a walk I would not let him have his way with me. If we then got married that would be different, of course.'

'Go on then John,' said Arthur with what passed for a smile,' 'Ask her now if she wants to go out with you. But understand as long as you are single you are not going to give her a bairn for us to look after, ruin her name, and you then sod of somewhere else.'

After six months walking her out, which sometimes he thought must be the equivalent to twice the length of Hadrian's Wall (with no prize for the effort at the end) John Byrne and Margaret Bevis were married.

The marriage took place in All Saints, Newcastle. As well as being attended by most of the Bevis family, John Byrne's aunt Matilda came down from Morpeth, together with his father William and wife Ellinor and with much surprise and appreciation, Rose Palmer. She was now a widow as John Palmer had passed on three years earlier. Matilda was still a beautiful lady, retaining her dark hair, with just a few flecks of grey. Jane Bevis, Margaret's mother, began to take a dislike to her as Arthur Bevis, thinking she was a widow lady, began to pay her more and more attention as his alcohol consumption increased.

Having initially given a flirtatious response to some of Arthur's attentive remarks, Matilda's experience of life saw that this could sour the atmosphere at her favourite nephew's wedding.

She pointedly went over to Jane Bevis and in a voice that could also be heard by Arthur, she said:

'It is a great pity that my husband, also called Arthur, was too poorly to come to the wedding. He would get on so well with your husband. He too likes the ladies, but we know how to keep those naughty old boys in their place. Do we not Mrs Bevis?'

Jane visibly relaxed.'My dear lady, come and sit by me. His attempts at flirting worried me at first, but I'm glad you have seen he is just an old rogue. He's been a hard working man all his life, who's always looked after me and our family.'

* * *

Being a skilled man the iron foundry management offered John Byrne a two up and two down house in one of the compact terraces which they had arranged to be built close by at the turn of the century. The rent charged was two shillings a week. He was fortunate enough to be allocated the house as an elderly worker and his wife had just been given notice to leave because he was no longer fit to work. Where he and his wife went to was not the concern of the company he had worked for over the past twenty years.

Following their marriage and prior to being given the company house John's landlady had allowed Margaret to move into his room with him – for an extra six pence a week.'But no bairns,' she insisted.'If you start expecting I will give you three months to find somewhere else as you have been a good tenant here and always paid your rent on time.'

Thus with the help of coitus interruptus, plus an ointment based on lily root and a certain amount of good luck it was just over a year before Margaret became pregnant. The timing with the offer of the company terrace house was opportune. In June 1811 their daughter Mary was born. Two years later Margaret delivered a stillborn baby boy. They grieved for some while but were compensated by the healthy development of their young daughter.

Four years later John Byrne, although not a regular drinker, went to the local tavern to celebrate the news that had come through coachmen from London that Napoleon had been finally beaten by the Duke of Wellington, aided by the Prussians and the Dutch, in a monumental battle in Belgium. He was still on his first pint of ale when he spotted an engineer who used to work with him at the foundry just after he finished his apprenticeship. He told John that he was glad to have got out of the 'hell hole' of the foundry. Starting on their second pint he shouted above the growing cheers and general noise of celebration, 'Let's go outside where I can give you details of what could be a good, independent job.'

Picking up his pint John shouted, 'Let's go then, I'm interested.'

It was a little quieter outside, although mothers and children were now in the street joining in the celebrations.'What's this interesting job?'

'It's a post windmill at Cut Bank by the Ouseburn in the city. The owner has never done anything to keep it going properly. I've looked at it and you could easily sort it out. There's accommodation attached where you can raise a family. The owner says all he wants is fifty pound a year rent and all the profit you take on milling corn is yours. That could be a hundred and fifty after you have given him his rent.'

'It sounds interesting,' John replied.'When I finish work on Saturday, about two, I will get the horse tram down to Ouseburn, have a word with the owner and then look it over.'

For the next three days – and nights – he thought about the mill offer and began to think that he might be wrong to take it up. His job was secure at the foundry, as was the house that went with it even though it was small, damp, and he had to wait for ever to get the leaky roof fixed. However, you had to take a gamble sometimes if you wanted to improve your lot. But again, there were now something like thirty wind or water mills in Newcastle. This meant a lot of competition and lowering of your price to keep a milling contract. He had not mentioned the possible change of career to Margaret, in case she accidentally let it leak out amongst some of the other women whose husbands worked at the foundry. Come Saturday he told her he was off to see a football match and would be back by six.

The address he had been given for the owner, Mr Abraham Taylor, was No. 10 Cut Bush. He had to walk past the windmill, which was No. 3, and was pleased to see that the sails looked in reasonable condition and the mill itself did not look as though it was about to fall down. He hesitated before knocking on the door of No. 10. Was he doing the right thing? Fortunately he found Mr Taylor in.

'I will be pleased to show you round the mill, young man,' he said in a pleasant tone of voice.'The living accommodation is near to the base of the mill, with a little garden round the sides where you can grow some beans and tatties.'

John first had a look inside the accommodation, which appeared to be weatherproof, had running water at the sink and a copper outside for washing clothes. With two bedrooms, one rather small, he thought that with a lick of paint it would be an advance on the company terrace house.

They went up inside the mill, with Abraham Taylor puffing up the stairs, as to be expected for a man well in his fifties. John could see that the mill stones looked to be out of alignment and several cogs, or teeth as some call them, were missing. He said:

'Although I am not a miller, but an engineer, any flour that the previous operator made must have been very coarse.'

'It was,' came the reply.'The man was an idiot and wouldn't learn.'

As they walked back towards Taylor's house John said, 'If I undertook to run the mill at the annual rent of £50 I would expect a written guarantee from you that I would remain the tenant for a minimum of two years. If you are happy with that my tenancy would not begin for another two weeks as I would need to give notice to my present employer and I could spend my spare time making the mechanical repairs we have noticed. Perhaps you would pay half the costs of materials, but not my time?'

They had reached No. 10 by then.

'John Byrne, I am quite happy with what you have said. You have obviously got a good head on your shoulders. Come in and my wife will make us a cup of tea, or perhaps we will toast the new tenancy with a wee dram. If you want to come round tomorrow or one evening in the week I will have the agreement drawn up.'

When he got home he told Margaret about the offer to run the windmill and that he would like her to come with him and see the accommodation. Nervously, he asked her:

'Am I doing the right thing pet? I am an engineer, not a bloody miller.'

'I am sure you are doing the right thing to become an independent man where hard work, which you never lacked, will give you a good profit. You have these bouts of a lack of confidence. Take me round there tomorrow when I have someone to look after the bairn and let me see where we will live.'

By the end of the first year John Byrne found that he had earned seventy pounds, after the rent was paid, which was about five pounds more than he earned at the foundry. By August 1817 he calculated that his earnings that year would be close on a hundred pounds. The second bonus he and Margaret enjoyed that month was the news from their doctor that their three-year-old son, Frederick William Byrne, was finally cleared of his asthmatic fever.

Chapter Eleven

The Toolmakers

It was the year after the ravages of the great Icelandic volcano eruption that Richard Lawson decided that there was no future as a farm worker. The name Lawson was linked to the Anglo-Saxon culture and became quite common from Yorkshire to Northumberland and the Scottish borders, both sides.

For several centuries they had worked on farms in the Cramlington area. Some of the sons had been soldiers or sailors, and all families, including their children, had made their contribution to the Black Death and the diseases that were rife in town and country up to the 20th century.

The alternative for eighteen-year-old Richard Lawson was to work down the nearby pit hewing out coal for no more money than a trained farm worker, or move nearer to Newcastle and get a job in one of the new iron foundries. He chose the latter because he knew it was at the heart of the newly born Industrial Revolution.

The small foundry he joined had only ten workers, including the owner, who concentrated on producing iron strip and bars, which were sold on in most cases to almost as small size iron manufacturers.

He found accommodation nearby and four years later was married with a son, Edward, who in his first year diced with death in the form of chicken pox and whooping cough. In 1801, when he was twelve , Edward joined his father working in the same small foundry. Father and son stayed working together for another four or five years.

Meeting up on a rare occasion with his brother at a family

wedding, Richard was informed that there was an opportunity to move to a house in Jesmond Vale which had a quarter of an acre piece of land at the back. The rent was nearly double that he was paying for the cramped accommodation he was used to ever since his marriage.'But,' said his brother, ' With all your experience you could have your own foundry there .'

That night he discussed the idea with his wife Sarah. They agreed that some additional source of income was needed if they started up a small foundry business at the rear of the house. It was decided that he would go the following morning to look at the house, its rear land and, importantly, to see if there was a tavern in the locality or even a small public drinking house. They found that there were no drinking establishments within half a mile and the house had a large ground floor front room with access at the back to the kitchen. Sarah already had long experience of brewing the Lawson family's beer requirements. The new pub in Jesmond Vale quickly opened with her as the landlady and was open between 10 am and 10 pm. The owner of the house had no objections as long as his rent was paid regularly.

Following the acquisition of a mix of second hand and new firebricks with family labouring and a hired foundry builder specialist, Richard Lawson saw the erection of the foundry to a scale of two thirds that of the one he had worked on for the last nine years. Two weeks before it was ready for operation he and his son left his long-term employer, accompanied by one of the remaining workers. They were already assured business from three of the former foundry's customers who were receiving a lower priority service because of the small volumes of their business. There was nothing unusual about the Lawson's small foundry business. They could be found all over Tyneside, Dudley and the West Midlands in general, Manchester, Glasgow and many parts of Britain in the first half of the nineteenth century.

The Lawson's business produced a good standard of living after a year or two, with Edward developing such a good eye for business that Richard let him make more and more of the company's decisions. This still left Edward some time to be 'walking out' with a local girl, Victoria Cummings, who he married in the spring of 1814. The marriage gave his mother the opportunity to say to Richard:

'As Edward and Victoria will be living with us for Edward to be near the works, my pub landlady days are over. We need to take that space back for them to live in.'

'You're nae telling me that I will be deprived of your homebrew ale, pet. It's the best for miles around,' said Richard, putting on an air of shock.

Sarah gave him a peck on the cheek, 'If you're too mean to buy it from the new tavern at the end of this road, then I'll keep brewing a pail or two for you and Edward.

For the next eighteen months Victoria gave a hand working in the foundry. In the summer of 1816 Catherine Lawson was born – the first of three daughters for Edward and Victoria.

* * *

At Cut Bank John Byrne and Margaret had just celebrated their tenth anniversary of taking over the windmill. He had found it hard work in handling – usually by himself – the two hundred weight sacks of corn. He was physically aided in this by not being over tall and having considerable strength in his arms – like most Byrne stock. But they had prospered and were even able to afford sending Mary and Frederick William to a local teacher for several hours a week.

It was a Sunday and for the first time in several months they had decided to go to church. Margaret preferred the Methodist Chapel but John Frederick said his family had always stuck by the Church of England. They had only been back about an hour when a messenger arrived with a note from his mother-in-law Ellinor. It stated that his father, William, had suffered a serious heart attack and was not expected to live.

He hired a horse-drawn trap and although he had not handled

a horse for several years, after an erratic start he made his way to Home Farm near Morpeth and arrived just before dusk.

He was met in the hall by aunt Matilda. She still stood tall and straight. He noticed that her dark hair was now almost completely grey. Those dark eyes that formed part of her legendary beauty were now red-rimmed through lack of sleep and the passage of tears.

'Oh John,' she said quietly as she hugged him, 'Your father's been asking for you. He will be so glad you have come. If it had not been for the new young doctor he would probably be dead by now. Willow tree bark has been used since Celtic times for steadying the heart's pulse rate. Now they have developed a way of extracting the salacylicate content in a pure form and it works even better.'

'You were always interested in these developments with nature's medicine, Aunt Matilda. I hope it continues to work.'

She led John into his father's bedroom. His mother Ellinor sat near him. His eyes were closed and he was breathing laboriously. Both hands gripped the edge of the blanket which he held to his chest. John noticed that the little finger on his left hand had curled back into his palm and on the right hand only his thumb and adjacent two fingers could be seen. It was the Viking Finger. Although he was now forty-one John had no sign that he would develop it and Matilda did not.

'Yes, John,' she whispered, 'Although as you know he could be such a kindly man, there was a time when those hands killed two men. One was a man who tried to rape me as we came up from Yorkshire.'

Making little sound, tears began to pour down Matilda's cheeks.

'You may have inherited your father's strength, but from what I have heard and seen for myself, it seems that the terrible temper has passed you by, dear boy. But for all that there are only two men in my life who I ever loved. One was my dear husband Arthur, who passed on two years ago, and the other was my brother William.'

At that moment William opened his eyes and said nothing for a few moments. He cleared his throat and in a weak voice he said:

'John, my son, I knew you would come. When I am gone I want you to see that Ellinor is all right and that nobody tries to take that frock and dress shop away from them. I know you have your mill to run and your family to look after but keep an eye on your aunt Matilda for me. Also old Mrs Rose Palmer who must be eighty by now. The old days are gone and any villains who try to rob our family can no longer be run through with a sword. Where a problem cannot be solved by our own young blood, then go to my lawyers. I am leaving them money to be on standby for legal advice.'

His breathing became erratic again and he started coughing and then closed his eyes.

Looking at John and Matilda, Ellinor said quietly, 'Would you mind leaving him now. After he has had a sleep before he seemed to improve for a while.'

'Of course,' said Matilda. Holding John's hand they left the bedroom.

He decided to stay the night in a spare room and set off back to Cut Bank around six.

Dawn was just breaking when he was awakened by the knocking on his door. Ellinor and Matilda stood there, both sobbing.

'Your father's gone,' cried Ellinor. 'It must have been around five o'clock, when I had fallen asleep in my chair.'

The funeral of William Byrne, the last Viking of the family as his sister described him, took place a week later. Some forty family and friends were there, including John's second cousin Bryan Byrne who travelled up from Church Fenton.

* * *

It was around this time that the most important development took place in the rise to dominance of the Industrial Revolution, and which within two decades was copied throughout Europe, America and the British Empire. This was the development in 1825 of the world's first steam locomotive that could carry people and/or heavy loads of goods.

George Stephenson, born in Wylam, Northumberland in 1781, built his first locomotive in 1814 and called it Blucher in honour of the Prussian general. It could haul eight wagons loaded with thirty tons of coal at 4mph. Locomotives of this type were immediately in demand to transport coal to the various iron foundries. With improvements on the rail tracks and development of the locomotives, in 1825 Stephenson's engine took 450 people twenty-five miles from Darlington to Stockton at 15 mph.

As steam power became popular more and more machines were crowded into each factory and ever increasing number of factories were crowded into each neighbourhood. This was, of course, not just in the North East, where there were more coal mines than factories but more so in the cotton mills and woollen mills of Lancashire and West Yorkshire and in the iron and steel factories in the 'Black Country' of the Midlands. In these mining and industrial areas the population increased much more rapidly than elsewhere. By the beginning of the 19th century for the first time the north became more populous than the south. This brought about the Reform Bill in 1832 which took Parliamentary representation away from 143 small boroughs, mainly in the south, and allocated most of them to the new expanded cities. But still the vote was only given to male property and land owners. Many of the factory workers, and even the miners of the North East, had been born in London and other areas of the south and they, or their parents, had gone to the north to get work. At least children below the age of twelve were no longer permitted to work in the mines, nor children under nine to work in factories.

Those of the Byrne family who had stayed with the two farms in Yorkshire had to battle with the consequences of the Enclosure Acts. These enabled the big landowners to take over common land as well as the strip farming land and squeeze out many of the small farmers. By 1850 there was only one Byrne farm left in Yorkshire. Most of the extended family had now moved into towns and cities to work in factories and those who had managed to achieve some education rose to business management, or manufacturing in a small way.

On a spring Sunday in 1832 John was helping Margaret to plant her early seed potatoes.

'Do you think, dear hinny, that we will still be here to harvest this crop? More and more factories have spread in and when they build the Ouseburn viaduct over the valley there will be no room for windmills along here. It's become the cradle of Newcastle's part of the Industrial Revolution.'

Margaret gave him a half smile, indicating her view of acceptance of the inevitable.

'It's the penalty a lot of people have to pay for this industrial progress. At least you don't have to go down the pit. You're a trained engineer and there are plenty of jobs for you now. I can always take in washing, I suppose.'

'There are no Byrnes to my knowledge who work down the pit. A few still farming, but most of them seem to be busy working in small units making tools. Even your cousin Alice's two lads, are making spanner sets. You told me that David, the eldest, is employing three people. I shall make some enquiries and see if we could do something similar.'

'Do that, John. And what about our Freddie?' Margaret asked.' He's fifteen now and young Maggie is twenty and about to be wed.'

'Frederick is a good strong lad,' said John.'At the moment he helps me out to lift some of the corn sacks and now I am wondering what I will do without his help. In his spare time he is being educated, and by who? By his big sister Maggie. She's the brainy one you ken and now she's off to pull pints with her new husband in the Bluebell Inn.'

Margaret butted in, 'Ah, you only know half of it. She is going to use a large back room in the Bluebell for schooling up to twelve children whose parents can afford two shillings a week for it. The busiest time in the Inn is evenings, when she is needed. And she could lay most men out who try to cause trouble, if of course her husband Alan needs her help.'

John looked at Margaret in amazement.'You women are ganging up on me and don't tell me the full story. You know my dear, our Mary reminds me of my aunt Matilda. Mary's not got her colouring, but she's bright, strong willed and always reliable, like my dear old aunt. She's not far off seventy you ken, but still going strong.'

John Byrne stayed as a miller in Cut Bush for almost another five years. The owner of the mill, Abraham Taylor, had died three years earlier. John had a good relationship with his son Alan, even though he had made a small increase in the rent which had remained the same since John first took over the mill. It was February 1837 when Alan Taylor gave him a month's notice as the City authorities had told him that the mill and adjacent house were among the buildings that had to go so that they could commence the construction of the Ouseburn Viaduct. The good news for daughter Mary and her husband was that the Bluebell Inn would remain, with the prospect of thirsty construction workers on hand to slake their thirst. Their first major visit was to celebrate the installation on the throne of eighteen-year-old Queen Victoria. Alan told John that he had been informed that if he wished to continue as a miller there was one to let at Benwell, to the West of the City, and one over the Tyne at Gateshead. John thanked him but told him that he had now finished with the physically demanding work of a miller, which was for younger men than he.'I am going back to engineering. That was what I was trained for. My son, now twenty, is in his fourth year as an apprentice to a steel manufacturing firm in Jesmond. My wife and I might move there, as it's less of a devil's kitchen than Ouseburn, and start something small in tool making.'

* * *

'There's one thing I am not doing, my hinny,' John said to Margaret.'I don't want us to be living close to our Frederick, otherwise he'll think we have come to keep an eye on him, to pressure him to doing what we want.'

'I agree with that, John. What I don't want is to be living in a pokey house, with a small foundry in the backyard like some do. With the savings you now have we could rent a nice little house in West Jesmond.'

'We must make sure that the landlord has no objections to a cat and a dog,' John muttered as he ran his fingers through the cat's fur.'Old Killer the cat and Marker the terrier have kept the mill and the house free of rats. It's a canny tradition with Byrnes. As far back as we know they've always had dogs and a cat.'

'Wey aye, my man,' said Margaret snatching the cat off John's lap.'Killer and Marker come with us, even if rats are hard to find.'

The first step they made was to inform Maggie (as Mary was now known to family and friends) and Frederick (he had come over on a Sunday to meet his parents and sister at the Bluebell) that their move was one of necessity. Frederick seemed pleased with the idea of his parents moving to West Jesmond. It would be near, but not too close.

Frederick suggested to his father that from what he could see in the area there were too many very small operations of less than three men, plus a wife or two, making tools. Prices were cut to the bone and it looked likely that new factory regulations now appearing on the horizon would kill off a lot of small operations.

'Push your engineering experience, Father, and approach some of the bigger tooling manufacturers, those employing at least ten people. You might even make a business deal with them.'

With the tax on newspapers now being lifted, the *Newcastle Journal*, published on Saturdays for one penny, was one of the few sources available giving details on houses to buy or rent. Catching a horse-drawn tram to West Jesmond John and Margaret visited two houses, both similar in being semi-detached with a large kitchen and eating area and a withdrawing room and two bedrooms upstairs. The one they chose to rent had a more solidly built lavatory which was nearer to the back door than the first house they saw. In North East winters this was an important issue, where some folk 'could die on the throne.'

John decided he would walk towards the Jesmond area where there were more small factories, including those built on to the house or in what was once a garden. When he came to the most promising area he would go into a tavern or inn to catch the midday drinkers and find out who were looking for skilled workers. Margaret decided to take the tram back to Ouseburn and prepare the tea of lamb chops followed by currant suet pudding.

John Byrne decided to go into an inn called the Northumbrian Arms. He thought it might be used by foremen, managers or even owners, rather than basic workers who were more likely to use the taverns, or public houses as some were now calling them. After talking to a few people at the bar, he sat down next to a man with a pint of Porter ale who was eating a pie.

'That looks edible,' he said.'I think I will get one myself. However, don't think me rude but I am a trained engineer and I am wondering whether you know of any of the foundries around here who might use my services?'

'Leave me to finish my pie,' came back the reply.'Get one yourself – they're quite good – and come back to me as I might be able to help.'

'If you are as experienced in tooling as you say you are then I do know that Lawson's Toolmakers are looking for a working manager. The old boy who founded it is dead, but they have grown under the son, Edward, and now have some thirty workers who need managing for best efficiency. I would take the job myself if I were younger, but I run my own little firm. That suits me.'

'Thank you for that information, and I am sorry to have interrupted your dinner. Can you tell me please where Lawson's are?'

* * *

They were in the same long road about half a mile from the Northumbrian Arms. For each pace John took he wondered whether he was doing the right thing. Was he suitable for an engineering job after twenty years running his mill. There again Margaret had to push him into taking on the mill as he lost confidence at the last moment. He rebuilt the mechanical operations of the mill, but that was far removed from toolmaking. When he got to Lawson's he wouldn't mention a manager's job but say 'I believe you are looking for someone with toolmaking experience.'

This lack of confidence was a characteristic that contrasted with that of his father, William, and his aunt Matilda and possibly his son Frederick. As for Mary she looked and acted more like Matilda every day. When they were alone there were times when Margaret would tell John that he was a kinder man than his father in that he would help anybody.'Whereas your father, like most of the Byrnes I have heard about, are kind and loving to their immediate family, but the rest can look after themselves. Frederick is going that way too. My father was like that in many ways and fond of talking about his Viking blood which would not let him go down the pit. Do you remember how at first he would scowl at you when he suspected you wanted to walk me out. You're a soft Saxon, my John, and I love you for it.'

He arrived at the factory of Lawson and Son and following the sign 'Enquiries' he walked into what was once the front room of the Lawson's house. An attractive young lady with light brown wavy hair looked up at him.

'Can I help you, sir?' she said pleasantly.

He though this must be part of the changes now happening in industry. Young women dealing direct with the public.

'I hope so miss. I am a skilled toolmaker and I was told you have a vacancy here for toolmakers.'

'Have you any references from a previous employer that I could show Mr Edward Lawson,' she replied.'He would probably want to see you.'

He handed her a reference that his employers at the foundry gave him when he left nearly twenty years ago. After she had taken it into a room leading from off of her reception area, she returned after what appeared to be a half hour or more to him but was only five or six minutes.

'My father, Mr Edward Lawson, would like to speak to you Mr Byrne. Would you please go in.'

He was met by a tall man around fifty, with dark hair just going grey, who offered him his hand.'John Byrne, please sit down. I am intrigued by the fact that in your reference it says that the iron founders where you worked after completing your seven-year apprenticeship were about to put you in charge of the tooling development section where you worked. How come you gave that up to run a windmill?'

'Well sir,' John replied, 'the reasons were rather complex. It starts with the fact that to get the mill running efficiently needed some engineering skills. I liked the idea of being my own boss and above all my wife and two young bairns had better accommodation to live in. And at that time being at the top of Ouseburn was an improvement on the devil's kitchen round the foundry.'

Edward Lawson looked at him for a few seconds while pursing his lips.

'I assume that at your age you will not be going to try yet another trade or way of life,' he said, breaking the silence.'We employ twenty tool makers here, plus two apprentices. Part of my time is taken up looking after a tooling firm over the Tyne at Gateshead that we have recently taken over. With the growth in business we could certainly do with two more skilled men here. However, what I am offering you is to be my manager. This means to co-ordinate their work with the orders that come in so that priority is given to those customers who are either good payers or, for example, require a higher technical skill from us that others can't give. I think you are a little on the reserved side but the men would respect you when they see that you really know a lot about tooling.'If you take this post your salary will commence at two pounds five shillings a week, rising to two pounds ten shillings after six months trial.'

John Byrne felt exhilarated at the offer but caution starting suggesting that he should ask Edward Lawson if he could go away and think about it. But he knew he would never have another offer like this at his age.

'Excuse my delay in saying yes to your generous offer. I was just taken aback by thinking I came here hoping to get hired as a toolmaker and now it is to be the manager. I will give you my best, Mr Lawson and will not let you down.'

The arrangement was made for him to start work as the manager in a week's time.

He went back to the new home in West Jesmond full of excitement and eager to tell Margaret of the excellent new job he had obtained. He opened the door and the first person he saw sitting on a chair was his sister Elizabeth who he had not seen for over a year. She had obviously been crying. Both of his children also stood there looking very sombre.

He looked quizzically at Margaret without saying anything.

'John, my love, it is double sad news. Both your mother Ellinor and your aunt Matilda have passed away. Typhoid fever has struck in Morpeth and the elderly and young bairns were those most hit. We know it has been rife here, but you would not expect it in ordinary country towns.'

With tears running down his cheeks John asked: 'When did this happen?'

'Our mother died on Tuesday and Aunt Matilda, still trying to fight if off, lasted until Thursday, yesterday,' said Elizabeth.'They want to bury typhus cases quickly so the funeral will be at Morpeth on Monday.'

It was not until John and Margaret had retired to bed did he tell her of the initial excitement he had had as he came through the door.

'You must look to the future, your mother and aunt would say. For the next few days the funerals must come first. Then you have nearly a week to concentrate on starting the new job. I am so proud of you, my love, for taking this job.'

Elizabeth stayed with them, as John planned that they would

all move together in a carriage late Sunday night to be at Morpeth early on Monday for the double funeral.

On Saturday, John and Elizabeth spent several hours reminiscing about the family's life since they were children and the story of the Byrne family in Yorkshire which had been passed on to them by their father and his sister, aunt Matilda. Margaret, Mary and Frederick were mainly only listeners to the conversation but joined in the occasional laughter at humorous incidents. It was following one of these breaks in the family story when Mary suddenly said, 'Aunty Elizabeth, from what has been said you obviously loved all the people in the family and particularly the children. Is their a reason why you never had any?'

'I did have a child, dear Mary. It was a little boy who was struck down by the measles when he was only three months old. Partly because of my husband Tom Wilson being away at sea – he's in Australia right now – I thought do I try for another baby next time he is home on leave? After all, that is what is expected of me to keep the Byrne and the Wilson families going. No, I thought, although I love other people's babies I wanted to pursue my own life. The two families will continue without my contribution. Now I am really too old to produce a healthy baby.'

'Aunty Elizabeth, I admire you for that. But now I am married I think with medical care improving I will aim for a boy and a girl and leave it there. I can't say no, because my father here might kill me.'

They all laughed.

* * *

On their return from the funeral John Byrne pointed out to his son the work that was now well under way in extending the railway for passengers as well as coal and goods north of Newcastle.

'I believe,' he said, 'that it will eventually go over the border to Edinburgh. As it is, the next time we want to go to Morpeth it will be by steam train.'

'That's true, father,' said Frederick William. 'There's a message for us that as the steam locomotives get more numerous and more powerful and the lines have to get more precise the manufacture of basic tools will go to large factories. The days of the small manufacturer can really only continue where they are designing and manufacturing specialist tools. Therefore I think you have made a good decision to take up this job with Edward Lawson.'

John replied, 'Let me see how I get on and after a while I will ask Lawson if I can take you on as you have good experience under your belt. Being your father it is not right that I should take you on without getting his approval. That would look like nepotism. It would certainly cause antagonism from some of Lawson's more senior workers.'

The six days at home in their new house enabled John Byrne to relax with a few carpentry jobs to do, together with digging over the neglected vegetable patch to let the forthcoming winter frosts break it into a fine tilth. He ceased worrying about whether or not he would be successful as Edward Lawson's manager. In fact he was eager to start.

* * *

On the Monday morning he was greeted by Catherine Lawson with an unforced smile before being taken into her father's office.

'Welcome ,John', said Edward, shaking his hand.'I have had a meeting last Wednesday with all the staff to explain why I have appointed you as a manager. I told them of your experiences but just made a passing reference to your time as a miller. I will be here today and tomorrow and am then going over to the Gateshead works for the rest of the week.'

Edward Lawson then handed him the information available on all their regular customers and a new orders file, which was always updated by Catherine.

'When you have updated yourself by reading through this', said Edward, 'I will take you into the works to meet our men. No doubt some might ask you an awkward question to see if you really are a toolmaker by training.'

John Byrne grinned. 'It's a natural reaction for them to take with a new immediate boss. I have regular talks with my son to keep up on tooling developments. He is twenty-six now and has worked in the trade since he was thirteen, when he commenced five years as an apprentice.'

Edward raised his eyebrows as he looked at John. 'Really? Well, we still need another couple of trained men. You must see if he is interested.'

John replied that he was not going to push his son into a job change if he was content where he was. Importantly, he said that he thought it best to see how he got on himself and whether or not after a few months he felt that some of the men might be disgruntled if he brought his son into the firm.

'You are probably right not attempting to bring your son in at present. But,' Edward added, 'we need an extra skilled man now. Prepare a draft on what experience we expect the applicant to have, but do not give a precise wage. Just say we are offering competitive wages. Then give it to my young Catherine. She will write it out neatly, check spelling and take it over to the *Newcastle Journal* for their jobs page.'

From the day he started working for Edward Lawson, John Byrne never once regretted his decision. Within six months of the first advertisement appearing in the press he had to take on another three employees – two skilled and one half way through an apprenticeship to be transferred to the company. Even more men were being taken on at the factory at Gateshead, which had much more room for expansion. The situation led him to recall what his son Frederick had said in regard to the future for small tool making companies. They could only exist for development of specialist tools and even there more and more work will transfer to the larger foundries to meet the ever increasing heavy engineering work in the North East and the Midlands. Much of it was being driven by the rapid expansion of the railways.

In January 1844 the inevitable happened. Frederick asked his father if there was still a vacancy at Lawson's Toolmakers. His employers had been suffering from loss of customers going to larger firms and in consequence was about to be taken over, although he was assured that his job was secure. John Byrne stressed that he would almost certainly be taken on, but he still thought the correct procedure would be for Edward Lawson to make that decision. The interview would take place on the next Wednesday.

Frederick followed the direction pointed by the freshly painted 'Enquiries' notice. As he walked through the doorway Catherine looked up, giving him a pleasant smile.

'Can I help you sir?'

'Oh, yes. My name is Frederick Byrne,' he replied with a slight stutter, not being used to meeting such an attractive young woman in a workplace. He was about to continue, when he was interrupted by Catherine's gentle laugh accompanied by a slight blush on her cheeks.

'I know, you have come to see your father and my father. I will immediately tell them you are here.'

As she walked to the door leading to the factory, she paused and turning her head towards Frederick she said, 'I knew who you were directly you came in because you look very like your father.'

Frederick was officially approved by 'the Governor', as Edward Lawson was now referred to, and found that there was little resistance among his fellow toolmakers to being taken on. Initially jocular reference was made to his father's position.

'Do you have to give your old man half your wages now he's got you this job?'

'No, only a quarter,' answered Fredrick.'I'm my ma's blue-eyed boy and she would stop his rations if he tried to take more.'

As acceptance grew into respect as they saw that he was an expert tool maker, the leg-pulling lost any maliciousness. After a few months the men noticed the growing frequency with which Frederick and Catherine took the opportunity to talk to each other. This inspired one of his critics to say:

' Fred, I bet the Governor has already spotted you two making sheep's eyes at each other. You might think you're a fine stallion right now, but he'll make you a gelding if you're planning to have your way with her.'

'In that case I will marry her. But I don't want to hear jokes about her which she can't answer.'

Then in a firm voice with a cold tone Frederick added, 'For me this is no longer a joking matter, if you don't mind.'

There were a few laughs from his workmates as they got back to work. However they knew he had influence which could affect their future employment. They accepted the subject was now closed.

On the Saturday afternoon after this incident Frederick went round to his parents. His mother was again cooking some lamb chops for tea and asked him if would like to join them as she had two more in the larder. To eat at his parents house was always better than what he could prepare at his lodgings and saved the expense of going out for a meal. He used this subject to move on to his objective of getting his father's view on asking Catherine Lawson to go out with him.

'Yes, Father, I would not mind paying to go out for a meal at one of the song and supper rooms that have recently opened in the city centre, as long as I had an attractive lady to accompany me.'

'Do you have the name of such an attractive lady?' asked his father, knowing full well who it was.

'It's Catherine Lawson. What I need to know is would this be right to even ask her as both of us work for her father. Just as important would you and mother approve whether her father said yes or no?'

'First thing to remember is that she must be mid-twenties, not a young girl of eighteen and she might just say 'No Frederick'. I have good reason to believe that Edward Lawson thinks well of both of us and is unlikely to sack either of us for you having the temerity to ask his daughter out.'

Margaret Byrne was smiling at her son as the conversation went on.' I agree with your father. You should speak to this young lady direct. That is the thing to do in this day and age. Before we were married father and I just went walking. Distance must have been from here to Edinburgh and back before he asked me to marry him. Now what are these song and supper rooms you want to take her to. It sounds like one of those places where the so-called gentry take wanton women for high jinks.'

Frederick explained that this was not what she feared. It was from song and supper rooms in London clubs that large music halls were being born. These were mainly being built onto existing taverns and were being visited by a growing number of working people as well as the middle classes. What Frederick did not know was that Catherine Lawson was engaged to be married some two years back, when it was then discovered that her would-be husband was keeping a mistress. This was the reason why Edward Lawson took the unusual step then of taking her into his business in order to take her mind away from the hurt she had suffered. The middle daughter Daisy was just as pretty as her eldest and youngest sisters but was a lesbian living with another woman in North Shields. On occasions when she visited her parents and her sexuality came into discussion she told them, 'I'm a Tom and I live with a Sapphist. There's nothing you or I can do about it.'

When Frederick asked his father how he knew all this, John said that Edward had revealed it to him one evening when they sat in the office having a few whiskies after the factory closed.

'Not a word about this to anyone outside this room Freddie,' said John.'But you will see that it is unlikely that Mr Lawson would object to you taking out his daughter.'

Leaving his timing until Wednesday, when Edward Lawson would be at the factory and near Catherine's usual arrival time, Frederick Byrne was standing in the office when she came in.

'Yes,' she said, 'I would be delighted to come with you this Saturday for the musical and supper evening. I feel sure my father would not object, but courtesy says that you should mention it to him.'

He did not object. He just added the rider, 'I expect you to act like a gentleman and look after my daughter.'

Choosing a private cab to pick Catherine up from her home, as they drove down to the city tavern he told her that he had never been there before and just hoped all would be to their liking.

They were taken to a table for two and chose their supper from a choice of three on the menu.

Catherine ordered a glass of German Hock – and proceeded to top it up with water. Although he would have preferred a glass of local brown ale, for this occasion he chose a red Burgundy.

The entertainment commenced with piano and violin playing some light pieces from Schubert.

As the evening moved on two singers, one lady and one man, moved from semi-classical songs to those more popular at that time. Many of these showed the influence of incoming Irish and Scottish workers to the Tyneside communities. In the half-hour before 10. 30pm, when Frederick had promised to call the cab to get Catherine home by the promised time of 11. 15pm, the singers were receiving encores for local songs such as Keel Row, Bobby Shaftoe and The Blaydon Races. They were both enjoying their evening together and begrudged the fact they had promised her father that she would arrive home so early.

At least they had the reward of their first kisses together in the back of the cab.

After six months and many kisses their wedding took place in the spring of 1840. In keeping with the tradition of a Byrne family wedding, music was provided by the bride and bridegroom. Catherine played the piano and Frederick accompanied her – or tried to – on a flute passed down to him by his father William.

The timing of the wedding was opportune, for over the next six months there were periods of considerable distress for both of them.

Chapter Twelve
Building Indian Railways

Just prior to the wedding Edward Lawson, now fifty-five, and John Byrne, three years older, put their heads together. They recognised a fact that many mentally active men of their age do not. Their mental and physical energy is slowly declining and for their company to continue thriving in a growing competitive era more young men must be groomed for top management.

On return from their honeymoon in the English Lake District, Frederick and Catherine would be based at the Gateshead factory where Frederick would be named as the assistant manager and be moved to full manager after twelve months. Catherine would continue maintaining records of all purchases and sales including chasing up of late payers. The two would be taking up residence in nearby Grensham Terrace.

John Byrne would become full manager of the Jesmond factory and a twenty-eight-year-old engineering employee, James Charlton, who had been with the company since he was thirteen would be appointed as assistant manager. As the Company chairman Edward Lawson would spend two days a week at Jesmond and two at Gateshead. A new development was that if a message had to be passed from one executive to another it would be taken by one of the apprentices on a bicycle, one being kept available at each factory.

The new management arrangements in the company's two factories worked well over the next three months. It was a hot July evening when everybody had gone home except John Byrne.

He was in the tool development section working on solving

a problem with the design for a new tool for railway engines. Although it was nearly 8pm windows were still left open in most areas.

He heard a periodic scratching noise coming from the front office, but thought it could be rats, who abounded in the area. This stopped and a loud banging started up.

'Christ,' he said to himself. 'I know what that is. Someone is trying to crack open the safe. And there's the men's wages for tomorrow in there.'

He grabbed a two foot bar of hardened steel to be used in making a tool and rushed through to the office. A man of average build and wearing a woolly hat pulled down over his ears was climbing out of the window. Byrne pulled him back and shouted in his ear.

'Sit there you bastard while I shout for the police. If you move I will hit you with this iron bar.'

He could see that the would-be thief was a lad not more than seventeen. With one eye on the lad John Byrne moved back to the window and began to shout:

'Police!, burglars here. Police...'

That was as far as he got when he felt a violent blow to his head, saw the office floor swimming and the boot of the young lad coming towards his head as he fell down and blacked out. The next thing he knew was that he was lying in a hospital bed surrounded by people he knew, but could only name one. This was Margaret, his wife. Looking at her he asked:

'How long have I been here? Who hit me?'

'It is over three hours since you were brought here,' Margaret told him.'Two burglars tried to break open the office safe but you stopped them. A gentleman who lives near the factory heard you shout for the police. As he knew where Mr Edward here lives he ran to his house and it was Mr Edward's youngest daughter who ran all the way to the police to get them to come.'

Mary Byrne, who was grasping her brother Frederick's hand, almost shouted as she bent over the bed.' 'Father, is your mind still wandering? Do you know who we are?'

Hesitantly, John Byrne said, 'I believe you are my daughter. Your name will come to me when I have had some more sleep. I know your young man, he helps me in the factory.'

With tears in her eyes, Mary moved close to her mother and whispered, 'Mother, he doesn't know our names and really who we are, except for you, his wife. I hope it is just the concussion and his mind will come back.'

'Yes, I hope so too,' said Frederick.'At least he believes you are his daughter. But I am only someone who helps in the factory.'

Edward Lawson smiled at Mary and Frederick and said, 'May I suggest that we leave your mother here for as long as the ward sister allows and let your father sleep. The three of us are doing more harm than good at this stage.'

As the three walked towards the door he turned to Frederick and said, 'I have a meeting with the Police Inspector at the Jesmond office at nine tomorrow morning. You might like to be there. Afterwards we must discuss what is to be done now that your father is likely to be away for some time.'

At the meeting with the Police Inspector they were told that they had arrested the young man who John Byrne first encountered at the break-in.'His name is Harry Charlton. He claims he did not hit Mr Byrne, which is probably right. We told him that it would help him when he appears at the next assizes here in Newcastle if he told us the name and whereabouts of the older man who bludgeoned Mr Byrne. I cannot give you that name until we have checked him out.'

As they made their way to the Jesmond factory Edward Lawson informed Frederick that until his father recovered, which he hoped he would, Frederick would have to remain running Jesmond with the help of the recently promoted assistant manager, James Charlton. He would now spend at least three full days a week at Gateshead, where at this time Catherine was running the factory with the help of the tool room foreman. Frederick agreed, 'as there was no choice at present.'

When they arrived at the factory the first thing he had to do was to solve the doubt in his mind that had grown in importance since they had left the meeting with the police. Although Charlton was a common name in Northumberland, was James Charlton related in any way to the Harry Charlton now held by the police? Everyone would know about the attempted safe robbery by now so he would see how he reacts.

With Edward Lawson sitting in the corner, James Charlton was called to come into the office and bounded in with enthusiasm. The conversation was obviously not what he had expected.

In a cold voice, Frederick Byrne said, 'Is Harry Charlton a relative of yours?'

James went white as he spluttered, 'Unfortunately he is a second cousin of mine who has already been to prison for some petty theft but fortunately my family has nothing to do with him, or his mother. His father is in Newcastle City Gaol still doing several years, I believe, for robbery with violence.'

'Tell me, James, when did you last see him to speak to, or send him a message', asked Fredrick?'

'It must be at least five years since I saw him and I have certainly never sent him any message.

Mr Byrne you have to understand that Harry Charlton's father Isaac is only a cousin to my father and not a brother.'

Frederick got up and walked over to where Edward was still sitting and they conversed quietly for a minute or so. Moving back to where a sweating James Charlton was standing, Frederick said,

'James you would have been utterly stupid to have been associated with this cousin in the attempt to rob our safe of the wages for everybody. As I do not think you are stupid, which is why I promoted you, I accept your explanation of the unfortunate family name connection you have with this petty thief. Now James, as you may have heard, my father Mr John Byrne was knocked unconscious by Harry Charlton and an older man and now suffers from memory loss which he may or may not recover from. I would ask you to work out a means of getting hold of the name and address of this older person, which we will hand over to the police without mentioning your name.'

Now looking very relieved, with his full colour returning, James Charlton replied, 'You can count on me, Mr Frederick, to do my best to do that. I owe it to you and your father, Mr John, who was always so good and encouraging to me.'

Having sent a cyclist with a message to Catherine telling her he would be late coming home, Frederick went to see his sister Mary at the Bluebell inn at Ouseburn. With a good turn out of customers she was helping in the bar. He asked Alan, her husband, if he would mind if he could speak to Mary for twenty minutes privately in the back room.

'Of course not and give my best wishes to your father John for a speedy recovery.'

Frederick told Mary that there was a good chance of being able to find the name of the person who had hit their father on the head with an iron bar and where he lived.

'If it turns out to be correct, Mary, do you think we should give him some extra punishment to what the law will apply.'

Mary looked at him for a few seconds before replying, 'You and I both know that when our dear grandfather William Byrne, the old Viking, was alive he would run him through with a sword.

But when he was dying he told you and me that he realised those were the old days and if people try to rob or harm our family we pay lawyers to deal with it. He even left a regular payment of three shillings a week for us to put aside for legal fees – not that that would go far nowadays.'

'Yes, I remember that well. Mary, you and I carry our grandfather's blood, for better or worse. Not like our dear father who is so kind and forgiving to everybody. I would suggest that if this man who beat him unconscious is found and by then father has not recovered his memory, then we do not kill him but see that he is given a beating and why. I would very much like to do this myself, but it is not fear for myself if I say that if I did and got caught the whole pack of cards around the two factories that

Edward Lawson and our father built up would come crashing down.'

'Freddy, I agree,' Mary replied quietly.'You know I am strong enough so I will do it myself.'

'I know you have the strength and the courage, but Mary you are not doing it !'

Frederick's whisper was almost a hiss.' If I won't do it because of the risk, you certainly will not. Your priority is your two young bairns. That's more important than punishment for the bastard who attacked our father. I thought you may know someone amongst your rougher customers who for a payment from us, which I will fund, will belt him good and hard on the head and say that's a present from friends of John Byrne.'

Mary smiled, thought for a moment and said, 'I think I know the man. He's a hard man but from what people say he is honest and not workshy. More important he thinks I am a lady from Heaven who looks after him when he gets a bit troublesome. If father's memory has not improved I will approach him carefully when we get a name and somewhere to find the villain.'

Nearly a fortnight had passed since the attempted burglary at the Jesmond factory. John Byrne had made only a slight progress in recovering his memory. However, there was an important development that morning when James Charlton knocked on the door of Frederick's office.

'I have just gained information through family connections that the man who struck Mr John was in fact Harry Charlton's father, Isaac Charlton, recently released from jail. As far as is known the police are not aware of this. Here is the address. As you will see he has gone over the river to try and hide.'

He handed Frederick a piece of paper on which a Gateshead address was written.

Putting the piece of paper in his top pocket he said, 'Thank you for that, James. Do not mention this to the police until I suggest that you do, nor to anybody else.'

He left the factory around five that night and left James Charlton to lock up.

In less than half an hour he was at the Bluebell Inn, where Alan was serving the early drinkers.

'Hello Alan, I just want a quick word with Mary as she has been to see our father this afternoon I believe.'

'Wey aye man, just go through. She's preparing our tea. It's belly of pork this evening.'

Frederick went through and talked to Mary for around five minutes about their father's unchanged health condition. Changing the subject he said, 'If you have spoken to the hard man, give him this piece of paper and these five one pound notes to make his visit soon as possible If he is successful there will be another fiver.'

Mary put the piece of paper and the pound notes in her apron pocket, and just said,

'It will be done, and soon.'

'Good. I must be away now. Catherine is expecting and is not happy with me being away so often.'

That night as they closed the inn Mary told Alan that she would have to go to see her father and also to try and calm down her sister-in-law the following afternoon and would not know what time she would be back.

Around noon the next day she shouted through to Alan who was cleaning the bar top,

'I am off now my darling I will try to not be too late,' and let herself out by the back door.

Alan did not see that she was wearing an old pair of his trousers.

After getting out of sight of the Bluebell she turned up an alley and from inside the heavy jacket top she was wearing she pulled out a working man's cap and bundled her hair underneath it. Anybody giving her a casual glance would think she was a man. She knew how to walk like one. Mary caught a horse tram to the City Centre and made her way to Mosley Street. She had been told that there was an information office there which cab drivers often went to in order to check the location of places in Newcastle and Gateshead. She found the street she was looking for.

As the next tram took her over the Tyne bridge, for the first time she began to feel nervous. 'There's no going back now,' she said to herself.

She got off at the new Post Office stop in West Street. As it was still only around half past two, she knew that she could not wait until it was dark, around nine pm. She would go and find the lodging house where he was supposed to be. As in normal times he rarely had a job, he might well be there now, waiting for a pub to open. She walked down West Street about 500 yards and took a turning into a maze of small streets and alleys. She thought '*that will help in my get-away.*'

She concentrated on trying to memorise where she should find the street she wanted. Turning another corner there it was and the house number was the second one along. She felt her heart racing. She said to herself,

'Let's get it over, if he is in we do it now.'

She knocked on the door of this dilapidated house. After a minute she heard someone walking slowly to the door. An unshaven man of around fifty in filthy clothes opened the door and said:

'What do you want?'

'Are you Mr Isaac Charlton', asked Mary in her deepest voice.

'I might be. Who's asking?'

Mary edged closer so that she was now half-way into the room. 'I have a present from Mr John Byrne'. With this she pulled from a trouser pocket a foot long piece of heavy pipe she had found in her husband's work shed and hit him hard as she could on the head. He fell to the floor moaning.

'Oh good,' she thought, 'At least I have not killed him'.

She pulled the door close and stepped out in the street. All she could see were two boys further down, kicking a ball to each other. She went round the corner she had come from and went up a deserted alley. She pulled her cap off, put it in her pocket and let her hair hang down again. She then pulled a light-weight skirt from the jacket top, rolled up her trouser legs to her knees and quickly pulled the skirt on. As this normally-dressed young working woman walked casually up West Street two men ran past her, stopping to say a few words to every tall man under thirty-five that they met. After a five minute wait Mary caught the tram back to Newcastle centre.

* * *

In December 1861 the nation was in mourning for the death of Prince Albert the Consort to Queen Victoria. He was only forty-two, the same age as Victoria.

In America a bloody civil war had broken out between the Confederate States of the South and the Northern States who were looking for an overall union and an end to slavery. Britain, although it had suppressed a major mutiny in India only three years earlier, surprisingly supported the rebels in the South, partly because of trade.

In Gateshead although the name of Edward Lawson still appeared on the entrance to the engineering factory, Frederick William Byrne, distinguished by his taciturn nature with most people, was in complete charge of the business. Following the Great Fire of Gateshead in 1853, which also spread across to Newcastle, he closed the Jesmond small factory and built an extension to the Gateshead factory on adjacent land where previous housing had been burnt down. James Charlton was appointed as manager and was still there when Frederick decided to sell the business in 1861.

The Great Fire succeeded a major outbreak of cholera on Tyneside in 1853 and one of its 1500 victims who died was Edward Lawson. Some say that with the passing of his wife and left to live alone, he no longer bothered to wash and clean himself as before.

John Byrne made a partial recovery from being attacked in the attempted robbery and would occasionally come into the Jesmond factory and sit down among the toolmakers and help efficiently with their work. His memory never fully recovered and in 1851 at the age of sixty-five he suffered a major stroke and died within a fortnight.

At his funeral tearful Frederick and Mary held hands throughout the service. Mary's husband Alan Smith held her other hand. He was the only person who knew the great secret this brother and sister shared. Even the deceased never knew of the revenge they enacted for the murderous attack upon him which stripped away the quality of his remaining years.

Isaac Charlton, the perpetrator of the attack upon John Byrne, recovered from the punishment inflicted by Mary. For seven more years he never worked and lived (mainly on drink) by theft.

As he lay in a drunken stupor he was one of the fifty-three people who were killed, mostly by asphyxiation, in the Great Fire of Gateshead.

Catherine also attended the funeral. She did so because she had always been fond of John Byrne from the moment he came into the Jesmond factory and asked if they needed a skilled toolmaker. One of the reasons why she married his son Frederick was because she thought that as he aged he would be as kind to other people as his father was. But he was not.

She noted the sobbing coming from Frederick and his sister and their hand-holding. Surely it was not all an act, she thought. This was partly caused by her dislike of Mary. At six foot she was taller than most men, let alone women. Catherine's opinion was that apart from her rather attractive auburn hair, she was a plain woman.

The seed that had taken root to cause the ultimate breakdown of her marriage was the ending of her work for her father's company. In some ways she was a pioneer for women to hold a decision-making job in mid-nineteenth century England. When she married Frederick the understanding was that they would delay having children for three or four years so she could continue to play her part in the growth of the company. Within six months of their marriage she became pregnant with her son

David Lawson Byrne, his name following the Victorian custom of using the mother's maiden name as the second forename. She felt that Frederick had planned this birth, in that he objected to using the growing number of birth control products and methods that were becoming more available. Just after David's second birthday they hired a nanny to look after him for three days a week, which enabled her to go back to work as her husband's secretary.

Then by early 1846 she found herself pregnant again. By the end of that year their beautiful daughter, who looked much like her mother, was born.

It was in the autumn of 1854 that, at Frederick's suggestion, they tried to solve their matrimonial differences by taking a three-day break. They hired a two-wheeled cart drawn by a small horse. It was late September with the trees starting to show their autumnal colours as they aimed for the upper Tyne valley. They decided to make their base for two nights at an inn in Hexham which had been recommended to them.

They had only got as far as Eltringham when they stopped by the river to enjoy the sight of two swans, and mallard ducks and coots in plenty. They could see fish as well, but what they were they did not know. One of the penalties of the industrial revolution was that for twenty miles or more from the sea the Tyne was now poisoned to all marine life. The first to go were the salmon that came in from the Atlantic to spawn in the upper reaches.

Having written to the inn at Hexham to make a booking, they arrived around 6 pm and checked in. Initially conversation flowed between them in apparent ease. Probably because neither cared to touch on the subjects that were driving them apart. They both agreed that rural Northumberland and Durham would be a natural home for them and many others now living in the industrial areas of Tyneside. The following morning they continued their journey up the Tyne, going across the remains of the great Roman wall and stopping at Barrasford. They managed to get a local meat and potato pie, which according to the innkeeper was said to be a speciality of the area. Frederick said to Catherine, 'Do you realise that if it was not for my grandfather William Byrne leaving Yorkshire I could now be running my own farm and you and our dear children would be breathing pure air for the betterment of our health and a longer life.'

'That's true, my dear,' said Catherine.'But now the Government has repealed the Corn Laws farmers cannot get a living in England for growing wheat and I am told they are presently not doing much better if they are rearing cattle or pigs. And the farm labourers can hardly exist with their wages. Freddie, apart from the foul air, we are better off trying to earn an improved life in industry.'

'You are right Catherine. You ought to be a country girl. What we must do is move to the western edge of Gateshead, such as just beyond Blaydon. We can still get into work, but live half the time in sweeter air. The railway line from Newcastle to Carlyle is now completed so we can find a house near a railway station.' Concern for each others feelings, if not quite a return to the love that once existed, was a promising reward for their three-day break. Then came the moment some six weeks later when Catherine realised that the only real outcome of the break was that she was pregnant for the third time.

In the August of 1855 David and Elizabeth had another brother. They christened him Edward John. Catherine had chosen the name Edward in recognition of her father and John in memory of the kind and gentle man who was Frederick's father. Frederick had no objections to the choice of names, nor to her wish that she would sleep in a separate bedroom in their present home until she had tried to obtain a divorce. He was taken aback by the mention of divorce. He just looked at her with tears in his eyes and slowly said,

'I am so sorry Catherine that I have driven you to this. I know it is mainly some fault in my character which I cannot handle properly.'

Vaccination, the liberal use of disinfectants in the home and installation of running water, ensured that the three children all lived beyond the age of five. The chances of children achieving this in the workers' areas of Tyneside were again drastically reduced as the evils of smallpox and cholera made their last appearance.

Catherine decided that with another body, even though a small one, now in the house it was time to remind Frederick of their plan to move home westwards to near a rail station. If he agreed to doing something about this it could lead to her no longer contemplating divorce.

'Business is bad,' was his response, 'and it's not the time to take on the extra cost. Things might improve by next year.'

Things did not improve at the factory. For one thing there was the growing strength of the Factories Act. This could be said to have been started by Earl Shaftsbury in 1833 when it was made illegal for children under nine to work in factories. By 1847 Fielden's Act limited the work of all young people and women to ten hours a day. Then by 1860 safety measures were applied to the operation of all equipment, particularly power shafts and gearing, for example. All these necessary steps taken to improve the lot of working people and the safety of their work environment added to costs. This affected the small firms more than the larger ones and was already beginning to show in the disappearance of some and the merging of others within larger companies. Blessed with foresight Frederick decided that he must look at selling the company while it was still profitable and try getting back into engineering. This could take some time.

With Catherine having to give up her post after five months of her last pregnancy, Frederick took on a twenty-year-old young lady of good education to fulfil some of the work that Catherine looked after. It was not long before she was secretly in love with the still handsome Frederick – and he knew it. Having no sexual relationship with Catherine for three months or more before Edward's birth, he felt considerable urges to possess Jane, his secretary. He even took her to high tea one evening to let her know his appreciation for 'good work in the office'. When he took her home in a carriage afterwards her surprise was apparent that all he did was to kiss her briefly on the cheek.

For the first two months after giving birth Catherine gave

Frederick every indication that she was not ready for him to make love to her again. That gave him the green light that he would now seek to seduce Jane. After increasing his display of affection towards her for a week or so he contrived an excuse, not that it was really needed, for her to work late at the office when everyone else was gone. As he laid her down on his cleared desk he whispered to her, 'I hope this does not lower my love for you but I think it best for me to wear this rubber condom. It would not be fair if I were to make you pregnant.'

Jane believed that this was because of his concern for her. Frederick, although he had become genuinely fond of her, believed that without this new style condom the arrival of a bastard child was the last thing he wanted if he was to preserve the marriage. The liaisons between them went on for several months. Jane was beginning to think that Frederick might just leave his wife, and as divorce was almost unheard of except for the rich hierarchy, they would live in sin.

Catherine knew when Frederick's behaviour meant that he was hoping for a return of their sexual relationship. Without resorting to verbal abuse she knew how to put on an attitude that said 'nothing doing'. After a while she realised that his attitude at night now said 'I'm not interested.'

As she thought about it, she recalled there was also the increasing number of nights when he would not come in until late. On two occasions it was midnight and he gave no explanations of why. She realised he was having an affair. This was a repeat of what happened with her first would be husband when she escaped marriage. Now, with Frederick, she had a chance, even though slight, of obtaining a divorce through his adultery. Prior to 1857 divorce was only granted by Parliament and it was for men only on the grounds of adultery. The Matrimonial Causes Act then made it possible in theory for wives to obtain a divorce if they could allege cruelty and desertion. Catherine made out a plan of campaign. With her work experience she obtained a similar post with a company that was a competitor of Edward Lawson Engineering, as it was now called. She would save most of the salary for future solicitors fees.

It was an early Sunday morning when all three children were still in bed. Frederick took Catherine up a cup of tea. Sitting on the edge of her bed, he said quietly, 'Catherine this is just not working. I have made arrangements for the sale of the business. Half of the money received will be given to you. When this is done I am going to India on an engineering contract for the new railways for a year. You will, of course, keep this house. Please do not speak ill of me to our children. You know I love them as you do.'

'I know that, Frederick,' Catherine said grasping his hand.'I sometimes think it is your only saving grace.'

Frederick was due to board a ship at London Royal Docks early May 1860 for his passage to India. In order to make the parting easier Catherine arranged to take the two youngest children on a new Thomas Cook five-day holiday to Scarborough. The journey would be by railway train to York then changing for the new line to Scarborough. Edward and Elizabeth's excitement at the news of this trip made it easier for them to accept their mother's explanation that, 'Daddy has to go away to India for a few months and when he comes back he will tell you all about its magic.'

On the last day of their holiday in Scarborough a report appeared in the local newspaper of a 'Historical Find By Newcastle Family'. It said that some boys and a young girl who had gone with their parents on a steam coach trip down to Osgodby had discovered the remains of a centuries-old rowing boat partly uncovered by last winter's storms.

'An archaeologist from Scarborough went down to examine it and said, 'It was definitely a Viking boat which could probably hold ten or twelve people. It has been partly preserved by being under the sand for centuries.'

* * *

On the day his two eldest children discovered the remains of the Viking boat Frederick was on the train to London to board his steam ship to India. The train took him to King's Cross and from there he took a cab to the Royal Docks at Wapping where he boarded the early version of the *Erl King*. This was a steamship that could be driven by screw propellers, but carried sails. They were necessary because there was insufficient space on the ship to carry enough coal to fire the boilers of the engines over a long distance, such as London to India.

The *Erl King* was carrying 350 passengers and its first port of call was Cape Town, where it would also take on more coal. She was also carrying eighty British soldiers who would be getting off at Calcutta together with cannons and other armaments. This supply of men and materials for Britain's Indian Army was part of the continual increase since the end of the Indian Mutiny three years earlier. If the Suez canal, which started being dug out that year, had been allowed to be completed earlier, it would have cut the voyage to India by more than half.

By the time the ship crossed the equator Frederick had come to recognise all of the passengers and to know a fair number of them. This included two of the Army's officers, who were allowed to go anywhere on deck and ate at a special table in the main dining saloon. The Tommies and their NCOs were quartered on the lowest deck of the ship, where they also ate, but were only allowed up on the lower stern deck for two hours a day.

The day after 'crossing the line' was Frederick's birthday. He must have casually mentioned the event the previous evening when having a few whiskies, because to his surprise at the end of dinner the waiters gathered round and wished him a 'Very happy birthday Sahib'. Two of the ladies on his table for ten even gave him a kiss on the cheek. They were mother and daughter and he had danced with both the previous evening. The unmarried nineteen-year-old daughter had made suggestive comments, which may have been made only in jest, on coming down to visit his cabin. He considered that any momentary pleasures that such a 'visit' would bring could mean that within a week of stepping ashore at Calcutta he could be dismissed from his new post for 'conduct unbecoming to a gentleman'. That was the story told to him in the gentleman's bar in regard to another compatriot landing in India to take up his job. Before falling asleep that night his mind recalled the birthday party of his sister Mary just a fortnight before he left England. It was held at the Bluebell on a Tuesday evening when the bar had been closed to all but a few special customers. Mary and Alan's two sons, George and Charles were there, with their wives. They were bakers specialising in cakes and now had two shops they owned, one in the Jesmond area – now becoming gentrified. Needless to say Catherine was not there, but her lesbian sister Daisy was – still smoking a pipe. Margaret, Mary and Frederick's mother was in attendance looking sprightly for a woman of over seventy, although she had become forgetful particularly in recalling names.

It was Mary's 50th birthday. She was still standing tall, with a few streaks of grey in her hair. Above all, she was as quick witted as ever with her great sense of humour.

Guests were well in to their food and drink and music and some dancing had started. Usually on such occasions, Mary would be playing the piano. When Frederick asked her why she was not playing she held up her hands and he could see that both little fingers were bending inwards.

'It's the bloody Viking finger that's struck half the Byrne family,' she said.'This only started about a year ago. It has a fancy name now, down to some French doctor called Dupuytren who has made a study of it. So they now call it Dupuytrens Contracture.'

Frederick recalled that Mary picked up his hands and feeling the tendons, particularly in the centre of his palms, she said quietly, 'Well my boy you are six years younger than me and your fingers are all straight now. But can you feel the slight hardness in the centre of your palms? That means a finger or two will probably start bending within ten years.'

His thoughts turned back to what his work in India would be

like. Had he done the right thing? As it was now past midnight his cabin was cooling off after the equatorial heat of the day.

A week had gone by after they had docked at Cape Town, where he had gone ashore for a few hours with Mrs Iris Benson and her daughter Rosemary as their chaperon and the ship was now using the sails as the wind had strength in that part of the Indian Ocean. The ship's routine, like its food, was much the same with dances held every other night to the music of the ship's band. He was always in demand for a dance, or two, with Mrs Benson and Rosemary being high on his list of partners.

With less than a fortnight to go before disembarking at Calcutta, Frederick was sitting in his cabin one afternoon reading up the information he had been given on the railways under construction in India. There was a knock on the door.'Come in,' he shouted. He looked up expecting to see one of the cabin staff, but it was Iris Benson.

'I trust I am not interrupting your work, she said.'Rosemary is not feeling well and is sleeping. I was feeling bored so I thought I would come and see you.'

He was sitting on the only chair in the cabin, so Mrs Benson sat down on the edge of the bed.

'Do you realise,' she said, 'that it will be another fortnight after you leave this ship before I get to Singapore and meet my husband.'

This confirmed to Frederick that Iris Benson had not come to see him for a conversation as such. After all, she was the same age as him, she was good company, her body was still in very good condition, and both suffered from sexual deprivation. Like the ship's boilers on occasions, they both needed to let off a bit of steam. Surely, he thought, if we confine it to this one occasion

I will not really infringe the code of 'conduct unbecoming to a gentleman' or in dear Iris's case unbecoming to a lady.

He locked the door and they both got into his bunk naked. As he was about to make entry, Iris whispered, 'Can I ask you for a favour? When you reach your climax could you please make a quick withdrawal. I don't want dear Charles to have reason to think

I had been naughty on my way to Singapore, and later present him with a little bastard.'

He developed a fit of schoolboy giggles at this request, which helped to extend their love-play.

When it came to the crisis moment he did what she requested.

He kept company with Iris and her daughter Rosemary until the final evening before reaching Calcutta, but it was confined to the dances and a farewell kiss.

* * *

As Frederick went past passport control he saw an Indian in Western dress holding up a placard with the message on it: 'Mr Byrne. East India Railway'. As it was in the middle of the monsoon season he carried an umbrella.'Good morning, sir. Welcome to India. Our gharri cart to take us to the head office has a good roof, so we will not get too wet.'

'At least it is warm rain and not freezing cold as in England,' Frederick replied, not really knowing what to say and how to address him.'

As if he had sensed Frederick's uncertainty he said, 'My name is Ajay and I completed my studies in engineering at Calcutta University last year. I am an assistant to Sahib Robert Maitland Brereton who designed and started all the work on the railway from here since 1857. My job is to turn all his orders and requests from English to Hindi where required.'

Ajay looked very pleased when Frederick complimented him on his excellent English, saying, 'Obviously Mr Brereton did well in making his appointment.'

As they stepped outside sheltering under Ajay's umbrella, the British troops who had arrived from the Erl King marched past wearing capes as some sort of protection from the rain.

'They will be going to Chowringhee, then up Park Street to the Maidan – our big park – so everybody can see they are here. They do a lot of this now. They will be based at Fort William.'

Ajay said this with no sign of approval or disapproval. Frederick decided to say nothing. After all, it was only three years since the Indian Mutiny was put down. Since then the British Army was equipped with Pattern 1860 Enfield Musketoon rifles, which were shorter than those used in the Indian Mutiny and more accurate.

The two-wheeled horse-drawn gharri cart soon passed the British soldiers and Frederick Byrne entered a world of which he had no prior concept. He had been to London once, York two or three times, otherwise his image of city life was confined to the mixture of prosperity and utter poverty in the streets of Newcastle-upon-Tyne. Here in India a number of boys in rags, some crippled, crowded round the gharri crying for 'Backsheesh! Backsheesh Sahib!' Twice he saw beggars leaning on sticks looking into corners where, according to Ajay, they would make themselves as comfortable as possible for the night. Each alleyway gave a glimpse of yet another world, one of teeming squalor. There were Hindu women in saris, both plain and expensive brilliant coloured ones, who even with umbrellas walked with an elegance that is the envy of many European women. As they got near to Chowringhee – the Oxford Street of Calcutta – he saw several small groups of young Indian men dressed European style chatting to each other. They seemed oblivious to the beggars, both old and young.

Accompanying the scene was an incessant background of noise. The multi-toned 'peep peep' of small horns on most carts rising above the babble of a myriad tongues. The clipclop of the horses hooves of the gharri carts carrying passengers to other parts of the great city.

They arrived at the East India Railway office where Ajay settled with the gharri driver, who seemed happy with his tip. Inside the entrance hall stood a tall Sikh. He greeted Byrne with the surprising announcement, 'Welcome assistant engineer Mr Frederick Byrne to see chief engineer Mr Robert Brereton.'

He had not been informed that he was going to be met on arrival at the company by the recognised head and thought the meeting would be somewhere on the railway line. He felt some anxiety as the Sikh led him in to meet the chief engineer.

'Good morning Byrne,' said the chief.'It is a tiresome voyage from England to Calcutta and you must be glad to have your feet on terra firma again.'

'I am certainly glad to be able to start work again sir, but I rather enjoy being at sea.' He added flippantly, not knowing what else to say, 'One of my ancestors must have been a regular sailor.' 'Ah well some of us have to be sailors,' the chief responded.'However, I hope you are going to show us that you are a useful assistant engineer in the construction of the railway, including bridges. I see that your engineering experience is almost completely confined to tooling and tool-making. Constructing this railway will be new territory for you. As you ran your own company, this experience of dealing with men will be useful. Our workers are overwhelmingly Indian. A mix of Hindus, Moslems and some Sikhs. Outside of work they do not always get on well together, but those that have remained with us do. We have got rid of trouble-makers and lazy blighters long ago. We are not part of the British Government, we just work for them. Therefore we believe in showing respect to those Indian workers who make the grade, including the few 155

young men who have some basis of engineering from their studies here in Calcutta. You have met Ajay. He is one of them. One of these days this railway we are building may well belong to India.'

Frederick made it clear that it sounded as if the company was being run in the same manner as he did in a small way on Tyneside, except there were no ethnic differences and only occasional arguments between Catholics and Protestants.

'I will be happy to work within the guidelines you have laid down for the company,' he added.

The chief nodded his head, with a slight smile.'

'You will be joining us tomorrow morning when we leave Howrah station to go as far as the line is presently completed. That is about five miles short of Benares, or Varanasi as the Hindus call it. It is probably the most ancient and sacred site in India. So far we have not started taking passengers, other than the Indian Army, of course. Tomorrow we will also take nearly a hundred high class Hindus, who will walk the last five miles so they can bathe in the sacred waters of the Ganges at Benares.

'We all stop at the hotel just up Park Street, so we will see you there for dinner and a chota peg or two.'

He was then taken into an adjacent room where two Scottish engineers were studying a large map of the rail route, completed and projected. Following the introductions they told him that the main hold-up they had at Benares was due to completing a large bridge over a tributary of the Ganges, both of which were flooded in the present monsoon season. As the monsoon usually ends at the end of September, in another month work on the bridge will speed up, Frederick was told. The next city to be reached was Allahabad and then complete the trackway to Delhi by 1864. Another railway line currently being constructed from Bombay should reach Delhi not long after this. Prior to dinner the chota pegs (small measures of whisky with soda water) were in some cases followed by burra pegs, which were considerably larger. Frederick confined himself to one of each. He noted that all dinner guests were European – as the Indians called all Britons or anyone who was white. When working on site though Indian assistant engineers, such as Ajay, always sat at the same tables as their white workmates. The next morning two gharris carried them over the Howrah bridge which crossed the Hooghly river, a tributary of the Ganges, to the station. Both were two of the largest engineering projects designed by the British. Byrne noted that the train was being pulled by two large R. W. Hawthorn engines with six foot diameter wheels, made in Newcastle. Apart from little over two hundred passengers the train needed the two engines to pull the large amount of rails, iron bridge supports and other equipment essential for the building of the rail track.

Some one hundred British soldiers were on the train when he joined and as far as he could see they did not include those who were on the ship. Last to join were the senior Hindus who were going to worship at Varanasi. They had brought their own food and their own cooking utensils for the long journey to Benares.

The vastness of India and its dense population was the foremost impression made upon Frederick on the almost two day rail ride until 'journey's end' near Benares. Whenever he looked out there was always some human figure in view. Sometimes it would be a farmer tilling his land with a wooden plough and oxen as his ancestors (and also Frederick's) had done for countless generations. Or there would be an old woman bent under a load of sticks, or two little children smiling and waving as the train went by, as children now do all over the world.

Early on the second day the train stopped at a station at Aurongabad. Here all the soldiers disembarked and unloaded some twenty horses, six cannons and other equipment. They were off across country to the larger city of Patna and from there, an officer said, they would eventually go on to Lucknow, a scene of cruel violence and a lengthy siege during the Indian Mutiny.

They reached journey's end where several large gharris were lined up to take the more elderly Hindus off to Varanasi to worship and immerse themselves in the holy, if rather dirty, waters of the Ganges. The younger and fitter ones set off with their umbrellas opened to walk the five miles.

Clad in tarred leather rain hats and cloaks the chief, followed by his engineering assistants who had arrived up from Calcutta, made their way to the bridge. It was a month before they could complete it and run a full train across it. By then the rains had finished for the next six months or more and the drive to Allahabad gained pace.

Frederick found the work challenging and inspiring, with the evening meals and a few chota pegs harbouring an atmosphere of relaxation and understanding of each other. This had never been a strong point of his and occasionally he would resort to his abruptness, including during the day when he thought a worker was slow in carrying out an order. As his time progressed the chief expressed his satisfaction with his work, particularly when Frederick came up with an idea inspired by his tooling experience of making an improved dog spike which was faster in fixing the rail to the sleepers.

After one year and one month the railway reached the spot in Allahabad where the junction station would be built. It marked the imminent end of his contract. The night before boarding the train back to Calcutta a party was organised to celebrate the achievement of completing another section of the railway that would cross India from west to south-east. Many burra pegs were drunk that night, including by Frederick and, unusually, Ajay. Refusing to accompany a fellow Tynesider to a brothel, primarily because he did not want to return to England with the pox, he crashed down on his bunk. His last thought was, 'By the time I get to Cal to catch my ship I might be sober.'

Frederick Byrne stepped off the train at Howrah station, where it all began for the East India Railway. He took a gharri cart to the docks to join his ship home. As they sped over the Howrah bridge in a cacophony of sound he could see the flickering lights from oil lamps down in the Chowringhee bazaar. He had spent only a year in the fascinating land of India but he had become conscious that he was in the presence of a deep seated culture. Perhaps because of his own ancestry he felt he could only be an observer, never to be fully enjoined within that culture.

Chapter Thirteen
Prosperity and Anguish on Tyneside

Frederick Byrne described his return voyage to London as 'pleasant'. If it was not for a chance meeting he would have been tempted to call it 'uneventful'.

The ship had started its return voyage from Singapore and on the second evening out of Calcutta he noticed that the social routine, as the food, was much the same as before. Tuesday night was a dance night. He had resolved to give this a miss, not least because the ladies at his dining table did not compare with the temptress Iris or her beautiful daughter Rosemary.

This was fate, he decided.

'I really must not allow myself to be involved with a woman, single or married, when there is a chance that when I get home Catherine may have dropped her idea of a divorce. It is only by returning to Catherine that I will be able to reconnect positively with my children.'

To compensate for the lack of exercise that regular dancing gives, he started each day with a walk of ten circuits of the promenade deck. After breakfast he would then spend a half hour in the rather rudimentary gymnasium with weight lifting and 'rowing' a mock rowing boat. He would then go to the bathroom at the end of his cabin deck and usually have to wait a while until the men's bath was vacant. He thought this situation could be improved.

'If they installed a shower sprinkler above the bath, as they often do in India, this would be very useful for those just wanting to rinse off their sweat. Also, it would save valuable water and speed up the time each person takes in the bath cabin.'

To while away his time he would also visit the ship's library and read various novels available. These included Sir Walter Scott's *Waverley Novels* and Charles Dickens' *Great Expectations.* It was not until he was but seven days from the London Docks did he get round to what became his favourite: Elizabeth Gaskell's *North and South* which contrasts the way of life in the richer South of England with the Industrial North.

After some of the excessive evening drinking sessions that went with working on the railway construction in India he decided to restrict his intake. He did not drink any alcohol during the day. With dinner he had a bottle of Saint Emilion Claret which consistently lasted him three evenings before replenishment. Down in the bar after dinner, or occasionally listening to the dance music or the weekly popular classical music concert, he would have two or a maximum of three single measures of a single malt whisky with water. The cheaper whisky blends he always drank in India were drunk with soda water.

It was in the bar that he met Tom Barley, an engineer who had worked on dock construction in Singapore for the past four years. Having been well paid he said that at forty-five years-of-age he would now retire. His wife Margaret, who was sitting next to him, said that would mean he would be 'under her feet every day while she tried to keep the house in order.' Tom Barley then made the telling point that made Frederick realise that being four years older than him his plans should give priority to the here and now. Tom Barley had said, 'I read an article in the *Singapore Times* just before we left that in Britain the life span of a man has now gone up from an average of forty years in 1800 to forty-five. If we had been farm labourers, miners or labourers in an iron foundry then the average life span was five years less. That's why I am retiring and with luck my lady Margaret and I can enjoy another ten years!

There was silence for six or seven seconds. Frederick then said, 'Your information is something many of us do not spend enough time thinking about when we are making our plans. I am glad you have mentioned it,Tom, for I must factor it in to what I decide to do with the life that is left for me. Please do not think that I am being ungentlemanly when I say that I would prefer not to discuss details at present.'

'We do understand and have no wish to intrude on your personal life,' Tom said. His wife nodded her head in agreement. She followed this up by asking Frederick, 'Do you play card games, such as whist, Mr Byrne? There are several teams of four who play regularly in the card room. There are three of us looking for a fourth to make up a team. Our third partner is Mrs Madelaine McKenzie, a widow lady who used to run her little school for British children in Singapore.'

'Well, that does not sound like a lady I could get into an amorous arrangement with and giving me more problems,' he thought.

Turning to Margaret Barley he said, 'I am not terribly good at whist and my wife invariably beat me when we played, but I would be pleased to make the numbers up and join you, as long as you understand you will probably be carrying a dead weight. Of course, I might improve by the time we dock!'

At 4.00pm the following afternoon he went to the card room and met Tom and Margaret. A lady about four years younger than Frederick joined them and he was introduced to Madelaine McKenzie. She was a pleasant looking slim lady with light brown hair and rather watery blue eyes, which suggested she may wear spectacles. She spoke with a gentle accent that was similar to his own but a little more like the Yorkshire accent.

'Do you come from Durham by chance?,' he asked her.' A good detection Mr Byrne. Actually, I was born and raised near Darlington.'

'As a Tynesider I am depending on you to raise the flag for the North East', said Frederick smiling at Tom and Madelaine.'Our good friends here from West London believe that all civilisation ends north of Cambridge.'

'Oh no,' said Tom. It goes up to York, on a good day.'

At the end of their friendly banter, which they readily pursued to hide their nervousness at wondering what they would be like playing as a team, they sat down to play. Frederick was not surprised to see that Madelaine was the best whist player and he was not too far behind Tom and Margaret. It was agreed that after dinner they would meet up again for a nightcap in the bar. Madelaine was at the same dinner table as Tom and Margaret. This was the routine for the last twelve days of the voyage back to London. During those evenings Frederick learnt that Madelaine's husband, Doctor Richard Mckenzie, had died in Singapore of typhus two years earlier after six months contact with his patients in the local hospital. It had taken another six months to sort out probate problems with his will, which eventually left his wife reasonably well taken care of. For this reason she had keep her little school of an average of ten pupils going as a source of income from the fees of the parents until her husband's money was released. As the days, and particularly the evenings, progressed before disembarking in London, Frederick became increasingly aware of how much he enjoyed Madelaine's company, which she seemed to reciprocate. On the final evening at sea he said to Madelaine, 'I am going to catch the first available train to Newcastle, which stops at York where I assume you will get off to catch the train there to Darlington. I will be only too pleased to accompany you to York and help look after your luggage.'

She smiled at him and said,' That will be a pleasure to have someone I know to talk to. Just think, Tom and Margaret will be sitting in their house in West London whilst we have only got as far as Cambridge, assuming the train does not break down.'

The following day Madelaine and Frederick were on the train and had just passed Cambridge when he handed her his card.

'Please do not think I am being presumptuous but here is my card. If ever you have a problem and your brother or elderly mother cannot help, then please write to me or send a telegram from your nearest Post Office. You will see that it is care of the Bluebell Inn, Ouseburn, Newcastle. As I am not sure where I will be living at present until I sort out some problems, that is the address of my sister and her husband who run the inn who would quickly find me.'

'I will accept what you say and that you are really not a problem drinker who lives in a bar,' Madelaine smiled. Putting her hand gently on his. She added, 'That is very kind of you, Frederick. I must say that I will miss your company. Here is my card. You must look me up if you are in the area.'

* * *

Although it was late March there was still snow upon the ground as Frederick Byrne got off the train at Newcastle main station just after 3. 00pm. He took a cab to the house in Gateshead. Hoping that Catherine was still living there he told the cab driver to wait.

He knocked on the door and waited a few minutes for someone to appear. He knocked again and the door was almost immediately opened by a young girl of around fifteen with light brown hair and blue eyes. It was a young version of Catherine.

'Hello Elizabeth, I hope you recognise me after my being away for nearly two years.'

'Of course I do, Father,' she said smiling.' Do you want to see Mummy? She was only saying yesterday that she expected you to call any day now.'

'Yes I would my dear, if she is in.'

Catherine appeared at the door of the drawing room. Eighteen years of on/off marriage told Frederick that she was slightly nervous.

'Hello Catherine, you look well and I am pleased to see you after eighteen months or more away in India.'

'You too are looking fine,' Catherine replied, 'and as handsome as usual. But I do not want to be sidetracked on trivialities when I need to explain to you the progress that has been made, at considerable expense, in obtaining our divorce.'

'So it is the end of the line then Catherine?'

'It is Frederick if you will sign this draft drawn up by my solicitors. There is a copy here for you to take away if you wish to in order to read every detail before signing. I am stating that we have reached an irretrievable breakdown of our marriage partly due to you having committed adultery on several occasions. We tried going away together to see if a reconciliation would work, but it did not. Now my solicitors state that the two years of living apart will soon be up by the time this reaches court and if you agree not to contest the divorce it will speed up the court's handling and reduce costs considerably.'

He listened attentively without interruption to what she had said and then asked her if he would be allowed to see the children once a week.'Secondly, does the divorce proceedings draft acknowledge that I have given the house to you already and half of the monies I obtained by selling my previous company Edward Lawson Engineering?'

'Yes, your points on the support you have given are all listed and it says that you can see the children whenever you wish.'

'In that case, dear Catherine, whilst I will take my copy away to read through before signing, I will not be objecting legally to this divorce. It is not my wish, but I recognise it is what you want.'

He extended his hand to her, which she took. He gave her hand a quick kiss.

Turning to Elizabeth, who was looking rather sad as she glanced at one parent and then the other, Catherine asked her if she would go up to the bedrooms and see if Edward John, now coming up to six would stop playing with his toy train. She returned holding the boy by the hand. He stared at his father rather nervously. Turning to Frederick, Catherine smiled as she said:

'Just look what you have left me with. He will look just like you when he grows up. The good thing is that he shows no sign of your temper as yet.'

Frederick's eyes moistened as he patted Elizabeth on the head and gently took his youngest son in his arms.

'What about his big brother David Lawson Byrne. Is he at work I suppose?'

He was amazed when he was told that twenty-one-year-old David had his own confectionery business, employing two girls and operating from a small frontage shop in West Street, Gateshead, and was getting married very soon.

As he left the house he told the cab driver, 'Take me to West Street here in Gateshead please. I am looking for a confectionery business. The name Byrne might be displayed'

He soon found 'Byrne Confectionery'. He paid the cab man for the afternoon's service and walked into the shop.

There was only a late-teenage girl behind the shop counter who was picking out a selection of sweets for a customer. He waited until she had finished serving.

'Is Mr David Byrne in at present?.'

'Could you tell me what your call is about, please sir?' said the girl.'He's cooking a new batch of confectionery right now.'

'Please tell him it's his father, just returned from India.'

She blushed.'Oh, I will tell him immediately. I am sure he will want to see you.'

The young lady delivered his message and within ten seconds the door to the back room opened and there stood David with a large ladle in his hand and a big smile upon his face.

It was two years since Frederick had seen his eldest son and he noticed that he looked very much like his own father John, and with the same friendly but cautious manner. David expressed his sadness that his parents marriage had broken up but added that he thought 'it was an accident waiting to happen'.

When Frederick asked him why he had not gone into engineering after studying it for three years at college, David told him, 'I realised that if you want to have your own business then the days of the small toolmakers business or supplier of special components are going. You knew that when you sold up Edward Lawson Engineering. I am not cut out to be one of hundreds working for a big company – I suppose that's in our blood of being small scale farmers for seven hundred years. As some people are slowly earning more money they will enjoy the luxury of taking home a bag of humbugs, toffees or chocolates. That will provide me with a fair living. The only expansion I visualise, or want, would be two branches across the water in Newcastle and one perhaps in Durham.' 'David, I think your plan is right for you,' his father replied. 'I need to get a job myself, which at my age means I must market my experience in building railways and bridges. I have made sure your mother will be all right financially but still have some funds left over from my work in India. Therefore, if you need some financial help to tide you over in your business, but not to save you from immediate bankruptcy if you understand me, then I will always help.'

As he shook Frederick's hand to say good bye, David said let me introduce Sophie Thompson. 'She's the one who deals with the customers and keeps them coming back. She's so good at it that I have decided to marry her.'

Frederick smiled as he shook her hand and said, 'I am pleased that my son David has good back-up who knows that the customer is always right.'

Noting that she looked as if she was already pregnant, he added, 'I am sure you will be both a good wife and a mother.' His next visit was to his sister and her husband at the Bluebell Inn. They agreed to let him have a room for a short period (which he insisted on paying well) until he knew where he would be working for the next few years. Mary told him that they found their work hard going to be open for fifteen hours a day and aimed to retire in two years.

Two days later Frederick was reading an article in the *Newcastle Journal* about the engineer Thomas Brassey who had been responsible for the construction of one third of the railway lines and bridges in Britain so far. The article stated that he had great faith in the experience of engineers and construction labourers from the North East and usually went out of his way to choose them for new contracts. Frederick was not surprised to see a small advert for 'engineers with railway experience' from Brassey's company on the same page of the *Journal*.

He wrote to them giving considerable detail of his recent work in India for East India Railway, with an outline of his experience as 'owner and managing director of a Newcastle and Gateshead tooling engineers'. He stated that while he would work on any contract in

England, Wales or Scotland, he would prefer North of England projects. He ended by saying that he did not expect to receive a salary of less than £700 per annum, which is what he earned in India.

After ten days he thought that as he had not even been given the courtesy of a reply this meant he had either asked for too high a salary, or perhaps they thought that his address of 'care of the Bluebell Inn' was not becoming a would-be executive. Then on the eleventh day a letter arrived from Thomas Brassey himself. He offered him the post of assistant executive director for railway bridge construction on the new railway to be constructed from Hull to Doncaster. This involved bridging two of the rivers feeding into the Humber and the Stainforth and Keadby Canal near Doncaster. He wanted Frederick to meet him on the following Monday before noon at his temporary office in the Paragon Station Hotel in Hull and therefore write to him first class confirming he would be there.

He arrived in Hull the evening before his appointment and stayed at a cheaper hotel than the Paragon Station. Following an hour-long discussion with Thomas Brassey and one of his company directors he was offered the post, at the salary asked for. Construction would not start for another few months in early 1863, but work was well under way with final planning and preparing the ground of the route. He started the following week and booked in at a long term rate at the cheaper, but quite satisfactory hotel. Following dinner on two successive nights he sat in his room and prepared a long letter to Madelaine McKenzie, in which he explained in detail that he now knew that his marriage was finished and he would soon be divorced. He ended by asking if he could visit her one Sunday.

Within four days he had received a reply from Madelaine. Early that Sunday he caught the train to York and then changed for Darlington. It was one of many visits over two years or more in which the couple developed a solid friendship. It was not until early in the second year was the friendship consummated.

* * *

It took up to April 1866 before Catherine finally received the divorce. She and Frederick celebrated it at the fifth wedding anniversary party of their son David and his workmate and soul-mate, Sophie Thompson. Their five-year-old son Brian Lawson Byrne was also there. Byrne Confectionery was now well established in Gateshead and a branch shop had recently been opened in Jesmond, with a £100 loan from Byrne senior which David was religiously paying back. Having replenished her glass, Catherine turned to Frederick and said, 'Although you could tell that you are Edward's father he looks less like you now and certainly shows no sign of your temperament.'

'I believe you are right, Catherine, but I will still love him. My sister Mary and I might be the last of the Byrnes to show the Viking attitudes from way back and the bent fingers in our blood. It's been diluted by all you good Saxons and Celts who came into the family.' They both laughed.

Mary came over, asking what they were laughing about. He told her that they believed the Viking traits within the family seemed to be diminishing and that they were the only two who became ill-tempered and cantankerous.

'It's you who is cantankerous,' said Mary.'But one advantage seems to be that although we are not frightened of hard work, we seem to keep fitter than most as age creeps upon us. Look at my dear Alan over there. He can hardly stand since he had his heart attack. They called it a stroke.'

Frederick butted in.' Did he continue with that latest salicylate medicine which is supposed to help people with heart conditions?'

'Yes he has,' Mary replied.'Without it he would probably be dead. Really it is just a refined treatment from willow bark by the Germans which the old Celts in Britain used centuries ago.'

Frederick, Mary and Catherine then circulated among the party guests, until music began for all to dance to. Catherine played the piano, David the flute, and Elizabeth sang in a sweet clear voice.

A year later the same number of family members turned up at

David and Sophie's home. This was for the belated christening of David and Sophie's son, Brian Lawson Byrne. They had hid Sophie's pregnancy in her bridal gown and when Brian was born they felt they could not face any lectures from the vicar on the christening of a child conceived out of wedlock. When they finally decided to get him baptised, the local vicar only smiled. Thus the occasion for a party. Missing was Mary's husband Alan Smith, finally taken by a major heart attack two months previously. His place was taken by his son George, now a foreman in one of the iron foundries. Mary and Alan's younger son Charles was a soldier in the Durham Light Infantry who had been given leave to attend his father's funeral, but not for a cousin's christening. Charles had his mother's auburn hair and the typical Byrne heavy build.'Best place for him is in the Army, where they will control his temper,' said Mary.

There were just two non-family guests at the christening. One was Madelaine McKenzie and the other was Clive Ashley, a friend of Catherine. Everybody except Frederick and Catherine's middle sister Daisy liked him. Daisy thought he was 'an upper crust suppressor of farm labourers.' Frederick aligned himself with this because of his own family origins of small landowner farmers always having to look out for their few acres being stolen by the landed gentry to which Ashley belonged. Perhaps his dislike was also due to his jealousy at Catherine having so easily replaced him, including in bed.

Interestingly, everybody, including Catherine, took to Madelaine McKenzie, as Madelaine did with Catherine.

Chapter Fourteen

The Final Rise and Fall

By the age of ten Brian Byrne was showing interest in anything to do with engineering. By the time he was twelve he would spend nearly all his spare time at the engine sheds at Gateshead cleaning down engines and parts that had been dismantled for repair. His father David, supported by Sophie, could see that he had no interest in working for the family confectionery business.

Wisely, they agreed to pay the fees for him to go to a mechanical engineering college in Newcastle for three years, with the potential of an apprenticeship with a local firm afterwards.

David and Sophie were very content with the stability and gradual growth of their confectionery business, with a fourth shop recently opened in Durham. Unlike Brian, their eldest daughter Alice was very interested in the confectionery trade and started serving in the Gateshead shop on Friday evenings and Saturdays from the age of eleven. In consequence David said to Sophie one evening, 'We must do everything to keep her interest going. She can then look after the business when we are old.'

The children's grandfather, Frederick William Byrne, who would visit them three or four times a year, warmly supported Brian's choice and his parents approval of it He was now nearly sixty and more irascible than ever. He and Madelaine McKenzie never married but she still looked after him with calm. She was there, holding his hand, when he wept in church at the funeral of his former wife Catherine. The only occasion when she lost her tranquillity was at the funeral of his sister Mary. A wake was held at the Bluebell Inn where a regular customer of long standing used inappropriate words in reference to Mary as being 'more like the blokes than a woman'.

With staring eyes and face turning red Frederick grabbed a water jug, hit the man on the head and as he fell to the floor he kept kicking him and growling unintelligibly.'Please excuse my father!' cried David as he helped pick the man up, 'He is distraught at the death of his sister. I will pay any hospital treatment you may need.'

Madelaine pushed her way through the crowd and grabbed Frederick's arm.'You are coming away with me now!'

He followed, looking puzzled and now grey-faced.'What happened? Did we have a fight with that man? Was he rude about Mary?'

He was rarely seen by the family or former friends after that. Two years later in 1873 he died quietly in his sleep, whilst Madelaine held his hand. When his will was read out it was revealed that he had more money saved than most believed.

He left £100 each to Madelaine, David, Sophie, Elizabeth (married six months previously), and to Mary's two sons George and Charles. To Alice, daughter of David and Sophie, he left £250. To his youngest son Edward John Byrne and his grandson Brian Lawson Byrne he left £2,000 each kept on interest in his bank until each reached the age of twenty-one.

Brian Byrne successfully completed his apprenticeship as an engineer at a ship builder in Wallsend, and stayed with them until he was twenty-one. The previous year he had followed the Victorian era habit of the Byrnes of early marriage. The strange coincidence was that his wife Joan's maiden name was Byrne. Her father said that in his family the legend was that they had come from Yorkshire just after the country had been afflicted with the eruption of the great Icelandic volcano. As they got into bed on their wedding night Joan said to Brian, 'I might well be your very distant cousin, but I don't think it is close enough to mean that our children will be idiots.'

'Brian laughed, then said, 'If it *was* true, we would be six or seven generations apart, which would not affect any bairn.'

By the autumn of 1882 Brian and Joan were able to feel confident that their eight-months-old son William John Byrne was far from being cerebrally affected.

Now that he was twenty-one Brian could make use of the £2000 he had been left in his grandfather's will. Joan suggested that he should take it all out and see what engineering business he could take over for this considerable amount.

'Probably a dead horse company,' said Brian.'One that could pay me a pound a week more than I am getting now and would survive for perhaps five years before it collapsed or was absorbed into a large firm. I want to wait until I have learnt as much business experience as engineering knowledge. Then, perhaps in three to five years we will know when the time was right – and strike!'

'After all,' he added,'the wage I am getting now at this new firm is not too bad. To make things better for you I will arrange to draw out £50 a year from my inheritance which will cover us on the extra rent for a better house in Jesmond.'

Eighteen months later in a normal birth Joan delivered a baby girl. They called her Anne, after Joan's mother. She was a normal nine-month-old baby but then began to develop breathing problems. Anne was not quite two when she died of a form of tuberculosis.

* * *

Despite the enjoyment they were given by the good health and physical and mental development of William John, both parents had still not got over the loss of their little girl. With Joan's eager prompting Brian followed up a contact given to him by a work friend which meant they would have to move to Manchester. The job offer was to work on the construction of a factory for a company called Lever Brothers.

It had been formed in 1885 by William Hesketh Lever and his younger brother James to manufacture soap in bar form. The factory was being built between Bolton, where both the brothers were born, and the South-West of Manchester. Brian Byrne was offered a salary nearly fifty per cent higher than what he was getting in Newcastle, plus free accommodation in a house with running water.

By early 1887 the factory had been running efficiently for more than six months, with Brian Byrne being kept busy as the maintenance and production engineer. The second event that year was the birth of another son, Richard, whose health was watched intensely by both parents . The third event was William Lever's purchase of fifty-six acres of land on the Wirral where Port Sunlight would be built.

After a year of non-stop working Brian had played a major role in the installation of the manufacturing machinery and servicing it to overcome teething problems. His salary had already been advanced again and during the ceremony to mark the official opening of the Port Sunlight factory he was presented with a cheque for a £500 bonus. It was typical of the generosity that William Hesketh Lever always showed to his employees.

Another bonus was that William John was bright as a button and had just started at a nursery school. The second child, Ellen was a healthy three-year old girl and Richard Frederick had reached his first birthday and also seemed set for good health. As for Joan, she had never been happier, particularly when attending social dinners and dances (usually funded by Levers) in her best dresses. Often, Brian was so tired he wished he could be at home in bed. In such spare time as he had he would go through the business pages of *The Times* and *The Daily Telegraph*. The objective was to see if there were any announcements, or box advertisements, from overseas companies looking for UK agents, particularly for machine tools.

He now had nearly £4,000 in his bank account, including the endowment from his grandfather. It was a Sunday morning after another one of Joan's Saturday night social dinners in Manchester City Centre. There in *The Times* was just what he had been waiting for. A German company manufacturing wood working machinery, including powerful chainsaws, was looking for a British engineering company to act as their British agents. They gave a telephone number as well as the postal address. Not having access to a telephone – he could hardly ask his employers if he could use theirs to seek another job – he wrote to them immediately. Detailing his engineering experience he stated:

'We are in the midst of acquiring a London engineering company and could start as your British agents from this base in about a month's time. We will have a sub-branch based in Newcastle upon-Tyne to cover the North of England and Scotland.'

On the same morning he saw an advertisement in *The Telegraph* from a Belgian confectionery manufacturer, Confiserie Bon Bon also looking for agents in Britain. Again this had a telephone number. He decided he could use the firm's telephone to speak to his father about this, and suggest that they offered to be agents in the North of England and he would 'soon be able to act as agents in London and the South of England.'

For either aspect of Brian's plan to become a reality he knew that it was now urgent to acquire a manufacturer's premises, whether it was in engineering or not, in the London area. He would add the Lever Brother's office copy of *The Engineer* to his reading list.

On the Monday morning he asked the office manager if he could use one of the company's telephones to speak to his father on family business. After ten minutes two operators managed to put him through to David Byrne in Newcastle. He explained the advertisement being put in *The Daily Telegraph* by the Belgian confectioners for a British agent. David said, 'It sounds interesting but I have not get the energy to handle that. Our Alice will, She is twenty now and this will appeal to her. She's at the Gateshead shop and I will get her to telephone you back as soon as she can get a connection from the local switchboard.'

Making his apologies to Lever's office manager, Brian waited some ten minutes until the firm's telephone operator said, 'Your sister is on the line Mr Byrne.'

He suggested that she try to get hold of a copy of *The Telegraph* and then telephone Confiserie Bon Bon in Belgium and, if she felt capable of running the agency, she should tell them she is interested, but the premises for London and the South will not be ready for a month. He told her that he felt sure her father and mother would attend any discussions if the Belgians sent anybody over to discuss it with her. If not, he would come up himself to help her but he knew little about confectionery. Alice added that if she got through on the phone, using the 'school girl' French she had learnt, then she should write to him immediately.

As he had seen engineering businesses for sale in *The Engineer* every week, although the majority were in the Midlands and the North, Brian Byrne decided it was time to take another action step. He made an appointment to see William Lever at his office in Port Sunlight the following afternoon to hand in a month's notice. He told William Lever, 'I am not going to a competitor of yours sir. I feel that my job of getting the equipment working at the original Bolton factory, then Warrington, and working with your Chief Engineer to get Port Sunlight up and running is now done.'

'That is basically true,' William Lever replied.'You have done a good job here and as our Chief Engineer is getting on a bit, I thought that when he retires, probably not before five years, you would take his job. Whatever you want to do I will give you a good reference.'

Brian told him in general terms how he planned to take over an engineering firm in London that needed resurrection.

Lever smiled and said, 'Your good wife Joan will be happy to be near the bright lights of the West End. My wife will miss her company in the social life of Manchester.'

Although Brian still gave his full attention to his remaining work for Levers, he now took the opportunity to scan the firm's copy of *The Telegraph* and *The Times* every day and *The Engineer* on Fridays. After a few days he noticed a box advertisement in *The Times* from a 'small specialist engineering company' in Bermondsey, South London, who wanted to sell their business and property for £5,500. He waited until Friday's *The Engineer* which said that their 'speciality' was braking systems for railways and trams. He took time off to go to his bank in Manchester to see if he could negotiate a loan of £900 (he thought this more likely to be accepted than £1000) towards the purchase of the company and its buildings and equipment. Having been told that it was likely but they would examine the proposal further, he then went to a shop where customers could pay for use of their telephone cubicles. He managed to get through to a Mr Arnold Robinson who said he was the proprietor and managing director of Robinson Engineering. He accepted Brian Byrne's proposal to come to Bermondsey on the coming Saturday and view the factory.

That night he discussed his plans with Joan. She wanted to go to London with him that Saturday. He had to explain to her that although Bermondsey was less than two miles from London's West End it was a working class area, like most of Gateshead and Newcastle.

'Oh,' she said, with an air of disappointment.'Will we have to live there?'

'Yes, but only until I have made the business take off. Then, Joan, we will live where you choose, but I think Buckingham Palace is now full up.'

When Brian had finished his phone call earlier to Arnold Robinson he took the opportunity to use the telephone cubicle to speak to his sister Alice. She was very excited. When she phoned Confiserie Bon Bon in Brussels the telephonist could understand Alice's primitive French and put her through to someone who spoke good English.

The same person had arranged to visit her and their parents at the Jesmond shop in a fortnight's time.

'The Jesmond shop is much more modern than the others,' said Alice, 'and the nearby Jesmond Dene area is an affluent looking part of Newcastle. It's more impressing than taking her to our Gateshead shop!'

As Brian Byrne expected by his voice on the phone, Arnold Robinson was quite an elderly man, probably coming up seventy.

The factory buildings were somewhat larger than he expected, but had seen better days, both inside and out. As he soon gathered in their conversation Arnold Robinson was inspired by Sir Joseph Whitworth, best remembered for the Whitworth screw thread and the promotion of true plane surfaces in engineering. As a result most of the lathes, turning machines and shaping machines in the factory were of the design period of 1855-65.

From what he had learnt at Port Sunlight and elsewhere, William Lever would have thrown them out.

Despite there being a ninety-nine year lease on the premises, plus a two-year tenancy on a three-bedroom house nearby, Byrne said that he found the asking price of £5,500 too high and suggested £4,700. Robinson came back with £5,000, which was accepted. Brian was to start coming in to the factory the following week with completion in a month.

Having had the good news from his bank that on sight of a copy of the agreement with Robinson Engineering they would grant the £900 loan, Brian, Joan and family moved to Upper Grange Road, Bermondsey. The house had gas lighting like most of the better properties in the area. Having given Alice his company telephone number, a week after his arrival she phoned him to say that the Belgians had been to see them. In the agreement signed by David Byrne and herself, Byrne Confectionary was now their official agent for the North and Midlands of England, with a view to extending this to the whole of Britain once the London premises was inspected and opened.

Bryan's first priority was to move some of the oldest machine tools out into the yard (where they were covered with a tarpaulin and later sold as a job lot for £150). The section emptied was then cleaned down and painted and a separate modern door installed and fitted with a Byrne Confectionery fascia board. The design was the same as the established notepaper. In late July the Confiserie Bon Bon sales director and their English translator together with Alice came and approved the new UK agent's office and depot. In a separate meeting afterwards Brian and Alice eventually agreed that

Brian personally would receive twenty-five per cent of the profit on sales to the Greater London area and the South of England. They phoned their father who, as expected, just said, 'That's all right by me. Just get on with it.'

Much to his surprise Joan actually committed herself to saying that the house was better than she expected.'But that does not mean I want to be here for more than two years when you have made more money.'

Brian smiled and said, 'We could make a bit more if you would give time to take over running the London depot here for the confectionery business, perhaps with a young girl assistant. My sister Alice would still be boss though when she comes down.'

'Yes, I will give that a try for a while,' Joan replied to his further surprise. 'But you must promise to take me to a good West End restaurant twice a month.'

Bryan Byrne's next priority was to call on all Edwards Engineering customers, including those they had lost over the last two years. In order to retain their custom he would often show them the reference given him by William Lever of Port Sunlight.

The same reference came in very useful when two months after moving into the factory he obtained an agency agreement with Schumann GmbH, a German machine tool company.

A year passed and, with Joan's occasional threat of quitting her Byrne Confectionery job (which a night out would usually solve) both businesses grew more and more profitable.

It must have been the result of one of these social nights out that Richard Frederick, their third son, was born, for he wasn't planned. Their two eldest sons were now mixing with working class children at school and sometimes being allowed by Brian and Joan to play with them in the street. They were distinguished by Joan deciding to dress them in green velvet suits, much to the distaste of the Cockney kids dressed mainly in their older brothers' worn out trousers and jackets and even boots if they were lucky.

Being older and more sensitive William regretted accepting

their offer of 'Do you want to play wizards.' William quietly said 'yes', but three-year old Richard bellowed 'Yes mate!'

The two boys from up North, in green velvet suits, were then pelted with horse manure.

William took Richard's hand and told him, 'Come on we're going home now to get cleaned up.'

Richard pulled his hand free and ran at the boy who had asked the fatal question. His little face was red with anger as he kicked him, tried to punch him, and shouted, 'Don't throw horses shit at me or I will get you when I'm bigger'.

All the Cockney boys laughed, and some patted him on the head as the Byrne's recently appointed house maid pulled Richard and William into the house.

It was coming up to Christmas 1890 when the solicitors for the owners of the house at Upper Grange Road said that the lease had already been extended by five months and they must leave by January 31st, 1891. As Joan was beginning to panic, Brian told her that looking to buy a house before Christmas meant that you could obtain a desirable property up to ten per cent cheaper than in the early spring.

One of the favoured areas among London's suburban middle class was Streatham. Brian took Joan to estate agents in Streatham who showed them a new house that had a kitchen, a pantry, large dining room and equally large lounge, plus a w. c. Upstairs there were three bedrooms, a large bathroom, and two box rooms – of possible use for house servants. Lighting was still gas, but it had the facility to connect to electric lighting when this became economically feasible. With a garden of nearly half an acre the estate agents said they could have this for £1150.

On hearing the price and then going over the property, Joan said quietly out in the garden,

'I must have this house. Don't you lose it by haggling over a few pounds like some East End trader.'

Brian glared at her.'I want to buy this house and not put myself in debt. If they see we are split they will see that and stick it out for the full price.'

They went back inside. Brian turned to the agents.

'If you want to make a sale with me then I am limited to one thousand. I will give you a banker's draft now for six hundred pounds, to be followed by the balance of four hundred on January 31st.'

The agents talked amongst themselves for ten minutes. The senior of the two smiled at Mr and Mrs Byrne, saying, 'You are a hard man to do business with Mr Byrne, but we will accept your offer on the understanding that you are limited to placing only one large bed, one table and three chairs in the house until we have the balance. We will put that in the agreement for you to sign.'

Ease of travel was another factor in Byrne's decision on the Streatham house. Brian could catch a train from Streatham Hill station to Waterloo East and walk to the factory from there. Access to the West End could be via Victoria or Charing Cross station or by tram from Streatham, not that this was favoured by Joan.

In June Brian, Joan and young William made their first visit back to Newcastle in four years. For Richard it was his first visit ever. The occasion was the marriage of his sister Alice. They went by train in a first class carriage, although Brian had said that 'second class was quite comfy and would save them at least five pounds'. Joan thought otherwise. They considered that the distance was too far for the baby son John so they handed him over to a reliable nanny they used on occasions.

There was a full turn out of the Byrne family at All Saints Church of England, Newcastle, as well as the local family of George Brandon, Alice's husband. At the reception considerable fuss was given to William and Richard, 'our lost Geordie boys' as Alice and Bryan's mother Sophie called them. The drink was flowing well when Alice's George said, 'I have been down to London twice now with Alice. To see the great sights was very interesting, but to live there would not be to my liking.'

'I could suffer a month or two', said Alice,' but I could not live in London full time.'

Richard had been listening intently to what was being said. Suddenly he piped up:

'I would like to live here but you all speak funny. You speak like Daddy.'

'Ere, watch it mate', said his big brother William, putting on a good Cockney accent.

Brian, unusually well under the influence, grabbed his sons and hugged them.'

Shall I tell you all something, my new friends and old, I was lucky in work when I went to Manchester. I was also lucky, with some help from Alice, when I went to London. But this is where I want to be and where I will return to. I hope Joan comes with me as there are plenty of good places to eat and to dance in Newcastle.'

Everybody clapped him, and some cheered, but Joan just gazed into space. His next visit to Newcastle was in the spring of 1900. It was to attend the funeral of his father David who seemed to have suffered from chest infections for the last decade. Joan said she would stay to look after the confectionery business in London. William John, now eighteen, accompanied his father. Alice's husband George had become a mainstay in Byrne Confectionery for several years. Because of David's lengthy illness no real business problems arose by his death.

Alice assured Brian that their mother Sophie was in very good health and wanted to keep active in the four shops

* * *

In 1902 Brian and Joan Byrne and their sons had been living in Streatham for eleven years. They had just had electric lighting installed, which was 'bloody expensive but will put a few hundred pounds on the value of the house' Brian told a friend.

Business turnover in their own engineering and as agents for the Belgian confectionery products remained good throughout the end of the Victorian period. The sole British agency for the German machine tools had done really well and was now Brian Byrne's main source of profit. In June that year Schumann GmbH invited Brian to bring his wife along to the annual meeting in Dusseldorf in early July and then stay for three or four days, at the company's expense, at a quality hotel on the Rhine.

Brian had over several visits found it easy to get on with the Germans in the company. This was Joan's first visit to the Continent and was pleased with the courtesy shown by her hosts. One thing that surprised them was that the Germans they came in contact with, as also their Belgian contacts, could not understand the celebration of victory over the South African Boers.

The two year conflict which ended that May was against Dutch, German and French origin immigrant farmers who could only win against the might of the British Empire by guerilla tactics. The Continentals did not approve of the concentration camps the British opened to accommodate Boer families after we had burnt down their farms.

For several months after their return Joan said how impressed she was with the fine country houses, with palatial gardens, where most of the Schumann directors lived.

'You are the MD of Robinson Engineering. I admit it is not as big as Schumann's but it is time now that we moved a little bit more out to a small country hall. I have seen just the place in Surrey in *The Lady* monthly magazine. They only want £3000.'

'Let me see the article,' growled Brian.

She watched while he read it all the way through. Without saying a word he folded the magazine back and returned it to her. She knew the signs. He was interested and it was best if she did not say anything more on it for a few days.

By the first week in December the Byrnes were living in Gaines Hall, some two miles from Esher in Surrey. The previous owner, an elderly Colonel who had a distinguished record for service in the Crimean War, had died and his wife was now in a ladies home. The son, who had no desire to live in the hall, accepted Byrne's comment that it needed some repairs, and sold it for £2,750. Emphasising the new installation of electric light, he sold the Streatham house for £1500.

He had no difficulty in obtaining a further loan from his bank to complete the purchase.

With William now working full time at the factory and having gained the respect of the workforce, Brian thought that now he was approaching forty-five he would take one day off a week and help with the local builders carrying out some of the repairs needed. They had also inherited a gardener, John Hartley, who originated from Scotland and with whom Brian developed a lasting rapport. By springtime 1903 Brian and Joan Byrne were ready to receive visitors. Family and friends from Tyneside made regular visits over the next few years. More regular were the friends, mainly from when they lived in Streatham, who lived in the greater London Area – and most approved by Joan. Brian also invited the works foremen and their wives once a year – not approved by Joan.

There were two important events in 1908. The first was that middle son Richard, now twenty, gave up working for the company and joined the army's Northumberland Fusiliers. The youngest son, John Alan Byrne, married Madge Hoskins, the daughter of good friends they had made when living in Streatham.

In early 1914 Elizabeth Hartley, the youngest daughter of John Hartley, joined the staff at Gaines Hall, dividing her time between being an assistant to the cook and helping one of the house maids.

She was an attractive seventeen-year-old with light brown wavy hair and blue-grey eyes.

The outbreak of the First World War was on July 28th 1914. By August 4th the German Army invaded Belgium and Britain declared war on Germany. Many people said it would all be over by Christmas. Brian and William Byrne certainly hoped so because they had immediately lost a considerable part of their income with the loss of their agency fees from Germany and Belgium.

As his father, with the support of two long-serving foremen of over military age, was able to run the curtailed business, William John Byrne, volunteered to fight for King and Country. He joined the Northumberland Fusiliers and was disappointed not to be in the same battalion as his 'regular' brother, now a sergeant.

After three months training he was sent to France. His first action was at the Second Ypres battle in the late spring of 1915. On the second day he became a victim of the German's first gas attack. After a month in hospital back in England he was told that his lungs were permanently affected and although he might feel better for a few years their capacity to function properly would fade with age. Throughout the rest of the war William spent much of his time at home in Gaines Hall, where he liked to help John Hartley, and went to the factory every other working day. In 1919 he married Elizabeth Hartley, with the full approval of his father, but not his mother.

Richard Frederick Byrne was in the 1st Battalion of the Northumberland Fusiliers based at Portsmouth when war was declared. Three days later they were in France and as part of the British Expeditionary Force immediately moved to the front to aid the French army in trying to halt the German advance. In the resulting Battle of Mons, Richard was awarded the Military Medal for bravery in the war's first British bayonet charge. He was promoted to Sergeant. It was the professionalism of the BEF at Mons that led the Kaiser to describe them as 'this contemptible little army'. It reflected his irritation that his army of close on a million professional soldiers was being held up by one of only a tenth of the size.

On Christmas Day 1914 Richard Byrne was in one of the groups of British and German soldiers exchanging gifts. With his very limited German he told them he had been along the Rhine near Dusseldorf with his father. One of them gave him a handshake and said, 'I'm from Dusseldorf. I hope I see you on your next visit.'
In the football match that followed, and which the Germans won, Richard was selected and played with too much vigour, particularly after the Germans scored. The joint referees sent him off for 'foul

play', which was greeted with ironic cheers and laughter by English and Germans. The man from Dusseldorf patted him on the back and grinned.

In late July 1916 Sergeant Richard Byrne was killed leading a bayonet charge on the Somme.

* * *

In Swanley, Kent, most people were hoping to see just an inch of snow that the BBC weather man on the wireless had more or less promised them for Christmas Day, 1931.

'Don't believe their nonsense, they make it up,' shouted John Byrne's mother Joan. Like many deaf people she was unable to speak in a normal tone.

'When we had the hall in Surrey it would snow every Christmas. The servants kept the pathways clear. Oh I do miss those days, which all ended because your stupid father lost all his money in the great stock market crash here and in America.'

'I know she is your mother,' whispered Madge to John but she is intolerable. Thank God she is only staying another two days.'

Their two children Margaret and Kenneth and cousin Daphne pretended they too were deaf and did not hear what Grandma Joan was moaning about. Sat on the floor they continued to play snap. Their frequent bursts of laughter were ignored by grandma.

Still keeping his voice down, John took Madge's hand and said, 'The Byrne family have certainly produced some odd characters, often being transported to a fantasy world, but never one so selfish as Joan Byrne. When my brother William died I was rummaging through various papers he left. Among them was an account of family origins written by the William Byrne who walked from Yorkshire with his sister around 1790 and founded the family in Newcastle. Although he gives no figures or records to prove it he says the family's origins came from a Danish Viking and a Saxon girl in York about the time of William the Conqueror. Although the descendants were said to be hard working and honest every other one had the Viking fingers in middle age and atrocious tempers. As the descendants continued to choose Anglo-Saxon and Celtic origin partners there were fewer berserkers. My great-grandfather Frederick William was one, and his sister Mary, but both learnt how to control it, and my brother Richard showed he had it as he put the fear of Christ among the Germans as he led that bayonet charge against them in 1916.'

'It seems to me,' said Madge, 'the new generation may have produced one more berserker. That is young Edward William Byrne over at Ranmore Common.'

'Madge, recently I have thought that myself. He will either end up in the House of Lords or get to see the inside of Dartmoor prison."*

---

* I Must offer my gratitude to Steve Blake for his invaluable help in checking the proofs of this novel. Any errors that have got through are down to me and not him. – John Bean.